Bits of Business

Also by the author in reading order:

Destiny: Union Station
Date Night on Union Station
Alien Night on Union Station
High Priest on Union Station
Spy Night on Union Station
Carnival on Union Station
Wanderers on Union Station
Vacation on Union Station
Guest Night on Union Station
Word Night on Union Station
Party Night on Union Station
Review Night on Union Station
Family Night on Union Station
Book Night on Union Station
LARP Night on Union Station
Career Night on Union Station
Last Night on Union Station
Independent Living
Soup Night on Union Station
Assisted Living
Freelance on the Galactic Tunnel Network
Con Living
Empire Night on Union Station
Space Living
Traders on the Galactic Tunnel Network
Orphans on the Galactic Tunnel Network
Swap Night on Union Station
Slow Living
Artists on the Galactic Tunnel Network
History Night on Union Station
Bits of Anarchy
Double Living
Bits of Flower
Synergy on the Galactic Tunnel Network
Substitutes on Union Station
Bits of Catalyst
Elder Living
Royals on the Galactic Tunnel Network
Deal Night on Union Station
Intellectual Property

Bits of Business

Book Four of EarthCent Metaverse

Foner Books

978-1-948691-96-3

Copyright 2025 by E. M. Foner

Hardwick, Massachusetts.

One

Mouser returned the soldering iron to its holder and then held his right hand parallel to the workbench to observe the tremor. "It's getting worse," he said in disgust. "I suppose it doesn't matter if I lose the ability to resolder surface mount chips since I already can't get the tiny screws back into the circuit boards."

"Go see the Farling doctor the next time we rendezvous with Flower," Hercules said. "The worst he can do is insult you for growing old at an age when the advanced species are barely out of childhood."

"Getting medical help from aliens is a slippery slope. That's why I have a NAT in place for if I reach the point that I can't make my own decisions."

"NAT?"

"No Alien Technology," Mouser explained. "The hospitals on Earth probably ignore medical orders, especially if you're brought to the emergency room by an ambulance, but a lawyer on Flower told Sophie and I that NATs are effective on Stryx stations and most alien worlds."

Hercules grunted something noncommittal and then lifted his chin toward the headset that the ship's mayor had just finished working on. "Is it fixed?"

"You'll have to plug it into a charger to find out."

"The battery was nearly full when virtual reality fritzed."

"Then it still is," Mouser said. "But the battery mechanically disconnects when you open the injection molded visor body. The way to reset the breaker on the standard virtual reality headsets is to plug them in, but I don't think I have a cord that matches the port on this one."

"I didn't bring the cord," the big man said after patting down his pockets. "It must still be plugged into the transformer you gave us to run the coffee grinder that Rayne picked up on Earth."

Mouser opened the drawer where he kept spare parts for the small appliance repairs that came in, rummaged around, and came up with a cord that terminated in a square connector. He plugged it into his universal power supply and fit the square end into the port of the headset. "Unbelievable."

"What?"

"That cord is from a battery-powered carving knife made on Earth around fifty years ago that somebody brought in for repair. Your mentioning the coffee grinder made me think of it."

"You couldn't fix the knife?" Hercules asked.

Mouser shook his head. "Between my time and the replacement parts, I would have had to charge at least ten creds, and you can buy the Dollnick version with a lifetime warranty for half of that. The owner asked me to recycle it for her, and I kept the cord since I didn't have one with that connector. I should have remembered, but like you pointed out, I'm getting old." He unplugged the cord and passed the headset to Hercules. "It only takes a second to reset the breaker. Try it."

Hercules donned the headset and pressed the power button on the side of the visor with his right index finger.

The triumphal sound that leaked out of the headphones informed Mouser that the repair had been successful.

"Great," Hercules said. "I promised the journalist from Colony One that I'd review the story she's put together about the renovations we've been doing on the Miklat and she gave it to me on this thing. I was afraid I'd have to tell her that I broke it."

"I was wondering where you got the headset," Mouser said. "Are you talking about Reba?"

"That's her. She joined the ship with the Colony One lottery winners we picked up at Earth last year but she's officially on board as working press. Reba sent me the last few issues of the Colony One Post and it's a real change from the Galactic Free Press."

"Good or bad?"

"Just different," Hercules said, removing the headset. "They only report on space news, if that's a thing. It was full of first-person accounts about life aboard the Miklat, but there was also some reporting from Flower and other ships where Colony One members are living. And lots of funny stories about alien encounters that may be exaggerated, though it's hard to tell."

"If you forward me a copy, I'd be interested in taking a look," Mouser said. "I only know Reba because she stopped by my repair booth to present her press credentials. She seemed disappointed when I explained that being the Miklat's mayor is largely a symbolic post that I ended up with because I was the last chairman of the Rules Committee on Bits."

Hercules took a few swipes and taps at the smartphone he was wearing in a forearm bracer. "Done. I sent you everything she sent me."

"And what did you think of her story about the work Colony One members have been doing on the Miklat?"

"It was just starting to play when the headset failed. What was the problem?"

Mouser laughed. "Beats me. I reseated all the connectors and redid the four joints that were soldered by people rather than manufacturing robots. It's from the generation of hardware that replaced the headsets that we use today."

"That seems backward," Hercules said. "Why did Flower settle on the older ones?"

"Because they were available as new/old stock in quantity, and the retail packaging is nearly indestructible so the visors were in excellent condition. I imagine if you wanted to replace the next generation headset that you're holding your only option would be finding one on the used market."

"I don't remember these at all, and I'm even more surprised that you never worked on one before."

"They stopped making them a couple of decades before I was born because the cheap holographic equipment that the Hortens and Dollnicks unloaded on Earth provides a superior experience for a fraction of the price," Mouser said. "The reason that the older virtual reality headsets Flower is pushing are catching on is essentially a marketing trick—presenting their weakness as a strength. Thanks to their limited processing power, they were designed for avatar conferencing, which saves a ton in Stryxnet charges. But you could get the same savings using holographic equipment if you just cut way back on the resolution."

"I wish Flower had let sleeping dogs lie because Rayne has been spending a couple of hours a day in avatar conferencing the last few months," Hercules said. "She's gotten caught up in trying to make a success out of the

Miklat's business incubator, and that means a lot of Stryxnet marketing presentations. I'm beginning to think that she married me for my babysitting talents."

Mouser laughed. "Sarah must be thirteen by now and I wouldn't be surprised if she believes that she's babysitting you while her mother is busy."

"You may be right. The truth of the matter is that I have less free time than I'd like these days because some of the Colony One immigrants are workaholics, and it wouldn't look good if I didn't keep up. When we pick up the next batch of lottery winners, they'll outnumber us by two-to-one."

"Us?"

"Everyone from Bits," Hercules explained. "I don't know why the Zarents want me to continue as their head foreman for renovations when most of the people doing the work these days are from the Colony One movement."

"You know how aliens are," Mouser said. "They already have two years working with you and they don't want to have to figure out the body language of a new human. Besides, you're still one of the biggest men on board and they probably think that gets you respect from the workers."

Hercules glanced at his phone for the time and groaned. "Nobody will respect me if I'm late for my own meeting, so I've got to run. Thanks for the repair, and if you want to try out the headset, I'll bring it to our weekly game before I return it."

"That's a good idea. I'm sure Shadow would be interested in seeing the technology, especially since Flower has been talking about manufacturing more of the old virtual reality visors when the stock runs out."

After Hercules left, Mouser glanced at the electronic whiteboard he used to schedule repair jobs. The screen didn't show any pending work.

"Is something wrong?" a voice asked in strangely accented English.

"Belle," Mouser greeted the Gem clone. "I was sure I had a few more repair jobs scheduled, but I just remembered that I finished the last one right before Hercules arrived."

"I thought that was him walking away," Belle said. "He must have the widest shoulders of any Human on the ship."

"Any humanoid on the ship."

"I take it you haven't met the Verlock who joined the business incubator from that last academy world we stopped at. And he's a bit below average for their species."

"I haven't had much experience with Verlocks," Mouser admitted. "Are you wandering around the bazaar for exercise, or did you come to bring me a repair?"

"Plus one." Belle reached into her fashionable purse and brought out a device that looked like an old ballpoint pen with a clicker for a retractable tip. "In addition to the exercise and the repair, I came to talk to you. But first, can you fix this?"

"A digital recorder disguised as a pen? Where did you pick this up?"

"Earth, it's the only place I've seen them. But I thought it came with a lifetime battery and—"

"Nothing on Earth comes with a lifetime battery, except maybe that one model of LCD watch with the three buttons that they've been making for the last century and a half." Mouser unscrewed the barrel of the pen and shook out a cylindrical object. "Yeah, they sold it with the cheapest battery on the market. I've got a replacement that would probably last a year if you aren't recording around the clock."

"Never mind," Belle said. "I only bought it for the novelty and that's already worn off. I'll go back to recording interviews on my reporter's tab."

"So that covers the repair and the exercise," Mouser said and gestured to the other stool at his workbench. "Have a seat and let's hear why you really came."

"I spent my morning at the annual meeting for the local chapter of Colony One. I'm doing a story for Gem Today about how a group of Human space fanatics, funded by a former independent trader who stumbled on a solid gold asteroid, have adjusted to the reality of living and working on board an old Dollnick colony ship."

"Are your sisters interested in that sort of thing?"

"I don't see why not, and if I never wrote any articles, my cover story of being here as a journalist would start wearing thin," Belle said. "Your name came up at the meeting."

Mouser raised an eyebrow, a skill he'd practiced for his role as a gamemaster. "Just in passing?"

Now it was the Gem's turn to make a face, though Mouser was unable to read anything from it. "The members of Colony One are interested in taking a more active role in the management of the Miklat, within the bounds set by the Zarents, Kruik, and the co-captains, of course. Somebody pointed out that you're the closest thing to a civilian authority on board."

"If one of them wants my job, it's theirs for the asking," Mouser said.

"You would pass your authority to some random human you know nothing about?" Belle asked.

"What authority? I announce the stops and cut ribbons for grand openings."

"But you meet with the co-captains every week."

"Their idea, not mine. I just nod and try to look like I'm paying attention."

"The police chief reports to you," Belle pointed out.

"After Drake and Sabina got married, it would have looked funny if he continued to report to her," Mouser said. "I agreed to do it as a favor, and Drake spares me the sordid details of whatever it is that he and his men have to do to keep people from getting the Zarents angry at us."

"The Oners formed an exploratory committee with the goal of selecting their candidate for mayor," the clone said with a straight face. "First, they intend to petition the Zarents for the right to hold elections."

Mouser wilted. "Something tells me that I'll be getting an invitation to speak with First Engineer Miklat in the near future."

"As the First Engineer is the leader of the Zarents, it does seem likely," Belle said, struggling to keep in her laughter. "I suspect he'll want you to explain the Human version of democracy."

"Maybe the Grenouthians made a documentary about it that he can watch."

"I've seen that one, and I think it would be better if you explained it yourself. The documentary wasn't very complimentary."

"None of them are," Mouser said. "All right, thanks for the warning. And speaking of edutainment, I've been asked to evaluate a Grenouthian role-playing game to see if it can be adapted for our market. I've been studying the gamemaster manual for the last couple of weeks in my spare time, and I told my group that if we don't start playing, I'm going to forget what I've learned. Any interest in joining us?"

Belle hesitated for a moment. "Are you talking about *Speed Trader* by any chance?"

"That's the one. Have you played it?"

"We had to ban it in Gem space after it almost led to a second revolution. It's hypercompetitive, which isn't a good match for a cooperative society of clones."

"But you'll be playing with humans," Mouser pointed out. "According to the manual, it works best with eight to twelve players, so I'm hoping to get Shadow's sister, her boyfriend, and a few others interested. You could bring a friend."

"The usual time on Saturday in your workshop?" Belle asked as she got to her feet.

"If you come at noon, we'll have pizza."

After the clone left, Mouser vacillated over whether to start stripping components from consoles in the recycling pile or to invest some more time in studying the translated gamemaster manual for *Speed Trader*. He settled on the latter and immediately regretted it when the electronic bookmark took him to the beginning of the rules about private promissory notes where he had left off. He was still puzzling over the difference between unintentional and fraudulent default when he caught somebody approaching out of the corner of his eye.

"Please be here to see me," he called to Rayne when she was still five steps away. "This manual is making me question my sanity."

"I am coming to see you, but I have to stop into the retro gaming cooperative first," she replied, veering toward the booth across from Mouser's that took up several vendor spaces.

"Nobody there," Mouser informed her. "They're sponsoring a tournament today, and all the cooperative members who aren't helping run it are playing in it."

Rayne changed directions without losing momentum and took possession of the chair that Belle had recently vacated. "I'm so out of the loop," she complained. "Back on Bits when everybody needed me to disburse funds, I knew everything that was going on. After we moved here and I took over managing the bazaar, I could have drawn a map of the vendors with my eyes closed."

"And then the Colony One lottery winners joined the ship and you let the co-captains talk you into taking responsibility for the business incubator. Hercules stopped by earlier and he said you bring the job home with you."

"It wouldn't get done otherwise, and the Zarents want alien businesses for the incubator," Rayne said. "That means if I want to schedule Stryxnet visor meetings, two-thirds of them are going to happen outside of regular business hours."

"Are the Zarents unhappy with the business that Shadow and Nigel are building around their xenoarchaeology game?" Mouser asked.

"It's not that. Part of the idea behind the business incubator is to give the Zarents a chance to raise their profile as a sovereign species on the tunnel network, and the other part is to make efficient use of the alien living accommodations left behind by the misfits from the Wanderers who remodeled a deck to suit themselves," she reminded him. "The Zarents were happy to have Shadow and Nigel create a magnet business to get the ball rolling, but it would be a waste of resources to bring human businesses into a live/work space that's set up for aliens."

"You discriminate against humans?"

"Our people can get the perks, but they'll have to accept space on another deck," Rayne said. "The space we gave Shadow and Nigel had been completely gutted, so there was no loss of alien habitat."

Mouser nodded. "All right, that makes sense. I knew from the grand opening that it was built to order, but I hadn't realized that the space was gutted before they began."

"It had been abandoned for thousands of years, if not longer, but that's not what I was coming to talk to you about. Do you have any experience with Horten Haptics?"

"Just the odd bits and pieces that trickled in from pirates back when we were still living on Bits. The tech was too advanced for me to be able to repair any of it. I suspect that the gear the pirates sold us was harvested from a quality rejects dumpster behind a factory rather than looted from merchant ships. Why do you ask?"

"I got a query from them asking whether a new division of an existing business would qualify for the incubator benefits. I checked with Snap, and the Zarents are fine with the idea, so I'm putting together a presentation to try to close the deal."

"Why would a major Horten conglomerate want to start a new division in the Miklat's business incubator?" Mouser asked. "I can't believe that the savings on rent and utilities are worth the effort. Are they hoping to get engineering help from the Zarents?"

"The new division intends to produce hardware for the human market," Rayne explained. "They already sell to humans, but the equipment is designed for Hortens, and even though we have similar body sizes, what goes on beneath the skin is very different. By doing the research and development on the Miklat, in addition to the incubator perks, they get access to human gamers for testing."

"I should have thought of that. What can I help you with?"

"I've been bluffing to this point in the conversation. I don't have a clue what haptics do, other than the fact that you wear them. I'm not even sure I'm pronouncing the word right."

"Human-made haptic technology has been around in a crude form since before the Stryx opened Earth," Mouser said. "Imagine a glove with little actuators sewn into the fabric, so when you shake hands with somebody in virtual reality, you would swear that you could feel the other person's grip. Or a tactical vest that employs dozens of motors to create vibrations or thumps so you feel when your virtual opponent has kicked you in the side or shot you in the back."

"Why don't I remember everybody on Bits using it?" Rayne asked.

"Haptics went out of fashion after alien holographic entertainment systems flooded the market. It turns out that immersive systems using scents and sounds can create a more powerful sense of reality than touch alone."

"So why didn't people revive haptics when you and my parents moved to Bits to preserve Earth's gaming culture?"

"The gear was always expensive, not to mention heavy," Mouser said. "I remember trying a full-body suit when I was a teenager that could make you feel like you'd been punched in the stomach, but it cost more than I earned in a year doing electronics repairs. It seems to me that the market for them was businesses working with motion capture since the haptic suit has to be able to track body motions accurately."

"But half of the game development work on Bits involved motion capture," Rayne protested. "Hercules was always—what?"

"There are cheaper ways to do motion capture than putting on a full haptic suit. By the time Hercules started working in the field, motion capture was done with lasers in special booths."

"I must be losing my memory to have forgotten about that, but wouldn't haptic suits be better if you could use them anywhere?"

"Cost," Mouser reminded her. "And even the well-built suits had problems with wearing out, not to mention what happens when the user gets carried away and falls on the floor or runs into a wall. But I imagine that whatever technology the Hortens are using can stand up to serious abuse."

"The Horten I talked to said that they could probably offer humans a lifetime warranty due to our," she stopped and made air quotes, "longevity issues."

Two

"Gorgeous," the leader of the Frunge delegation said. "I've never seen such lovely copper vessels, but what are they for?"

"Fermentation," Sabina replied, managing not to wince at the grating alien sounds produced by the external translation pendant she wore while showing the ship to visiting dignitaries without implants. "The brewer had the vessels made special by Flower's Frunge blacksmith and they were just installed last month."

"I could tell from the quality they were made by one of our smiths, but how did a brewer qualify for space in the Miklat's tech incubator?"

"The business incubator isn't limited to tech companies, even though our first success story is ReVisor, the maker of *Rescue Dig*. We'll be stopping in their development lab at the end of the tour."

"Can we see the Frunge living space?" asked a serious-looking young alien with close-cropped hair vines. "You've already convinced me that the Miklat has more than enough surplus power to run my metallurgical lab, and the support from an engineering-oriented species like the Zarents would be invaluable, but I can't ask my employees to relocate unless the living conditions are acceptable."

"Of course," Sabina said as she consulted the map on her heads-up display for the shortest path through the maze-like business incubator which had served as the multi-species deck for outcasts when the old colony ship had been part of a Wanderer mob. "First Agronomist Miklat has made restoring the Frunge garden one of her priorities."

The alien delegation followed the Miklat's co-captain through a side corridor to a small plaza where a dozen stone tables with inlaid boards for various games formed a circle around a fountain. A young Zarent apprentice riding a unicycle whipped by on the way to his next task, and a human couple sitting close together to study something on the same screen were working at one of the tables, but the plaza was otherwise unoccupied.

"What percentage of the business incubator's space has been leased?" the head of the Frunge delegation asked.

"We only started advertising last cycle, so less than twenty percent," Sabina said, hoping that the alien wouldn't press for details and force her to admit that less than ten percent would be an equally true statement. "But applications are coming in from around the Tunnel Network."

"Are you intentionally replying in generalities or is it a flaw in Humanese? The translation I heard suggests that the occupancy could be as low as zero and that you may have received as few as two applications."

"I haven't updated my translation pendant recently, so that might be it." Sabina waved open the door to the Frunge living section and practically ran inside to forestall further questions. She felt a slight tug as something snagged when she ducked through the arbor at the entrance, and all the platinum blonde hair that she'd stuffed into her captain's hat rather than braiding it that morning came cascading down.

"Gross," the Frunge immediately behind her said. He reached up to retrieve the elaborate hat modeled after the headgear of an admiral from the sailing ship days of the British Empire. It had snagged on a twig, and he extended it in the co-captain's direction while averting his eyes. "I'm going to have nightmares."

"Dzar," the head of the delegation scolded him. "Remember your manners around primitive species."

"Sorry," Dzar apologized, but his eyes were already on the manicured hedges that were often substituted for trees on spacecraft to create privacy barriers in Frunge gardens. "This is nicer than I expected."

Sabina stepped out of the way, put the hat on the ground, and then used both hands to gather up her hair. When she had it all piled on the top of her head, she kept it pinned with one hand, then used the other to work the hat back over her hair, pulling it down tight. Then she reflexively pointed at her ear to let anybody looking her way know that she was communicating over her implant.

"Dewey brought a surprise," her identical twin and co-captain informed her.

"I'm with the Frunge delegation," Sabina reported tersely.

"Rayne is on her way to take over," Katya said. "Kruik tells me that you're in the residential gardens, and Rayne will probably have to drag the Frunge out of there to see the rest of the business incubator before they return to the surface."

"I suppose they can't think any worse of me as they've already seen my hair loose."

"Provincials. I bet if you give Rayne your hat when she gets there the Frunge won't even notice that you've left. You're probably the first human they've ever seen in person."

"Rayne won't wear the hat, but I'll give her my external translation pendant in case she's forgotten hers," Sabina said. "See you on the bridge."

"We're not on the bridge. Meet us on the docking deck at Dewey's ship."

Sabina watched the Frunge exploring the garden and decided that her sister was right and that Rayne would have her work cut out for her getting them to leave. A few minutes later, a woman in her mid-thirties ducked through the arbor.

"Rayne," Sabina greeted her. "Thanks for filling in. Do you—" she broke off as the business manager for the Miklat's bazaar deck fished an external translation pendant on a thin chain out of her blouse and let it hang on her chest. "Great. The delegation wasn't interested in visiting the facilities for any of the other species. There's one hot prospect who wanted to see if the residential gardens were good enough for his employees, and Shadow is expecting to give them a tour of ReVisor if you make it that far."

"Shadow won't be disappointed if the Frunge use up the rest of their time here," Rayne said. "Go. Katya said that it's important."

Sabina noted that the head of the Frunge delegation was lying on a mossy bed with her eyes closed and decided that she didn't need to announce her departure. Five minutes later, she found herself strapped into one of the jump seats on the bridge of Dewey's ship as it left the Miklat. Sabina gestured at the back of the command chair that wasn't occupied by Dewey and shot her sister a questioning look.

"Thomas," Katya said. "THE Thomas."

"Oh." Sabina mentally reviewed everything she knew about the deputy director of EarthCent Intelligence, who she'd never met, and realized it didn't amount to anything more than the fact that like Dewey, Thomas was an artificial person.

As soon as the ship was out of the way of any shuttles entering or leaving the Miklat's core, it decelerated to a stop, leaving the occupants weightless.

"Right," Thomas said, spinning his seat so that he was facing the sisters at the back of the bridge. He took an alien device from his belt pouch, pressed the button, and it began to glow an eerie green. "This is as secure as we can manage. How did you get away from Flower, Katya?"

"I guess the dissidents from Bits rubbed off on me," Katya said with a straight face. "That and Nigel is seriously not into getting stuck at Human Empire headquarters for the rest of his life. As soon as he finished teaching the xenoarchaeology seminar at the school of government, we grabbed a Drazen ship to Corner Station, saying we were going to visit my mom. Then we threw out our return tickets and rendezvoused with the Miklat at Horten Forty."

"So Samuel didn't get a chance to tell you about our new push."

Katya shook her head. "Assuming you're talking about something in the intelligence game, no. Vivian brought up the subject when we were reminiscing about our co-op jobs for aliens, since she worked for Drazen Intelligence, but nothing about her plans for the Human Empire."

"Our assumption is that they'll simply inherit EarthCent Intelligence along with the diplomatic service, and

Clive is talking about retiring when that happens, so he doesn't end up working for his daughter," Thomas said, flashing a grin on his perfect features. "But before he goes quietly into that dark night, he wants to make an effort to lay the groundwork for a clandestine service that the Human Empire can grow."

Katya and her twin exchanged a look. "Don't we already have one?" Sabina asked.

Thomas sighed. "I was the first agent hired by EarthCent Intelligence and I've been with them even longer than Clive. We made the decision upfront not to hide any of our activities from the other species, and it's paid dividends in the relationships we've been able to establish with alien intelligence agencies, despite our having very little to offer in return."

"You're talking about the spies hosted on Flower?"

"And the Miklat, though I understand that the arrangement here is less formal."

"We only have the three, and Belle is the only one who's officially on the payroll of an intelligence service," Sabina said.

"Belle indeed works for Gem Intelligence, and she has an information-sharing arrangement with the alien station chiefs on Flower, though I wouldn't be surprised to hear that the other species have undercover agents on the Miklat," Thomas said. "Bindaal is an officer with Vergallian Fleet Intelligence, and while she may claim to be detached from active duty, they never retire. Kyor is a relative of Myort, who is both the cultural attaché and ambassador for the Huktra embassy on Earth. I have my doubts about Kyor's independence."

Katya laughed. "Let that serve as our aptitude test for intelligence work," she said. "We took their word for who they were."

"It's not like we asked them directly," Sabina said, looking thoughtful. "We knew that they were working together, and since they didn't present credentials, we just assumed that they were freelancing. I wouldn't be surprised to learn that they've lied to each other about their status in order to bypass their rules for inter-agency cooperation."

"That hadn't occurred to me," Thomas said. "Dewey?"

"I'm not listening in," the other artificial person said. "I've set my name as a wake word, but I'm running a visor simulation and doing some beta testing on the latest update to *Rescue Dig* for Shadow."

"As long as you're not listening, would you be offended if I asked if your first loyalty is to humanity or Flower?"

"I wouldn't be offended at all," Dewey replied.

"Then I won't ask," Thomas said, winking at the twins. "In any case, Clive sent me to ask you to keep your eyes open for likely prospects to work as true undercover agents, and that goes for your husband as well, Sabina. We're especially interested in people who have experience in industrial espionage, so if your police catch anybody…"

"You're recruiting criminals?" Sabina asked. "Is that wise?"

The artificial person shrugged. "Reformed criminals? We need operatives with useful skills who we can keep at arm's length. Our training camp on Union Station has never been secret, so the identities of our agents are all blown before they even start working for us. We may try to change that when the Human Empire takes over, but keeping it a secret from the advanced species?" He shook his head.

"Drake won't like playing nice with criminals. He's about as square as they come."

"That's what makes him a good fit for the Miklat's police chief, but if you explain what we're looking for, he might surprise you."

"So what are we supposed to do if we come across a likely prospect," Katya asked, leaning forward against the four-point safety harness and frowning. "We know that our communications aren't secure. Do you expect us to run them as agents ourselves?"

"We're still working on that part," Thomas said. "The first step is to find people, and that may not be easy." He produced a couple of programmable creds and gently pushed one at each of the twins. In the absence of gravity, the coins floated in a straight line and were easily caught. "Each of those coins has a five thousand cred balance, unlocked—that should be enough to convince a likely candidate that you're serious and to lie low until you can send us a hand-carried note. Be circumspect."

"What if one of your new super-agents gets in over their heads and needs help?" Sabina asked. "Are you giving them any way to confirm their identities if they show up here or at an EarthCent embassy?"

"Fast-talking." The artificial person looked surprised when the co-captains laughed at his words. "I was being serious. If we tell every embassy employee what to look for, word will inevitably get out."

"EarthCent security sucks, and we're on a tight schedule," Dewey spoke up.

"And you're not listening."

"Right."

"Then take us back, and we'll keep our eyes open," Katya said. "But I'm going to be honest with you. If you want special operatives, I think you'd be better off going through the rolls of the independent traders who already work for EarthCent Intelligence on a casual basis and figuring out who the risk-takers are. That should be easy enough to spot from their travel patterns, assuming you keep track."

"We do, and it's being done," Thomas said. "Clive thought it was important to keep the two of you in the loop, and since I was coming to talk to you anyway, we thought it couldn't hurt to kill two birds with one stone."

"You mean that asking us to recruit secret agents is secondary to letting us know that you're trying to stand up a more traditional agency to hand over to the Human Empire should Sabina or I ever find ourselves stuck in charge."

"Kruik is ready to bring us back to the Miklat," Dewey announced. "Everybody still strapped in?"

The Zerakova twins reflexively checked their safety restraints, even though they hadn't released them in Zero-G, and Thomas began turning his chair back toward the main viewscreen before halting midway and saying, "One more thing. Have you been keeping track of the aliens moving on board the Miklat?"

"Kruik maintains a database of everybody on board," Sabina replied. "I'd be surprised if we have more than a few hundred inhabitants from all of the advanced species combined, but that could spike in a hurry if the business incubator takes off."

"Our analysts believe that the Miklat will prove a magnet for oxygen-breathing alien intelligence agents, including from non-tunnel-network species," Thomas said.

"Your regular stops at Farling Four, Union Station, and the rendezvous with Flower mean that residence on the Miklat will be highly attractive to those tasked with watching the Farling Empire, as well as to intelligence services within the Farling Empire watching the tunnel network members."

"We only have two stops scheduled at Farling Four in the next eight months, and we only visit Union Station twice a year."

"You're thinking like a human," Katya scolded her sister. "A few months or a year to the aliens is like a few weeks to us."

"And the regent of Farling Four hasn't approved any requests from the tunnel network species to establish regular passenger liner service," Thomas added. "Working on board a passenger liner is one of the standard cover jobs for anybody tasked with running agents."

"How is Tunnel Trips progressing with starting a passenger service?" Sabina asked.

"The Rainbow Five is currently on a shakedown cruise, and they've managed to piece together enough temporary gate leases to set up a schedule that will meet the milestone requirement for the Human Empire. The lead analyst on our Farling desk speculates that M793qK may have instructed G32FX to hold off on granting an elevator hub gate at Farling Four to any other species in anticipation of giving the first one to Tunnel Trips."

"We're going to end up looking like Farling client species if we're not careful," Katya muttered.

"This didn't take as long as I expected," Sabina said, making a subtle hand signal to let her sister know they could discuss the Farling issue later. "I wonder if Rayne ever got the Frunge to leave the garden."

Even as Sabina spoke, Rayne had given up on her attempt to wake the guests by coughing and began clapping as loudly as she could.

"Is something wrong?" the leader of the Frunge delegation asked sleepily.

"I was trying to warm my hands, but as long as you're up, why don't we continue with the tour?" Rayne suggested. "I'm sure you have questions that could be best answered by somebody who has been running a business in the incubator."

"If we must," the alien grumbled, and let out a cackling sound. The other members of the delegation set up such a groaning that Rayne imagined she was walking in a wintery forest with creaky trees, but the Frunge all rose to their feet and fell into line behind the leader.

"We only have forty minutes left before your shuttle is scheduled to return to the surface, so I thought I'd bring you directly to ReVisor," Rayne said as she backed through the arbor. "The business is a partnership between a hacker from Bits and a Verlock-trained xenoarchaeologist."

"What do they revise?" Dzar asked. "Is it an editorial business?"

Rayne blinked. "No. ReVisor is just a made-up word they were able to trademark and my translation device should have sounded it out rather than—" she interrupted herself and shot the entrepreneur a sharp look. "I would have noticed if it had substituted a Frunge word. You understand English!"

"It would be crazy to move my business to a location where I couldn't speak the language," Dzar said. "I bought a course through the Open University extension for alien languages and memorized the rules and vocabulary. But I have a lead ear, so I doubt I can pronounce any words in Humanese that would make sense to you."

"Try me."

"Borscht."

"That was perfect," Rayne said. "I didn't know that Frunge were fans of cold beet soup."

"I don't know what beets are, and I was trying to pronounce the fifth element in your periodic table," Dzar said in Frunge. "We use it in my business."

"Boron?"

"That's the one."

"Then you got it half right, which isn't bad for a first attempt," Rayne said. She glanced over her shoulder to make sure that she was still moving in the right direction and spotted Drake standing at the intersection of the corridor coming from the human zone of the business incubator where it crossed the corridor leading to the plaza. "There's the Miklat's police chief if you have any questions about security. He has an implant."

"I thought all Humans had implants," the leader of the Frunge delegation said. "We heard that you need them to do basic math."

Rayne brushed back the hair that covered the translation device she wore cupped over her ear. "I used to be the treasurer for my community on Bits. If you want to test my basic math skills, I won't be offended."

"Say we're fifty steps away from the police chief and we approach him at two steps per second, while he waits for one second and then comes toward us at three steps per second. How many steps from where we started will we meet?"

"Twenty-one," Rayne said after a brief pause.

"Twenty-one point two," Dzar corrected her.

"I had nineteen point two," the leader of the delegation admitted.

"You forgot the two steps we take before he starts," one of the other Frunge told her.

"Drake," Rayne called before the Frunge could get any deeper into the weeds. "Sabina had to attend to some ship's business and I was the last-minute substitute. Did you plan to meet her?"

"I'm checking the deck for potential camera locations," Drake said. "Industrial espionage is practically a game on the tunnel network and the Zarents want the incubator to provide the highest level of security."

"You've hired the Grenouthians to design a system?" Dzar asked.

"I guess I misspoke, but between Kruik being on duty around the clock and whatever the Zarents come up with, I'm sure it will be the next best thing."

"But why would they send you to scout camera locations?"

"At the moment, ninety-nine percent of the sentients on the Miklat are humans or Zarents, and I'm sure you can guess which group is more likely to cause problems. Most of my career has been policing humans, so I'm familiar with how they interact with advanced surveillance systems."

"Will you object to my bringing my existing security system when I transfer my research facility to the Miklat?" Dzar asked.

Rayne heard the "when" and did a private fist pump.

"I'd need the details so I can check with Kruik and the Zarents," Drake said. "As long as the system doesn't put the ship or inhabitants in danger, I don't imagine it will be a problem."

"The security system won't present any danger to the ship. As to would-be thieves, it would depend on how hard they push and how well prepared they are for the consequences."

"I'm not familiar with advanced security systems myself," Rayne said, "but I would be concerned about unintended consequences, like somebody who's had too much to drink entering the wrong office, or kids fooling around."

"They'd never get past the door," Dzar assured her. "The first level of our security system would foil any attempt from Drazens, Hortens, or Gem, not to mention Humans. It's mainly the Dollnicks, Vergallians, and non-tunnel network species that concern me."

"Not the Grenouthian and the Verlocks?"

"If they don't know about the metallurgical process I've developed, it's because they forgot millions of years ago," the Frunge entrepreneur said. "If they want my ideas without paying, they could find them, and better, in their archives."

Three

"I can't come down to the planet today," Shadow told Delphi apologetically. "I know I said I would, but Nigel was down there yesterday and he invited a Dollnick to interview for the office manager job."

"I can't believe that Nora quit on you," Delphi said. "She really seemed to love the work, and I know you paid her well."

"Her boyfriend is a sales rep for Drazen Foods and they just granted his request to open an office on Farling Four. She's going to manage it for him."

"Is Drazen Foods giving him exclusive rights to the territory?"

"For five years," Shadow confirmed. "They're going to be rich."

"Well, between that and it being a chance to go into business with her boyfriend, I guess I can't blame her," Delphi said. "But why a Dollnick? He can't be that successful if he's willing to work for humans."

"She. Kruik explained that it's not normal for Dollnick females to be out wandering around the galaxy by themselves, and I got the impression that he'd feel better having her on board than bumming around the Farling Empire."

"Does she have any experience running an office for a business?"

"Nigel said she'd be perfect for the job," Shadow said. "Given that everything he knows about business he learned from me in the last year, that's not saying much."

Delphi laughed. "He probably thinks that an office manager with four arms can do twice as much work as a human, though when it comes to Dollnicks, he'd be right. I worked all day yesterday to get the containers that were waiting for us in orbit stowed away, and tomorrow I'll get the deliveries sorted, so today is my only chance to get to the surface. If you finish up early, come down and meet me."

"Will do. And I'm sorry if I screwed up your plans."

"Nothing special. I'll spend the morning shopping in Human Town, and if you make it for lunch, maybe we can visit the caverns with the singing crystals everybody talks about."

Shadow almost told her that he'd heard the caverns were a tourist trap, but something told him she probably didn't want to hear that, and since both of them were operating on imperfect information, there was no point getting into an argument about it. He cleaned up the breakfast dishes after Delphi left, strapped on the forearm bracer with his smartphone, and checked the time.

"Ulah has arrived," Kruik informed him via the cabin's sound system.

"Thanks. I was about to head to the office." Shadow started for the door, and then checked his pockets. "I don't remember if I left my external translation pendant at the office or if I brought it home again by mistake."

"It won't be necessary. Ulah has been living in Human Town for several cycles."

"She can speak English? Maybe that's why Nigel wants to hire her."

"Ulah understands Humanese," Kruik said. "I haven't heard her speak it. Some Dollnicks find your words extremely difficult to pronounce."

"Maybe I'll finally get some use out of my implant," Shadow said, jogging for the lift tube. "I doubt I've needed it three times in the six months that I've had it."

"You told me that you purchased the implant to keep Delphi company when she got hers."

"M793qK was having a two-for-one sale when we rendezvoused with Flower. And I guess I use it all the time if we count talking with you in my head."

"There is that," Kruik said, and the lift tube capsule started for the business incubator deck without waiting for Shadow's instructions. "If I may make a suggestion…"

"Sure."

"Don't ask Ulah about her family."

"Got it. Do you think she's a runaway?"

The capsule lurched as if Kruik was so surprised by the question that he had a physical reaction. "Dollnicks don't run away from the nest, and she's old enough to have completed her basic education. While it's not normal for a young female to strike out on her own, it's not unheard of."

"Her basic education?" Shadow asked. "Are you talking about grade school?"

"A comparison would be forced at best, but I would estimate that Ulah's education is equivalent to thirty-second grade."

"You mean she has a few doctoral degrees and she wants to work as an office manager?"

"Human and Dollnick educations don't have direct equivalents," Kruik continued via Shadow's implant as the young man left the capsule on the business incubator deck.

"Preparing young people for life is a serious business, and the older the civilization, the more material there is to digest, not to mention the physical training. Making efficient use of four arms requires a great deal of practice."

"I guess," Shadow said, not bothering to try to subvocalize since there was nobody nearby. "Where is she now?"

"In a lift tube capsule traveling out a spoke of the next ring aft. You'll have two minutes to prepare for her arrival."

Shadow waved open the door to ReVisor and wasn't surprised to find that he was the first person to arrive. He glanced at his smartphone again and it was just after 8:30 A.M. on Human Standard Time. He went straight to the desk of the previous office manager and was relieved to find that she had cleaned up the cubicle, but when he sat at the desk to check the drawers, something occurred to him.

"Uh, Kruik?"

"Yes, Shadow."

"How tall is Ulah?"

"Your height," the Dollnick AI responded. "Females are shorter than males, and she's still a few years away from her final growth spurt."

"Then the desk will work for her?" he followed up.

"The standard height for Human desks is a bad compromise. Dollnick-made desks are fully adjustable, though most office workers settle on two height settings, depending on which set of arms they're using."

"Wouldn't it be easier to adjust the height of the chair like we do?"

"There's only one ideal setting for the height of the chair seat, and that correlates with the length of the user's legs from the knee down," Kruik explained. "Attempting to compensate for a universal desk height by adjusting the chair is just bad engineering."

Shadow grunted, knowing he wouldn't win any engineering debates with the alien artificial intelligence. He caught a movement in his peripheral vision and looked out through the glass wall that separated the ReVisor offices from the corridor and saw a tall, slender Dollnick with a giant backpack approaching.

"Did she bring all of her stuff with her?" he asked.

"Ulah was leaving Human Town whether or not Nigel had offered her the job interview. If it doesn't work out, she'll either find something else or get off at another stop."

Shadow hastily rose to greet the Dollnick at the door and was surprised when she offered him a handshake, extending her upper right arm.

"I'm Ulah," she chirped in a voice that reminded him a little of a parrot from a pirate movie. "Are you Nigel's partner?"

"Shadow," he replied. "Yes, it's a partnership, but we give employees points in the products they work on, just like the system we had back on Bits."

"I'm not familiar with Bits," she said, shrugging her way out of the giant backpack and setting it on the floor. "Is it a habitat?"

"The world where I grew up, but we were renting and the Hortens took it back," Shadow explained. "Everybody there worked in software development, mainly games, but we also did most of the work for Earth's smartphone industry, which was given protection from alien imports when the Stryx opened Earth. Do you like games?"

Ulah made a face, but Shadow didn't have a clue what the expression was meant to convey. "Engineering games," she said after he failed to react. "The Human games I've tried were either about killing things or farming. Nigel said that you create educational games and that your flagship product is based on xenoarchaeology."

"It's our only released product," he said. "I'll give you the grand tour, though there isn't much to see other than desks."

"I'd like to see one of the visors that your product uses to create virtual reality. Nigel tried to describe it to me, but I have to admit that it didn't quite make sense. It sounded like a step backward from holograms."

"More like three steps back," Shadow said with a grin as he led her into the testing room. "But Flower was able to get patent protection for virtual reality headsets as a repurposed technology, and that helps create a moat for our brand. Are you familiar with business?"

Ulah let out an amused whistle. "I've been trading my way around the tunnel network for the last six years and I'm saving up for a ship." She looked at the headset that Shadow extended to her. "Oh, that's surprising."

"Yeah, it's kind of low-tech. You can adjust the pupillary distance with the button on the top. I'll hand you the wrist controllers after you put on the headset."

The Dollnick settled the visor over her eyes and started with surprise when the screens activated. Shadow hesitated a moment over which of her hands to give a controller and then went with the lower left. Ulah reached with her lower right hand, and he deposited the second controller.

"Just two?" she asked.

"I could give you another two, but the headset would interpret your motions as if they were on your ankles," Shadow said. "If you load *Rescue Dig*, it's set up to work with Dollnicks using six controllers, but you're looking at the default demo for humans."

The Dollnick started working through the calibration exercises for virtual reality, and Shadow took the opportunity to add water to the office coffee machine and start it brewing. He had seen so many people work their way through the demonstration exercises that he could tell exactly how far along Ulah progressed, and it was apparent that she was mastering the basic controls faster than anybody he'd seen. He almost forgot that he was watching a Dollnick until she removed the headset with her top hands without putting down the controllers.

"What an interesting experience," Ulah said. "And your educational products all run on these visors?"

"So far," Shadow said, and then took a shot in the dark. "Did Nigel tell you about the position we're attempting to fill?"

"Chief administrator."

"Okay, that's not far off. We're looking for an office manager."

Ulah nodded. "Somebody to run everything. I can do that."

Shadow accepted the headset in return and put it back on the shelf, followed by the controllers. "Yes and no," he said. "An office manager does sort of run everything, but only as the representative of, uh, the people who are in charge."

"I assumed I would be answering to the owners," the Dollnick said. "Are you suggesting that there are multiple levels of management and that the office manager is at the bottom?"

"It's more like the office manager is in charge of everything that doesn't relate to the products," Shadow explained.

"Why would your business be wasting time on anything that's not related to your products?"

"Okay, that wasn't a good description either. Your job would be making sure that everybody else has what they need to do their jobs."

Ulah let out an untranslatable whistle. "You mean a prince's administrator. Yes, I can do that."

"Do you have any experience in an office environment?" Shadow asked.

"No. Is that required?"

"I hadn't thought about it before I asked. Are you familiar with bookkeeping?"

"I learned the Princely Standard in school," Ulah said. "Quadruple entry bookkeeping."

"Probably twice as good as ours then," Shadow said. "Do you have any experience purchasing advertising?"

"No, but it sounds interesting. Would I be doing that?"

"Our last office manager took it over when our marketing manager left."

"How long did these managers work for you?" Ulah asked.

"Uh, the office manager for almost a year. She was our first employee. The marketing manager was more like six months."

"Did they have any experience before you hired them?"

"Good point," Shadow said. "They were friends of friends and needed jobs. I guess if you want to give it a try, you can start as soon as you're ready.

"Then I'll start today," the Dollnick said. "If you don't have anything else that needs my immediate attention, I'll start by creating hiring guidelines for you to follow in the future."

"Great. I'll get you settled in, and then I'm going to run down to the planet to meet my girlfriend."

"Will anybody else be coming in today?"

Shadow grimaced. "Most of our programmers come in before noon, but starting late and staying late is kind of a tradition for those of us who grew up on Bits."

"I'm sorry," Ulah said. "Did I get you out of bed early?"

"No, I'm ownership. I can't even remember why it used to be so important for me to come in late."

While Shadow was getting ReVisor's new office manager settled in, his girlfriend was disembarking from the shuttle on the surface of Farling Four. She joined the crowd walking toward the maglev station, but then her eye fell on a floater limo parked right next to the train stop. An alien who reminded her of a shark that had somehow grown a pair of stubby legs and left the ocean was standing next to the back door of the limo holding up a sign that read, 'Delphi.'

"Me?" she asked herself, but the tooth-baring grin of the driver gave her pause. Without pointing at her ear, she subvoced, "Kruik? Are you still in range?"

"Until the shuttle departs," the Dollnick AI replied. "Is something wrong?"

"There's a shark-like limo driver holding up a sign with my name on it."

"He's Oosh, they're very reliable. Talk to him."

"Will he understand me?"

"If he's been sent to pick you up, I'm sure he'll have active translation technology."

Delphi approached the alien, who folded up the sign at her approach and opened the rear door of the limo.

"Are you sure you're here for me?" she asked. "I'm the Miklat's loadmaster, not anybody special."

The Oosh bared the rest of his teeth, unfolded the sign, and showed her the back. She saw a sketch of herself done in some sort of pastel that she would have paid at least twenty creds for if it hadn't been folded. "G32FX requests your presence."

"I'm getting in the limo," Delphi subvoced. "The driver says that G32FX sent it."

There was a brief pause, and then Kruik said, "Confirmed. Remember, he's the planet administrator now, and as the loadmaster, you're an official representative of the Miklat."

"Thanks for the extra pressure," Delphi muttered as she got into the back. As the driver took the limo through a wide circle away from the maglev rail, she found herself sliding off the seat. "Hey! How come there are no safety restraints?"

"Look up," the Oosh replied.

Delphi looked up at the roof of the limo and saw a heavily padded U-shaped yoke. She had to kneel on the seat to reach it, and as she pulled it down, she felt a subdued ratcheting and noticed that it wasn't pulling back against her. She squirmed around so she'd be facing forward and then pulled the yoke down the rest of the way. It settled comfortably over her lap.

The speed of the floater kept increasing until the surroundings were just a blur. Then, almost as quickly, it began decelerating, and without the yoke, she would have been on the floor. An ornate gate in a high wall opened to admit the limo, and it came to a halt in a courtyard that was mainly a garden. The safety yoke released of its own accord. Delphi began searching for the button or touch panel that operated the door, but before she could find it, the Oosh driver opened it from the outside.

"G32FX will be with you as soon as he's free," the alien said. "There are refreshments for you at the table in the glade."

Delphi thanked the driver, who was already getting back into the limo, and then took the garden path he'd indicated, which led into a particularly dense area of vegetation. A small table with a single chair was set up on a large flat stone, and there was a bowl with fruit. She was just finishing off an apple that must have been grown locally when a familiar Farling entered the glade.

"Delphi," G32FX rubbed out on his speaking legs. "Thank you for coming. I was beginning to think I'd have to send somebody to fetch you from the Miklat."

"Really?" she asked. "What for?" Then her eyes narrowed. "Do you want me to smuggle cargo containers or something? I may be the loadmaster, but Kruik knows everything that enters or leaves the ship."

"Nothing so sinister. I have a business proposal for you."

"But I'm not a businesswoman. I mean, sure, I still get a royalty stream from my ringtones, but my mother set up that deal."

G32FX's wings popped partially out of his carapace in amusement, but he quickly controlled himself. "The business I have planned isn't related to any of your prior occupations, but I promise you it will be both educational and profitable."

"And legal?" Delphi asked.

"As the administrator of Farling Four, whatever I do here is legal by definition. I can't speak for the rest of the galaxy, but I'm not aware of any laws that prohibit simple trade."

"I don't have any experience in trade."

"But nobody on the Miklat is better placed to retrieve shipping containers on short notice for prospective buyers. I need somebody I trust who can show the goods and keep records, in return for which I'm willing to pay you a five percent commission."

"Human agents get fifteen percent."

"Humans are idiots, present company excepted," G32FX rubbed out on his speaking legs. "I'm not talking about five-cred, ten-cred deals. Five percent of the value of the merchandise I'm sending along on my personal account would pay for your retirement."

"Oh." Delphi absent-mindedly ate a grape. "I'd have to ask the co-captains."

"I already discussed it with Katya when she came down for the official visit yesterday. She and her sister will handle outside sales for five percent, including a few of the high value scientific interest items with fixed pricing."

"But they already have jobs."

"So do you and I," the Farling pointed out. He picked up a banana with one of his upper limbs and used it to point at a black rock that in addition to looking out of place in the garden gave the impression of somehow being out of focus. "What do you think that's worth?"

"The blurry black rock?" Delphi went over and crouched to study it, but being up close didn't reveal any details. "There's something weird about it."

"You can't see the controls at all?"

"Rock controls?"

G32FX rubbed out a sigh. "That's the whole problem with Human evolution right there. You're overoptimized for survival and breeding."

"Clearly, because I don't have a clue what you're talking about," Delphi said.

"Evolutionary Game Theory—I would have thought somebody who grew up on Bits would be familiar with it."

"I've heard of Game Theory, but I haven't studied it. Shadow talks about it sometimes."

"Of all the species I've encountered, Humans are the easiest to fool because you can't see the truth if it's in front of your face," the Farling said. "It's a genetic flaw that I could show you if I'd brought my holographic projector."

"And you're saying that it's because there wasn't any evolutionary reward on Earth for seeing the truth," Delphi surmised.

"Exactly. While working on Earth for M793qK, I developed a morbid interest in your mating habits and discovered that you've evolved to reward dishonesty. I have a theory that your evolution hit a dead end as soon as you developed language and began lying to each other, but I've been too busy to write it up."

"But what does that have to do with my seeing controls on a blurry rock?"

"You can't see them because your vision system didn't evolve to show you a true picture of your surroundings. In order to conserve the limited processing power of your brain, your visual cortex filters out some fundamental information about the universe to reduce your reaction time should opportunities to eat or breed arise."

"That's ridiculous," Delphi said, running her hand over the rock. "I can't feel any controls either."

"What do you feel?" the Farling asked.

Delphi started to answer and then frowned. "Nothing," she admitted.

"The controls are right there but your eyes don't see and your fingers don't feel."

"Is it dark matter?"

This time G32FX's wings came all the way out, and he beat the air in amusement. "The stuff that according to your physics makes up over a quarter of the energy-mass in the universe? Next you'll guess that it's dark energy, which takes up over two-thirds of the missing energy-mass required to make the math for your conception of gravity work. No," he said, pulling in his wings. "The controls are holographic, but at frequencies you can't see. You can think of the rock as the inverse of a Verlock heat stone. If there's enough demand, I'll see about having the controls updated for your visual range."

"It's a cooling stone?"

"Of a sort. Do you know how Verlock heat stones work?"

"I thought it was a big secret."

"No, most of the advanced species could make them, but the Verlocks can do it cheaper so there's no point," G32FX explained. "It has to do with their choosing to live places that have a surplus of heat which they can lock into a dimensional matrix and—the important thing is that the cooling stones can keep a modest residence at a comfortable temperature for years. If you return them for the deposit, the cost is well below any cooling method that requires the purchase of energy to operate a heat exchanger."

"You want me to demonstrate products that I can't operate?" Delphi asked.

"Don't worry about that. The interface is intuitive and anybody who can't figure it out shouldn't be buying the things."

"I guess if it's okay with Kruik and the Zarents. I mean, it's their ship."

"The Zarents are enthusiastic about being part of a new trade route," G32FX said. "I have six containers in orbit for you to load tomorrow, so put them somewhere you can get them out again on short notice."

"Fine," Delphi said, wondering what she was getting herself into. "Do you have a contract prepared?"

"You just agreed to it. Don't worry. Should a question ever come up, I have perfect recall."

Four

"Why isn't anybody eating the pizza that I made?" Lisa asked plaintively. "It's healthy."

"I think you have your answer right there," Mouser told Shadow's older sister. "I don't have any objections to vegan food in principle, but the fake cheese doesn't work for me."

"The tofu isn't a substitute for cheese. I've reimagined what pizza can be."

"I had three pieces," Botan said, displaying the crusts on his recyclable plate as proof. "I think this was your best pizza yet."

"Then why are you throwing out the crusts?" Lisa demanded.

"Some people see the glass as half empty," Shadow declaimed from the relative safety of the other side of the long coffee table that Mouser kept specifically for gaming. "I miss the vending machine pizza from Bits, but I'm willing to make do with the combo from Big Tony's."

"Maybe Belle or her friend will be hungry," Delphi said.

"I'll bet the reason they aren't here yet is because they knew we were having vegan pizza. The nicest thing we can do for them is to finish it before they arrive."

"Is that why Rayne and Hercules aren't here yet? Have they stopped eating pizza?"

"They've started a cooking class together on Saturday mornings," Mouser explained. "Hercules said it was the only way he could come up with to stop Rayne from working seven days a week. I'm pretty sure they'll eat what they made before coming."

"What about Sarah?" Delphi asked when her boyfriend stretched for another piece of pizza.

"She likes vegan food," Shadow said. "I've seen her at the Vergallian place a bunch of times."

"Sarah stopped by my booth to apologize that she wouldn't be able to come to our gaming group for the foreseeable future," Mouser said. "She made friends with a Zarent apprentice and they're both shadowing First Agronomist Miklat on Saturdays to learn about the career path."

"Does she have to ride a unicycle?" Botan asked. "I've been thinking about adding a Zarent apprentice to my manga, but a girl who wants to be a Zarent might work better."

"I haven't seen her on a unicycle yet, but I wouldn't be surprised. At our meeting yesterday, the co-captains asked me if I'd noticed any of our population from Bits going native. I wasn't sure what they meant, and Katya explained that it's normal for people living on open worlds to start imitating the culture of their alien hosts."

"But the Miklat is a colony ship, and there are far more humans on board than Zarents," Lisa said.

Mouser shrugged. "Maybe going native has more to do with quality than quantity."

"Tell us more about this game we're testing," Shadow said after he finished the piece of pizza. "Can I revive my old assassin character?"

"He didn't read the player manual—again," Delphi said.

"It was only three pages," Botan said in disbelief.

"I'm allergic to instructions," Shadow said. "Somebody just has to point me in the right direction and I'm set. I have gaming in my genes."

"The game is *Speed Trader*," Mouser said. "Most people know about the Grenouthians through their news network and the humorous documentaries they produce about primitive species like us, but they also have more independent traders than any of the other tunnel network members."

"So the idea is that we're all Grenouthians and we go around trading and fighting. I can do that."

"It's about trading, not combat," Lisa told her brother. "If there was any fighting, I'd kick your butt."

"Grenouthian traders are also known as masters of the Pushing Paws martial arts style," Mouser told Lisa, who ran the Miklat's sole dojo.

"I know a little bit about that one," Lisa said, jumping up and demonstrating a series of open-palmed strikes and kicks, all of which fell just short of hitting her brother.

"Are you trying to knock some sense into him for not reading the player's manual?" Hercules asked as he and Rayne entered Mouser's new lab space on the light industrial deck.

"How did you know I didn't read it?" Shadow asked.

"You never do the prep work," Rayne said. "It's a wonder we haven't kicked you out of the group."

"I was just starting to explain the game, but maybe I should wait until Belle gets here," Mouser said. "I suggested she bring a friend since we're short-handed."

"Do we play in teams?" Shadow asked.

"It's every Grenouthian for himself, though you owe loyalty to your clan," Delphi told him. "But the game requires a minimum of eight players."

"Why?"

"Because those are the rules," Mouser said patiently. "All of the action takes place at trade fairs, whether on planets or space stations and habitats. Travel between locations is instantaneous."

"Do we all have our own spaceships?" Shadow asked.

"Yes, but they only matter in the sense that the hold serves as your storehouse," Delphi explained. "There's not much buying and selling for Stryx creds because everything is based on barter."

"Barter is better," Botan and Lisa chorused.

"So it's basically eight people sitting around a table trading stuff?"

"Eight Grenouthians," Mouser corrected him. "And everything happens on timers. I've been practicing with the gamemaster console in the evenings while watching immersives with Sophie."

"You don't find doing two things at once distracting?" Rayne asked as she helped herself to a soda from the small fridge.

"Sophie is on a Vergallian drama kick, so I assign a player timer and score to each character. It's not an exact correlation since the actors in the drama aren't playing a Grenouthian trading game, but I've gotten a lot better at toggling the timers, and I update the point total based on who seems to be achieving their goals."

"Are the timers to ensure that we all get equal time trading?" Shadow asked.

Mouser shook his head. "Time is money. Maybe not literally, since the trading between players is limited to barter. Your final score is based on the goods you've acquired free and clear divided by the time you spend trading for them."

"I wonder where they came up with that idea," Rayne said. "I know that the Grenouthians have a reputation for being quick about everything, but imposing an artificial deadline on making deals seems like a good way to force blunders."

"I've met hundreds of independent traders since I took over as Miklat's loadmaster," Delphi said. "Most of them tell me stories about deals they've made while I'm fishing containers out of the hold for them to restock inventory that's produced on Flower. It sounds like the ability to make fast decisions plays a bigger role in bartering."

"You're restocking traders directly from cargo containers that are en route?" Rayne asked. "Why aren't they unloaded into warehouse space?"

"It's the new version of Flower's dynamic warehousing scheme. I guess it's more efficient than moving the goods twice, and as long as we do it in the tunnels rather than at stops, it doesn't get in the way of loading and unloading containers for regular customers."

The door to Mouser's lab slid open and Belle entered, accompanied by a blue dragon variant. "Are we on time?" the clone asked. "This is my friend Kyor. She said she knows some of you already."

"Hey, Kyor," Hercules greeted the Huktra. "Taking a break from Club Ucerin?"

"Saturday afternoon is always slow for beer sales," Kyor replied. "Belle told me you were evaluating a Grenouthian game and I'm curious to learn more about how they think."

"From a game?"

"Games offer key insights into how sentients view themselves, and are especially useful calibrating concepts of fair play."

"I thought the whole point of games was that everybody has to follow the same rules," Shadow said. "The closest thing we had to a government on Bits was the Rules Committee."

The Huktra crouched on her haunches at the end of the oversized coffee table and curled her tail to reduce the chances of anybody tripping over it. "If a Verlock came into Club Ucerin and got drunk, their notion of fair play would permit me to inflate the bill or make change improperly. In their culture, anybody who drinks to the point of diminished mathematical capacity is a fool who deserves to be taught a lesson. If I did the same thing with Humans, Police Chief Drake would pay me a visit."

"In the old Gem Empire, fair play was supposed to be guaranteed by the fact that we were all clones," Belle said, taking a seat on the couch next to Hercules. "In practice, we still ended up with elites, which just goes to show that equality is a political rather than a genetic construct."

"Speaking of equality, I hear that you have competition for mayor," Kyor said to Mouser.

"The lottery winners from the Colony One movement have established an exploratory committee to select candidates if they can convince the Zarents that we need elections," Mouser said, arranging the materials from the game behind the Grenouthian tri-fold gamemaster's screen. "First Engineer Miklat asked for my input, and I told him that I'm fine with being voted out of office."

"By election, do you intend for the next mayor to be chosen by your deity?"

"You lost me."

"She's talking about Biblical election," Belle said. "I've been studying your religious traditions and election is at the core of your Old Testament."

"I'm pretty sure the Oners are talking about an Earth-style election," Mouser told the Huktra. "One sentient, one vote, and all of that. Did Belle give you a player guide?"

"Games are games," Kyor said, echoing Shadow. "I'll wing it. Just tell me how we start."

"Like this," Mouser said. He dealt each of the players a single card that was at least four times the size of a standard playing card, though not much thicker. "The column on the right shows the available goods, and you put them in inventory by dragging them to the left and assigning the proportion of cargo capacity you want to commit. If the combination of merchandise doesn't fit in your hold, you lose the overage. After everybody has chosen, you get one roll of the chance die," he continued, producing a large die with twenty numbered facets, "which is the multiplier for your initial cargo."

Botan picked up the die and squinted. "Point eight seven four?"

"I could find no explanation for the exact values, but they range from eighty-five percent to a hundred and ten percent."

"I dibs a hundred and ten percent," Kyor growled.

"You have to choose your cargo first and then roll the die," Mouser told her.

"I already chose my cargo, and I don't see why I should have to roll the die when the outcome is already known—unless it's been rigged."

"Don't you have that backward?" Shadow asked.

"It's just a twenty-sided die," Kyor said. "Didn't any of you practice rolling polyhedrons when you were young?"

"These aren't printed cards," Rayne said suddenly. "They're thin tabs with touchscreens."

"The Grenouthians do an impressive job with tech when they put their minds to it," Belle said as she studied her options for cargo. "Can you tell us where we'll be setting up shop, Mouser?"

The gamemaster swore under his breath. "Thanks, Belle. I knew I had forgotten something. If you want me to reset your cargo manifest so you can decide what to stock after you know where you're going, just pass it to me, Kyor."

The Huktra completed her study of the twenty-sided die that Botan had passed her and tossed it into the felt-lined box lid on the coffee table. It bounced a few times, rebounded off the edge of the lid, and came to a stop. "A hundred and ten percent," Kyor declared. "And I'll stick with the cargo I've chosen."

Mouser cleared his throat and attempted to produce the basso profundo of a barrel-chested Grenouthian. "The new production day is just beginning on Timble Orbital, and the docking deck area for visiting independent traders is empty except for a few early morning joggers. After completing your postflight inspection, you do a quick survey and find that there are seven other Grenouthian solo traders parked nearby."

"We stopped at Timble with Flower," Lisa said. "Everybody on board was in the immersive business. A video director I knew from Bits who got work there tried to hire me as a stunt actor."

"They offered me a job storyboarding," Botan added. "We thought about it seriously, but I didn't want to miss the MangaXCon on Flower."

"I'm loading my cargo space with holo memories of immersives," Shadow declared, tapping on his thin-screen.

"Coals to Newcastle," Rayne said. "Why would you stock up on the one item that they produce locally?"

"Do you think that people who live on farms don't appreciate a change of diet?"

"I can't believe that you and Nigel have been successful in business," Delphi said, shielding her thin-screen card from her boyfriend as she made her cargo selections. "Neither of you have any commercial sense."

"Why can't I stock our pickles?" Botan asked Mouser. "I see a full line of Drazen Foods products, and every other brand I can think of, but no B&L Pickles."

"They're listed under Flower Foods as a specialty brand," Lisa told him, displaying the selection she'd made on her card.

"You guys are stocking up on your own pickles?" Hercules asked. "You're going to end up competing with each other to get rid of them."

"But we make a royalty on every jar."

"In the real world. This is a game."

"He has a point," Botan said with a sigh, tapping at his card to make a change. "I'm dropping my pickle allocation to ten percent."

"I take it you don't want to hear the rest of the Timble description," Mouser said.

"We've all been there," Rayne reminded him. "Unless... Kyor?"

"You've seen one Grenouthian production orbital, you've seen them all," the Huktra said. "When do we go on the clock?"

"There's more than one Grenouthian orbital producing immersives?" Hercules asked.

"There are probably a dozen. They specialize by species, and if you're ever traveling off the tunnel network and you need a safe place to hole up and repair your finances, they always have background work for aliens with a modicum of theatrical talent."

Mouser cleared his throat. "All of you spread a blanket and begin setting out your trade goods, with a limit of three categories of items to keep the game moving. Lisa, what are you displaying."

"Jarred pickles, six complete pickleball sets, and yoga mats."

"You're nuts," Shadow told her. "Nobody is going to want any of that stuff. I've never even heard of pickleball."

"It counts as a team sport on Flower," Rayne told him. "It's popular with members of the independent living cooperative. My mom plays it with her boyfriend."

Lisa stuck her tongue out at her brother.

"Hercules?" Mouser asked.

"I spread my blanket with hand tools," he said. "I guess I was thinking that we'd visit a lot of tech-ban worlds."

"Belle?"

"I set out twelve nanobot emergency home surgery kits, five used Humanese copies of the *All Species Cookbook*, the edition with the pop-up ads, and ten Earth smartphones, the ones with the good cameras that actors can use to make audition videos."

"No chocolate?"

"I stock chocolate for me, not to trade it away," Belle said. "If I wrote the rules for this game, whoever ends up with the most chocolate would win."

"Shadow?"

"Do I have to tell everybody?"

"They can't trade for what they can't see," Mouser reminded him.

"It's all gaming accessories," Shadow said. "Actors are always unemployed, so they play a lot of games."

"Delphi?"

"I display cans and jars of ethnic foods from Earth, the kind of stuff that's not easy to find out here, plus memory chits with the latest Earth music, and some street fashion stuff for girls, mainly hats and purses."

"Sounds like a sure winner," Mouser said, making a note on his gamemaster's tab. "Kyor?"

"Winter clothes for Humans, bicycle parts, and," the Huktra glanced at her thin Grenouthian tab again, "potted cacti."

"Potted what?" Shadow asked.

"Cacti, it's the Latin for cactuses," Delphi told him. "They're houseplants."

"I picked at random," Kyor told them.

Mouser shot the Huktra a curious look over his trifold, then shrugged and said, "Rayne?"

"I went with kitchen gadgets and place settings," Rayne said. "If I was moving to an alien orbital to try to find work in the immersives, I'd pack light and plan on buying household goods later if I could get a part."

"Botan?"

"Last place, as usual," Shadow needled his friend.

"I went with art supplies. It's what I know, and I won't mind getting stuck with them if they don't sell."

"I thought it was all barter," Lisa said.

"You barter with each other," Mouser told her. "You can also barter with civilians, but—"

"Civilians?" Rayne interrupted.

"That's apparently how Grenouthian traders refer to everybody who isn't a trader. If you sell for cash, you can use it to restock your inventory at the same wholesale rate you got when laying in your initial stock."

"We were paying cash?" Shadow asked. "I would have saved some if I knew that. I thought it was just stocking credits."

"Who needs instructions?" Delphi said, doing a fair impersonation of her boyfriend.

"All right, that's everybody," Mouser said. "The way this works from now on is that anybody who speaks up or who I ask a question goes on the clock until they're done speaking. Remember, your ultimate score will be divided by your cumulative time."

"Including table chatter?" Lisa asked in dismay. "Like, I can't tell my brother that he's doing it all wrong?"

"I'll ignore snarky remarks aimed at third parties that have nothing to do with the gameplay, but if you ever compete in a Grenouthian tournament, you'll be in trouble. Does anybody want to start, or should I—"

"I jump in front of a Human jogger," Kyor said. "Hey, Human. Buy a cactus."

"What do you do with it?" Mouser asked in one of his stock NPC voices with a little panting added for effect.

"You bring it home and talk to it. Ten creds."

"Does it talk back?"

"No, but it's a great listener. Just think how much you'll save over that therapist you see."

"How did you know I see a therapist?"

"You're a Human actor, aren't you?" Kyor countered. "And how much does the therapist charge?"

"I buy the cactus for ten creds," Mouser said and entered the transaction.

"The nursery on the ag deck sells them for one cred," Botan objected.

"The nursery doesn't have me," Kyor said. "I jump in front of another jogger."

"Hey!" Mouser said, trying his best to sound like a young woman. "Just because you have a big soft belly doesn't mean I want to run into it."

"You looked cold in that skimpy top. Couldn't you afford sleeves and some fabric to cover your abdomen?"

"It's a jogging top. Now, if you'll excuse me…"

"I bet you're cold in your cabin without any fur. I hear they keep the whole orbital at the same temperature because Humans were always playing with the thermostats."

Mouser exhaled loudly. "Now that you mention it, I do get cold in the evening."

"I have ugly Christmas sweaters," Kyor said. "Ten creds."

"They look warm," Mouser said, clearly wavering. "But ten creds."

"For two. Give one to your boyfriend and take a picture to make your friends jealous."

"I buy two ugly Christmas sweaters."

"Hey, you're buying everything she offers you," Shadow objected.

"I can't argue with her logic, and none of you are even trying," Mouser said. "And your chance has passed as the joggers all head for the showers to prepare for their workday."

"That's it?" Delphi asked. "We don't get a chance to trade again until lunch?"

"You can trade with each other. According to the gamemaster guide, that's where most of the decisive trades take place."

"I'll trade you bicycle parts for pickles," Kyor immediately offered Lisa. "Nobody is going to look at your pickles when Botan has them too, and Delphi is offering a full selection of ethnic foods. I'll give you four bicycle chains for the whole lot. They're dual-use technology."

"The bicycles I've seen only have one chain," Lisa said.

"I meant you can use them for bicycles or fighting. Haven't you ever trained with bicycle chains in a dojo?"

"Really?" Lisa grimaced, but the idea had struck her fancy. "I'll trade you a case of pickles for one chain. I don't want all four."

"Two cases," Kyor said immediately.

"What is it with you and doubling or halving the price? I'll give you one case plus four jars."

"Two cases."

"She's baiting you into talking, and every second lowers your final score," Shadow reminded his sister.

"Two cases," Lisa conceded. "At least I traded something."

Five

"Why not come with me?" Sabina asked her husband. "The visitors from Verlock academy worlds never cause trouble, and you haven't been off the Miklat in months."

Drake paused his struggle with the top button of his uniform shirt, one of the few tasks where dexterity of the fingers on his artificial arm fell short. "I'd have to change. The Verlocks might not take kindly to a visitor wandering around in a police uniform copied from twentieth-century Earth."

"Just take off the shirt and leave the hat. Uniform pants are generic, and it's going to be T-shirt weather. It's always T-shirt weather on Verlock worlds."

"I never worked one," Drake said. Undoing the buttons was easier than working them through the buttonholes, and he stripped off the shirt. "How much time do we have?"

"Kruik will hold the shuttle for me, but I don't like to abuse the privilege, so we should get going as soon as you're ready," Sabina said.

"Then why are we standing around?" Drake took off his police chief hat and sailed it at the hook on the wall, where it failed to catch and dropped to the floor. "It will still be there when we get back," he said philosophically as he followed his wife out of their cabin. "And why did I think that it was your sister's turn to go down to the planet this stop?"

"It is, but Katya has morning sickness."

They entered the lift tube, and the capsule started moving before either of them gave the destination. "And you want to compete. Now I understand what happened to all my jockey briefs."

"Boxer shorts are healthier," Sabina insisted. "My mother sent two dozen pairs in the diplomatic pouch and there wasn't enough room in your underwear drawer without getting rid of the old briefs."

Drake sighed. "Is your mother going to let us name our children when they come along, or is that another one of her ambassadorial powers?"

"If you think she's bad from a thousand light-years away, imagine living on the same space station. I swear she had the Stryx station librarian reporting to her on our movements."

"I can't even imagine growing up under a microscope like that."

"Well, I'm exaggerating for effect," Sabina said. "I'm trying to talk Katya into going to Corner Station to have the baby because the alternative is Mom coming here."

"Does your sister get a choice in the matter?" Drake asked.

Sabina thought for a moment, and then said, "No. Neither do we."

"Then that's something to look forward to."

The lift tube doors opened on Miklat's innermost cylindrical deck, and both the capsule's passengers unconsciously clicked their heels to activate built-in magnetic cleats before shuffling out. "There's Belle,"

Sabina said as the clone disappeared up the ramp into the shuttle. "She never misses visiting the stops."

"I imagine it's part of her job for Gem Intelligence," Drake said. "And didn't you say she has a reciprocal agreement with the intelligence agents on Flower?"

"Yeah, but I'm kind of surprised that more of the species haven't sent agents to join our ship, for the recruiting opportunities if nothing else. We stop at twice as many worlds as Flower each circuit, and we don't go back to the same stops every time the way she does."

"But the human populations on the worlds we visit number a tenth of the total that Flower reaches on half as many stops. It makes sense that the alien intelligence agencies would be more interested in the larger communities."

Sabina stopped abruptly at the foot of the ramp and gave her husband an incredulous look. "The alien intelligence agents aren't spying on us. They're spying through us."

"I don't get you," Drake said, nudging her to get started up the ramp. "Don't they recruit human agents to report on what other humans are doing?"

"Yes, we're like a secondary effect. Haven't you ever watched an old Earth movie where the hero figures out that trouble is coming because all the birds in the jungle have gone silent?"

"I take it we're the birds in this scenario."

"You can learn a lot about what aliens are up to by keeping track of how many of us they're hiring and what they have us doing," Sabina said as they entered the shuttle. "I want to sit with Belle and catch up."

"Am I invited, or is it a girls-only thing?" Drake asked.

"I was giving you navigation instructions. I'm not starting to sound like my mother, am I?"

"I don't know her well enough to say."

"Wrong answer," Sabina told him as she stopped at the row where the Gem clone had taken a seat. "Feel like company?"

"Co-captain Zerakova," Belle greeted her. "Chief Drake. I've been meaning to ask you both whether I need to change the way I address you now that you're married."

"She's stuck with Zerakova because I don't use a family name," Drake told Belle. "And plain 'Drake' without the 'Chief' works for me."

"You brought a carry-on," Sabina observed. "Are you planning on staying over?"

"We're only here for two days and I just woke up, so I won't be sleeping again until after we leave," Belle said. "I thought I'd try my hand at a little trading."

"What brought that on? I don't think I've ever met a Gem trader."

"The home office sent me some samples of nanobot products to rep. Now that our homeworld is moving away from the cloning economy, we need to ramp up our exports, and nanobot technology is the only product category where we can compete."

Drake finished strapping his safety harness into place and then leaned forward to address the clone. "I'd heard that the Gem fell behind the rest of the tunnel network in terms of technology, but you must still be tens of thousands of years ahead of us."

"The Human market is highly competitive because everybody is dumping their old technology on you," Belle explained. "The Old Gem Empire was so focused on cloning that we didn't generate surplus goods, other than the nanobots which were our only source of foreign exchange. It just doesn't make sense to build new factories to produce obsolete goods for the Human market."

"I never thought of it that way," Sabina spoke over Kruik's public address message that the shuttle was about to depart. "But how will that help you with marketing nanobots to the Verlocks? Isn't their technology millions of years in advance of yours?"

"I have little doubt that in their past, the Verlocks have manufactured nanobots far superior to anything we can produce. But the funny thing about technological advancement is that nobody bothers preserving obsolete tools and products because they no longer serve a purpose. I suppose they may have some old nanobots in museums or antique collections, but all the advanced species pride themselves on recycling."

Sabina thought this over for a moment before replying. "Maybe humanity hasn't been using complicated technologies for long enough to have run into that sort of obsolescence on a grand scale. I imagine that if we wanted to reproduce the tools and goods that existed a few hundred years ago, it would just be a question of searching through enough old books to find accurate descriptions."

"I suspect you're underrating craftsmanship," Drake said. "That kind of knowledge is often passed down in families and may never be committed to writing. You could probably produce a facsimile of ancient technologies based on incomplete records, but it might not be accurate."

"Both of you might be correct," Belle said. "In the case of the Verlocks, their record-keeping for the technological innovations of the last few million years might be good enough to reconstruct a past era, but that doesn't mean it would be economically efficient to do so. Take surgical nanobots," the clone continued. "The Verlocks have developed non-invasive surgical procedures using wave interference and manipulator fields, not to mention preventative medicine that allows them to avoid most situations that require corrective surgery. There's no reason for them to maintain a medical nanobot industry if there's next to no demand. And since my homeworld's industry focused on nanotechnology for tens of thousands of years, our products are inexpensive and rock solid, even if they aren't cutting edge."

"Why did the Gem invest so much time in nanotechnology?" Sabina asked.

"Because it's very useful in the cloning process."

"Is there any demand for your cloning talents on the tunnel network?" Drake asked. "I seem to remember that some of our food crops are produced entirely through cloning. Banana trees come to mind."

Belle grimaced, a facial expression that Gem and Humans shared in common. "Cloning is accepted in corners of agriculture, but any contribution we could make is seen as tainted by the fact that we used cloning for sentients. It's one of the instances where the advanced species put their principles ahead of profits."

"Do you have any experience trying to sell products?" Sabina asked.

"Does information count?"

Drake closed his eyes and drifted off as the Gem intelligence agent and his wife began a long dance of questions and answers that might have eventually ended in a trade. As soon as they exited the shuttle for the planet's surface, he regretted that he hadn't taken the time to change into shorts.

"I have to check in with the academy head," Sabina told him. "Do you want to come along, or should we meet somewhere for lunch."

"Is it going to take that long?" Drake asked. "I thought these visits were mainly formalities."

"You're forgetting how slowly Verlocks speak, especially if they aren't used to talking with aliens."

"Aren't there around thirty thousand people on this world?"

"That doesn't mean the academy head speaks with them," Sabina pointed out, and then shook her head. "I should have worn sandals."

"Let's get inside before we give our lungs a coating of volcanic dust," Drake said. "Is that a subway entrance?"

"They have them on every Verlock world," Sabina confirmed as they walked across the tarmac behind the Gem. "I think they've standardized as a species on levitated trains using magnetic monopoles."

"You'd think they'd have figured out escalators by now."

"Climbing up and down stairs is good for you, and the dust storms would probably ruin the machinery."

"There's a protective field over the subway entrance," Belle said over her shoulder. "You didn't feel it as we passed through?"

"I didn't, and I thought I was sensitive to electromagnetic fields from the years I spent working on Drazen worlds and Frunge habitats," Drake said.

"I thought you worked on Horten habitats," Sabina said.

"Those too."

Belle stopped to wait for them at the bottom of the stairs. "None of those species are anywhere near the

Verlocks in terms of field technology," she said. "The Grenouthians and the Verlocks are on a level of their own among the oxygen-breathing tunnel network members."

"Does anybody else come close?" Drake asked.

"The Huktra, maybe? But I'm not sure of their tunnel network status, and I can't get a straight answer out of Kyor for some reason."

"Here comes a train car," Sabina said, moving toward the platform. "I love public transportation on academy worlds."

Drake followed his wife and the clone onto the monorail car, and then it struck him that they were alone. "Where are the rest of the passengers from the shuttle?"

"You slept through the announcement," Sabina told him. "After dropping us here, the shuttle headed for the southern hemisphere, where there's a tropical resort with a permanent outdoor fair. It attracts a lot of independent traders from around the tunnel network."

"You didn't want to try your luck there?" he asked Belle.

"I have to stop in the academy, which is the closest thing to a government on this world, and register as a spy," the clone explained. "And we already sell plenty of turnkey nanobot solutions to independent traders for resale. It's the government and industrial markets I'm trying to open."

"Next stop, Dormitory," the train car's public address system announced in English.

"It must have heard us talking and adapted," Sabina said. "I wish trains everywhere did that."

"Smoothest riding maglev I've ever been on," Drake said as the car came to a halt. "The Frunge ones make me feel queasy."

"The Frunge like the rocking motion," Belle told him. "It's not a design flaw."

The rail car gathered speed again after a young Verlock shuffled on board and sat as far as possible from the three visitors. "Next stop, Academy," the PA announced.

"Why did they do it in English with a Verlock on board?" Drake asked.

"That wasn't English," Sabina told him. "Haven't you set your implant up to flash a message on your heads-up display when it's translating and blocking the source language at your auditory nerves?"

"It seemed like more trouble than it's worth."

The car soon came to another stop, and all four passengers disembarked. Sabina pointed at her implant for a moment and Drake assumed she was checking the public information channel, but then she nodded, and he realized that she was holding a subvoced conversation.

"The academy head is waiting for me, and you're welcome to come along, Belle. He said he hasn't met a Gem since your revolution and he's curious to see if you've changed."

The clone gripped her sample case and puffed three short breaths as if she was working herself up to an act of physical courage. "He can make a slide from my skin cells if he'll place an order for nanobots," she said.

The elevator took them deeper into the planet's crust, and Drake wished for the second time in ten minutes that he'd changed into shorts. When the doors opened at their destination level, he judged that the temperature was about the same as the sauna room in the Miklat's public baths, except it was a dry heat. A surprisingly slender Verlock with smooth skin was waiting for them.

"Sab – in – a?" the young alien asked.

"That's me," Sabina replied. "Do you work for the academy head?"

"Intern," the youngster said. "Follow – me."

It took the party from the Miklat at least twice as long to get to the academy head's office with the guidance of the slow-footed Verlock than it would have taken without, but Drake was impressed by both Sabina's patience and her subtle quizzing of the intern. By the time they were ushered into the older Verlock's presence, they'd learned that he had only been the academy head for a century and was still considered to be new on the job by some of the senior staff.

"Welcome – to – Nykest," the academy head said, shuffling forward to greet the guests. "I've – heard – good – things – about – the – Miklat. Will – any – Zarents – be – visiting?"

"I'm afraid they find extended stays in strong gravitational fields difficult, but First Engineer Miklat sends his greeting and invites you to visit his way," Sabina said. "This is my husband, Drake, who is the Miklat's chief of police, and Belle."

"I'm a games journalist for Gem Today and an intelligence agent," the clone said. "Do I need to register somewhere?"

"How – long – will – you – be – staying?" the academy head asked.

"Just until the Miklat departs. Another forty-two hours."

"No – registration – required." The Verlock turned ponderously to open a large cabinet and took out a chest that wouldn't have looked out of place on an old sailing ship. "I – have – something – to – show – you."

Sabina nudged her husband and winked at Belle. "Would it be a math puzzle?" she asked.

"How – did – you – guess?"

"It looked about the right size," she said, rather than telling him that the head of every academy world they'd stopped at had tried to sell her a math puzzle.

The Verlock took almost ten minutes to set out all the obsidian puzzle pieces, and then he used them to demonstrate a few simple calculations that went right over Drake's head. Whether or not she understood them, Sabina nodded along and made the appropriate comments, and although she managed to work the Human Empire into the conversation several times, their host failed to react.

"There," the academy head declared after completing a particularly tricky manipulation in which three-quarters of the puzzle pieces seemed to have vanished. "An – elegant – proof – of – the – multiverse."

"Could I see that again?" Belle asked. "There was a moment there when you were doing the partial differential integration that I lost track of your bounds."

"That's – what – makes – it – a – puzzle. If – you – take – it – home – I'm – sure – you'll – work – it – out."

"I wish I could afford such a functional work of art, but I know without asking that it's beyond my means. Unless..."

"Unless what?" Drake supplied the prompt when the Verlock took too long to respond.

"Unless a barter arrangement is possible," Belle said, balancing her sample case on the edge of the Verlock's desk and flipping down the side. "Have you ever used Gem nanobots?" She charged ahead with her pitch, removing one of the clear jars that might have come from a baby-food factory on Earth, except for the contents. "This one contains self-assembling measuring devices for those hard-to-reach places that are difficult to image."

"Interior – spaces?" the Verlock asked, clearly intrigued by the idea of generating data to crunch.

"Precisely. Cup your hands." She poured the silvery contents into the academy head's cupped hands, and the lack of leakage indicated that the nanobots were preferentially clinging to each other. "Go ahead, enclose them entirely."

"Interesting."

"Now. Hold still for five seconds, and then release the nanobots on the table.

The Verlock followed Belle's instructions, and the result was a metallic casting of the space that had been formed by his hands. "Now, here's the trick," the clone continued enthusiastically. She picked up the casting and placed it on top of the open jar, where it sat for a moment before the shape dissolved back into a metallic liquid, all of which clung together and refilled the container. Instead of replacing the lid, she tilted it toward the academy head and began tapping on the glass with a finger.

"Surprising!" the Verlock exclaimed as various diagrams and numeric notations appeared inscribed in the surface of the liquid. "Volume, longest – dimension, shortest – dimension, average – distance – from – implied – center – of – gravity. Can – it – measure – between – any – two – points?"

The clone winked and poured the nanobots out of the bottle again, and they immediately reassembled into the prior casting. "Touch the two points," she encouraged him.

The academy head studied the shape for a moment, looked at his own hands as if to calibrate, and then carefully poked the nanobots in two locations. Belle picked up the casting and put it back on top of the jar, and after the nanobots slumped back into place, a string of characters appeared engraved in the shimmering liquid.

"Twelve – decimal – place – accuracy," the Verlock said approvingly. "Even – trade?"

The clone smiled and handed over the lid of the jar. "You can recharge the nanobots in sunlight or with an infrared lamp, but they will become sluggish after a few hundred uses."

"Expected. If – I – want – to – order – more?"

"The product code is on the lid. I'm just a spy with a sample case, but my commercial sisters can provide any of our nanobot products in quantity."

While the Verlock showed Belle how to fit all the puzzle pieces back in their chest, Sabina took out her smartphone and began playing a game. Drake wondered if the heat had gotten to his wife and tried to get her attention, but she waved him off. Just as the Verlock closed the lid of the puzzle chest, a blue crystal rose out of Sabina's purse and levitated over the desk.

"Projection?" the academy head inquired.

"Projector," the Miklat's co-captain said. "Can you turn off the lights?"

"Off," the Verlock intoned, and except for the glow from the phone, the office was plunged into the sort of darkness that's only possible deep underground.

"I haven't had much opportunity to practice with this, but I thought you'd find it interesting," Sabina said. "I'm told that it displays gravitational distortions, starting with the immediate area, and then extending out into space for up to ten light-milliseconds, depending on the settings."

All of a sudden the room was filled with holographic grid lines, describing a sheet that appeared to be almost perfectly flat, though it seemed to jitter at a low frequency.

"Approximately – sixteen – cycles – per – second," the Verlock declared. "That's – expected – for – background – gravitational – waves – in – this – volume – of – the – galaxy."

Sabina tapped at her phone and moved a slider, and the grid lines grew denser and took on a slight hemispherical shape. A few small depressions or spikes became apparent, and the academy head nodded, apparently familiar with the local distortions. Sabina continued moving the slider, and the grid continued to morph. Then a slight mound formed and began slowly rippling across the projection.

"One – of – the – moons – passing – over," the Verlock said. "Impressive. Not – Human – technology."

"No, it's from the Farling Empire," Sabina said. "One of their species is very interested in gravitational mapping devices and is willing to sell them barely above cost to anyone who will share the data for scientific purposes."

"On," the Verlock said, and the room illumination returned to normal. "Cost?"

"Cost plus. I don't know anything about the technology, I'm just representing a friend, but my understanding is that the crystals contain a microscopic black hole and are very difficult to grow. Does a hundred and thirty thousand creds for a set of crystals sufficient to girdle a planet this size sound excessive?"

"Yes." After a long hesitation, the academy head added, "I – would – need – to – see – the – goods – and – warranty – information – before – paying."

Six

"Thanks for lunch," Shadow said, getting up and pushing in his chair. "I have to—"

"Sit," his sister interrupted him from the kitchen area. "There's a dessert."

"Is it healthy?"

"Sit," Lisa repeated, and this time her words carried a tone of command. "We have an announcement."

Shadow let out a theatrical sigh and looked to his girlfriend for support, but Delphi was sitting next to Botan and reading through the manga artist's latest episode.

"It's banana-carob bread," Botan told Shadow. "It almost tastes like chocolate."

"It tastes exactly like chocolate," Lisa corrected him as she set a plate with artfully arranged slices of the dessert bread on the table. She glanced at Botan, who nodded in return, took a deep breath, and said, "We're getting married."

"All of us?" Shadow asked hopefully.

"You wish," Delphi said without looking up from the manga. "Congratulations, but it's hardly a surprise."

"It will be to my family," Botan said. "We aren't telling them."

"Ever?"

"Not until the deed is done and I'm safely knocked up," Lisa said cheerfully. "One of Botan's manga subscribers from Earth sent him a copy of his biography that she found on a Japanese matchmaking site."

"Your family is hardcore," Shadow said in admiration. "If I told my folks I was marrying an alien, they'd be, like, 'I hope you'll both be very happy.' And then they'd go back to whatever game they were playing."

"Are you worried your parents will try to interfere?" Delphi asked Botan.

"It's more my grandparents," he said. "I still can't understand why they ever left Japan to move to Bits in the first place. They don't even like programming that much."

"How long have your parents been married?"

"Almost forty years, I guess. I came along pretty late."

"Is it possible that your grandparents left Earth because they didn't approve of whoever your parents were dating back in Japan?" Delphi asked.

"You think they arranged a marriage between my parents and then dragged them to Bits so they wouldn't have any choice?" Botan asked. He sat back as if stunned. "That would explain a lot. My parents never talked about how they met or ended up together."

"Yeah, I think that a private marriage makes sense," Shadow said, reaching for another piece of banana-carob bread. "I bet that one of the co-captains would do it for you on short notice. How complicated can it be? You just jump over a sword or something."

"He's thinking about that game with the sailing ships," Delphi explained, setting aside the proof sheets of manga and taking a slice of the dessert. "The one with all of the fighting."

"The fighting is the good part."

"We're going to have a real wedding, so we can send Botan's family a holographic recording," Lisa said. "You're going to be the best man."

"Me?" Shadow asked. "Are you inviting the folks?"

"No, because that would just set up a classic family feud," Botan said. "Besides, your parents stayed on Flower, and we don't want to wait until our next rendezvous."

"Do I have to wear a tux? You know that I hate—"

"You'll wear what I tell you," Lisa interrupted her brother again. "We're going to do it on the ag deck as soon as the cherry trees blossom."

"That's so romantic," Delphi said. "What can I do to help?"

"We're using a planner for everything because we're both so busy and we don't know what else to do with the royalties from the pickle business," Botan said. "She's a new student in Lisa's dojo."

"A Colony One lottery winner?" Shadow asked in dismay. "But they're on the other team."

"There's something deeply wrong with you," Lisa said. "Just because there are more Oners than Bitters living on the Miklat is no reason to start competing."

"They started it. The Oners are trying to arrange an election so they can take over the ship."

"Mouser is hoping that the Zarents approve making the mayor an elected position so he can lose and step down," Delphi explained. "Shadow is the only one who will be disappointed."

"Wait until they want to put in their own captain," Shadow said darkly. "They joined the Colony One movement to get a ship and the Miklat is still eighty-five percent empty. In a few years, instead of being outnumbered by two-to-one, we could be outnumbered by twenty-to-one."

"You're right," Lisa said sarcastically. "We should attack them now."

"If I learned one thing from playing war games since I was old enough to hold a controller, it's—"

"That you should quit while you're ahead," Delphi interrupted, getting up from the table. "Congratulations on the wedding plans, guys. Shadow will be there wearing whatever you rent if I have to get Kruik to send a bot to help dress him. I've got to get a container out of the hold to show some traders."

"I guess I do have to get back to work," Shadow said, following his girlfriend's lead. "The new office manager we hired gets on my case if I spend too long at lunch."

"But you own the business," Botan pointed out.

"Try explaining that to Ulah. She claims to be fluent in English, but she hears what she wants to hear."

Lisa sighed and shook her head after her brother and his girlfriend left. "Shadow never was good at games where the players have imperfect information," she said. "He just assumed that our wedding planner is a Oner and went off on a rant."

Botan laughed and gave her a one-armed hug. "I work as closely with the Zarents as anyone on board, except maybe Hercules and the co-captains, and they aren't going to give up control of the Miklat to anybody. It took them millions of years to get to this point, and I can almost sense their confidence growing from day to day."

"I'd take them more seriously if they'd developed martial arts," Lisa said. "Maybe they wouldn't have been stuck doing ship's maintenance work for the Wanderers all those years if they knew how to take a stand."

"It's tricky on a unicycle. Even First Agronomist Miklat sort of leans back and forth when he's trying to stay in one place."

"You know that's not what I mean."

"I was kidding," Botan said, shouldering his backpack. "The Zarents do have a form of martial arts, sort of, but it's Zero-G wrestling, and you wouldn't stand a chance unless you can grow a half-dozen tentacles."

"Are you going to be back late again?" Lisa asked, looking pointedly at the backpack. "It looks like you're bringing dinner."

"It's snacks. I'm in charge of the new apprentices this afternoon."

"First Agronomist Miklat has made you responsible for the Zarent apprentices? She must really trust you."

"I think she does, but in this case, the apprentices are human kids who think they want to pursue a career in agriculture," Botan said. "Rayne's daughter is one of them."

"Don't they have to be in school?"

"This counts as school. The eighth graders get two afternoons a week of vocational training."

"Sarah is in eighth grade already?" Lisa asked.

"Thanks," Botan said. "I'd forgotten her name. I'll be home at the usual time."

Lisa took her time cleaning up the dining area because she didn't have any students scheduled for the next hour and then she jogged to the dojo and started doing warm-up exercises for the second time that day. Just when she felt ready to go, a Frunge female wearing her hair vines in a tight bun entered the dojo.

"Fonz," Lisa greeted her. "You're early."

"Early is on time, and it's Fonzil," the alien corrected her. "If you don't pronounce the last syllable, it means a type of bacteria that forms in waste digesters at a sewage treatment plant."

"You studied sewage treatment in school?"

"Of course. Don't Human children learn all about what happens with their waste?"

"I don't think so," Lisa said. "Out of sight, out of mind."

The Frunge's hair vines paled. "I worry that I don't know enough about Humans to act as your wedding planner," she said, beginning a set of deep knee bends that produced audible creaks. "I only worked as a part-time assistant to a wedding planner back home, and I got the job because she's my third cousin."

"Whatever you come up with will be better than my plan to get married in the dojo."

"But you weren't serious about that. You were just making small talk with a new student."

"I was a hundred percent serious, and Botan had already agreed," Lisa said. "He just wants to get it on paper that we're married, and he cares more about the calligraphy than the ceremony."

Fonzil straightened up, then bent to touch her toes, followed by putting both of her hands flat on the floor, and then leaning forward and lifting her legs into a slow handstand. "That does set a pretty low bar, and I do need to get a business started if I'm going to remain on the Miklat for long."

"I thought you were on your post-school tour. Isn't that like a vacation?"

"Most Frunge my age would rather be in school than anywhere else, but I'm more of the hands-on type," Fonzil said, leaning a bit to the side as she lifted one of her hands to transition into a one-armed handstand. "I was always more of a sports type, but I'm not quick enough to compete at the professional level."

Lisa's jaw dropped as the Frunge flexed her base hand and pushed up so she was eventually balancing on just her index finger. "But you're so strong. Surely you could compete at something."

"We're all strong compared to Humans. And I could get faster with training, but my reaction time is just average. There's no way around that one, it's who I am." Fonzil shifted her handstand to the other hand, repeated the index finger trick, and then returned to her feet. "All set. I've been looking forward to this lesson since you told me what to expect."

"I can't fight Cayl style," Lisa cautioned her. "I just learned the basic forms they go through at slow speed in their warmups, though it's top speed for me."

"That's more than I've ever seen offered in a Frunge dojo. My sensei wasn't interested in alien martial arts, she said they were just a distraction at our level. It's impressive how many styles you know."

"It's a video game thing," Lisa said, settling into the wide starting stance of a Cayl warrior. "I had a good gig standing in for aliens in games so I learned as much as I could about their martial arts to make it more realistic. Then on Flower, I had the chance to train under a Drazen who had worked in a dojo on a Stryx station, so he'd picked up all sorts of styles."

Fonzil kept her eyes forward on the dojo's mirrored wall to copy Lisa's stance. "I always wanted to see more of the galaxy, so when I was in my last semester at school and I saw a story about the Miklat on the Grenouthian news, I decided to learn Humanese and try living here. So far, it's exceeded my expectations."

"How long have you been on board?" Lisa asked, bringing her hands together in the initial pose.

"Two weeks."

While Lisa and her student exhausted themselves with the Cayl warm-up routine, Botan was following First Agronomist Miklat around a freshly plowed patch on the ag deck while the Zarent explained what she wanted the apprentices to do.

"I've chosen the seedlings and plants so that the children will see rapid progress before they go out on their long vacation," the Zarent spoke through the pendant she wore. "The climate on this section of the deck is nearing the end of the spring planting season on your planet."

"We won't be starting anything from seed?" Botan asked.

"Just the lettuce, radishes, and beets, and you can start those next time the students come. I want to give them a head start on the other vegetables, so the students will have produce for a farmstand their final week."

"I can't help noticing that you refer to them as students rather than apprentices."

"Apprenticeship is a contractual arrangement that carries with it a deep commitment to a future path," First Agronomist Miklat explained. "It wouldn't be fair to ask the children of your species to indenture themselves to a Zarent master for the next century."

"I guess it wouldn't make sense from a longevity standpoint either," Botan acknowledged. "And you think that operating the farmstand is important?"

"Anybody can grow vegetables. Growing food in an economically and environmentally sustainable manner is the challenge on a spaceship." The Zarent wheeled her unicycle around at the sound of boisterous children exiting the nearby lift tube. "You have the deck, Mister Botan. Niney will bring a floater cart with your plants," she added before speeding off.

"Botan!" a young teenager shouted, waving vigorously with both hands before turning to her schoolmates and saying, "I told you guys that we'd be apprenticing with a human. We learn too slow for the Zarents."

A light-haired girl who was as tall as Botan pulled at the seat of her coveralls as she walked. "Do everybody else's clothes fit? Mine are too tight."

"You probably grew another three centimeters since we signed up last month," the sole boy in the group said. "Give me a few years and then we'll see who's taller."

"The gloves are too big for me," the last girl said, pinching a fingertip with her other hand to show that it was empty. Her jet-black hair fell to her waist, and Botan winced, realizing that it could drag in the dirt while she crouched to plant seeds.

"All right, students," he said. "I'm Botan, and I know Sarah through her mother. Why don't the rest of you introduce yourselves, and then we'll do some safety checks before we get started."

"Davu," the boy said, offering Botan a firm handshake. "Do we really need safety training to plant seeds? I mean, I think we're all old enough not to eat the dirt or drink the fertilizer."

"Greta," the tall girl said. "My coveralls are too tight."

"We'll get you a new pair," Botan said. "I just ordered the next size up from Kruik over my implant, and when the bot brings them, you can change in the tool shed."

"Mio," said the petite girl with the long hair. "My gloves are too big, and you don't look Chinese."

"I'm Japanese, and those gloves might be the smallest size. There's a selection of spares in the toolshed, so we can check."

"I'll go," she said and took off running for the blue plastic shed before Botan could tell her to wait. He was about to call her back, but then a four-armed bot carrying a pair of coveralls emerged from one of the maintenance tubes and zipped toward them at breakneck speed.

"Those are mine," Greta told the bot as it came to hover in front of Botan. The bot hesitated for a moment, then it turned and floated to the girl and handed over the coveralls, which were wrapped in a thin film.

"Go ahead and change," Botan told her. "There's a recycling bin in the shed for the wrapping."

"Is the bot going to help us plant?" Davu asked. "Can we ride it?"

"No and no. The Zarents are the only ones who ride bots, and they have a special saddle arrangement."

The bot chose this moment to zip back toward the maintenance tube, almost as if it had been listening to the conversation, and decided to leave before its status deteriorated from delivery boy to mount. Sarah waved after the bot as it moved off, and then she asked, "Can we plant tomato seeds? I love tomatoes."

"First Agronomist Miklat wants you to experience harvesting and selling your produce, so we'll start you off with nearly mature tomato plants," Botan said.

"I don't want to work in a store," Davu said. "That's retail."

"Farmstands aren't stores. They're really cool, and all of your friends will be jealous."

"I used to go to a farmstand on Flower's ag deck for salad stuff," Sarah said. "Everything was super fresh. The salad didn't need dressing."

"I found a smaller pair," Mio announced, returning with a pair of brown gloves on her hands. "There weren't any white ones."

"It's not a white-glove job," Botan told her. "We'll just wait for Greta and—wow, that was fast."

"I'm in a dance group and we do fast changes all the time," the girl explained. "These fit much better. Thank you."

"You can thank Kruik. He always listens in on this deck, so don't say anything that you don't want an ex-military Dollnick artificial intelligence to know."

"I talk to Kruik all the time," Greta said, and the three other adolescents all nodded. "He's great."

"All right then," Botan said. "The first rule on the ag decks is that safety always comes first. When you're using tools, always pay attention to the pointy end, and when you're working around a bot or a floater, don't assume that it knows you're there."

"But they do," Sarah protested. "Or Kruik does. He wouldn't let a robot or a floater run us down."

Botan shook his head. "You're thinking about it wrong. When everything is going to plan, safety is just a word. It's when things go wrong that safety can save you or your friends from injury. We're going to be planting in a prepared field today, but if we were going to use a mechanical tiller or thresh grains, I'd have brought you safety goggles."

"What if we were planting magic beans?" Sarah asked.

"Definitely safety googles," Botan said solemnly. "Magic beanstalks grow so quickly that you can get poked in the eye."

"They'd never catch up with Greta," Davu said.

A faint beeping sound began somewhere over the deck horizon as Davu dodged a half-hearted swing from the gangly young woman. The beeping rapidly became louder, and a floating mass of vegetation appeared in the distance. As it drew closer, it resolved into a farm floater carrying plants and seedlings piloted by a young Zarent.

"Hey, Niney," Botan greeted the furry little alien riding in the pilot's saddle. "Everybody, this is Ninth Apprentice Miklat, who's studying agronomy. Niney, this is Sarah, Davu, Greta, and Mio."

"Pleased to meet you all," the octopus-like alien spoke through its translation pendant. "Will you be unloading the floater now? I could return for it later."

"We can unload it now. Come on, kids. Let's get all of those plants and seedlings on the ground and try to keep like with like. It's as good a way as any to find out if you have an eye for plants."

"I'll do the tomatoes," Sarah volunteered. "They're easy to tell apart from—what are those?"

"Peppers," Botan told her. "And let's try to unload the floater evenly. Two of you can work from each side and I'll take the front."

"Are you worried that an uneven load could cause the floater to tip it over?" Davu asked.

Before Shadow could answer, Niney let out a buzzing sound of amusement. "You could all stand on one edge of the floater and it wouldn't dip any lower," the little Zarent said. "But keeping an even keel requires more power, so it would be inefficient."

"The Zarents are big fans of efficiency," Botan told them. He started a timer on the smartphone he had strapped in a forearm bracer and said, "I estimate we can get everything unloaded in twelve minutes, but don't hurry so much that you knock things over before we have a chance to plant them in the dirt."

"Don't we have to take the seedlings out of the pots first?" Greta asked as she began removing pepper plants and placing them on the prepared field.

"Those pots aren't just biodegradable. They're made from compressed compost, and they'll provide all of the fertilizer that the plants need."

"We're handling poo?"

"Compost isn't poo," Davu told her. "It's peels and stuff that people didn't eat."

"Cow manure is good for plants," Mio said. "Back on Earth, they sold it in bags."

"Enough poo talk," Botan said, trying to remember if he'd had similar conversations when he was that age. Since the only fresh produce on Bits was grown hydroponically, he thought it was unlikely. "And move the plants a little further away from the floater or you won't have anywhere to stand before it's half unloaded."

The twelve-minute estimate proved optimistic, but in just under twenty minutes, the little Zarent was able to spin the empty floater around and head back up the circumference of the ag deck. The kids looked a little daunted by the amount of work ahead of them and Botan had to suppress a laugh.

"What?" Sarah asked. "Why are you grinning like that?"

"Because you all look like you think you're going to be here planting this lot for the next three days," he said.

"You'll have it done in three hours, and most of the time will be spent walking back and forth to get new plants. But we don't want to trample down all this freshly plowed soil by moving around at random, so even though this will be a mixed vegetable plot with variable row spacing, it will still have rows. To make it easy, we'll start at the side closer to the tool shed and plant a row of tomatoes—"

"Yay," Sarah interjected.

"—and then we'll work our way back in this direction. So everybody take a tomato plant, a gardening trowel, and follow me."

Botan's time estimate proved too conservative the second time around, mainly because the kids made the snacks and drinks he'd brought disappear about ten times faster than he'd expected. Once all the plants and seedlings were in the ground, he showed the kids how to attach a programmable sprinkler head to the nearest post.

"We use different methods of irrigation on the ag decks depending on what we're growing," Botan told them as he skimmed down the control pad to the setting for newly transplanted seedlings. "Vegetables and other short-lived crops are watered with programmable sprinklers, while we use semi-permanent drip irrigation tubing for trees and bushes. Because the ship is a closed system and all the water is eventually recovered, it's a question of what works best, rather than conservation."

"Poo water too?" Davu asked.

"Let's not go there," Botan said with a sigh. He activated the sprinkler, and it began shooting out high, tight streams of water that turned into droplets as they descended on the plants. "It might not look that complicated, but running a sprinkler in a centrifuge is trickier than you might think."

"Because there's no real gravity," Mio said as she struggled to remove her gloves. "How come the water doesn't just keep going up until it hits the ceiling?"

"I'm not a physics guy, but the way it was explained to me, everything in the ship becomes part of the system, including the air. Even though the water stream doesn't have gravity dragging it back toward the outside of the cylinder, it doesn't escape the centrifugal effect just because it comes out of the sprinkler, unless maybe you aim in exactly the wrong direction. The sprinkler programming takes care of all of that, but be careful if you ever try to use a hose because the water might not go where you expect."

Seven

Hercules tipped up the reading glasses that had become as much an affectation as a visual aid when a dozen foremen, most of whom he recognized as Colony One members and a few of whom he knew by name, crowded into the breakroom. "Is this a mutiny?" he asked mildly.

A tall man in his early fifties stumbled forward and then turned to glare at whoever had pushed him before replying to Hercules. "There was an election and I've been chosen to represent the renovation crews," Darryl said.

"Then why are you coming to me?" Hercules asked. "We all work for the Zarents, and I'm sure that First Engineer Miklat would—"

"No," a different man interrupted. "We aren't here to complain or anything like that. Just to clarify a few things."

"Darryl?"

The tall man cleared his throat self-consciously. "The thing is, all of us, I mean, the foremen here in the room, worked in construction back on Earth. We know enough to realize that when it comes to the real alien stuff, we're just following instructions, and that's okay. But the cabin customizations for humans are right up our alley, and we think we should have more input."

Hercules set aside the tab with the spreadsheet he'd been studying and rose to his feet because he felt awkward being the only one in the room who was seated. "The

Zarents want us to experiment with the cabins, which is why we aren't doing them all the same. You're welcome to try any customization within reason providing you can do it with the available materials in the allotted time."

"That's not what our corridor foreman says," a different man replied. "My crew did a few kitchens without the island, just to give whoever is cooking a little more room to move around. There's plenty of counter space, but he accused us of cutting corners and said he wouldn't sign off on the cabins until we put the islands back."

"Who was that?" Hercules asked.

"Captain Crunch. One of your lot."

"You mean, he's from Bits."

"All of the corridor foremen are from Bits," Darryl said. "Some of us have been working on the Miklat for a year now, but there seems to be a glass ceiling for Colony One guys."

"I never even thought about it," Hercules admitted. "When you guys joined the ship, First Engineer Miklat asked me to pick some guys to be corridor foremen for the new crews, so I went with the ones who had a track record." He picked up the tab and brandished it as a sort of display. "If you haven't figured it out yet, I'm just a figurehead for the human workers. The Zarents send apprentices out to inspect all the work that's been done, and then they send me these reports that make it clear who is doing a good job versus—" he paused for a moment, "—just average. I think the reason they insist that crews change members after every completed job is that lets them spot the weak links."

"So why didn't you promote any of us who have been working the last year when the new lottery winners joined the ship?"

"The spreadsheet gives all the workers an overall quality rating based on the inspection scores from the crews they've been on, and to choose the new corridor foremen, I combined that with experience. Since some of the original guys from Bits have been working renovations for twice as long as any of you, they ended up at the top of the sort. It just didn't occur to me that I was being unfair." Hercules thought for a moment. "I don't want to start taking corridors away from guys for the sake of swapping some of you in, but we'll be starting on the next deck in a few weeks, and those cabins are in much worse shape than what we've been dealing with here. I'll need to run this past First Engineer Miklat, but I think it would make sense to cut the number of cabins each corridor foreman is responsible for in half."

"You're going to have layoffs?" asked a short woman who Hercules hadn't noticed because she was standing behind a taller man. "We told Colony One that there's enough work for another twenty-five thousand people, and they're planning another lottery."

"He's saying that he'll double the number of corridor foremen and give all the new jobs to us," Darryl told her and turned back to Hercules. "Did I get that right?"

"That's the plan, but like I said, I have to run it by the boss. And as long as you're all here, I should give you a quick tour of the next deck so you'll know what you're letting yourselves in for. The Wanderers drew members from all over the galaxy, not just tunnel network species. The last species that lived there converted the deck into a sort of hive, and it's been abandoned ever since because it was just too much work to restore it to something that worked for humanoids."

While Hercules was showing the foremen around the abandoned deck, Mouser was entertaining a different delegation from Colony One in his electronics repair booth at the bazaar. The leader of the delegation, a woman whose copper-colored hair was brighter than any transformer winding, was clearly having difficulty believing the current mayor's ambivalence about reelection.

"But it's one of the top jobs a human could have—anywhere," she argued as if her mission was to convince Mouser to stay in place rather than to replace him. "There's the First Administrator of the Human Empire," she folded down the finger of one hand, "the—I can't think of anybody else. You have the second-best government job in space."

Mouser choked while swallowing and almost spit up a mouthful of the take-out coffee that the delegation had brought him as a consolation for taking up what the leader had called, 'His valuable time.' While he was struggling to breathe, the delegation's secretary, who was wearing a fancy Frunge business suit that practically screamed 'Lawyer' produced a tab and began reading off bullet items.

"First," the man said, "We've scheduled primary elections to choose our candidate. The Zarents agreed that it was the best way to proceed."

"They did?" Mouser asked in surprise.

"Third Educator Miklat might have said that we were free to do whatever we want, but the context was clear."

Mouser restrained himself from asking why the Oners would have approached the Third Educator to discuss electioneering and instead made a noncommittal sound that he hoped the lawyer would interpret as an invitation to continue.

"Second, our chosen candidate and his or her supporters will canvas the inhabitants of the Miklat explaining the Colony One platform and seeking their support."

"Makes sense to me," Mouser said, which was exactly the opposite of what he was thinking.

"Third," the lawyer continued, "there will be a series of debates in which the current mayor," he lifted his chin in Mouser's direction, "and our candidate will discuss the issues. We came to you today to negotiate how to choose the moderator or a series of moderators, and the rules for each debate. A three-debate series is the norm in the Colony One movement, where the first debate is based on a slate of pre-agreed topics, the second debate takes questions from the audience, and the third debate is a free-form affair in which the candidates pose questions directly to each other."

"You expect me to debate your candidate?"

"Of course," the woman said. "Elections are a serious matter. I understand that you were appointed to the position based on your previous leadership of the Bits community, and however you ran that planet is your business, but—"

"I didn't run it at all," Mouser objected. "Bits was an anarchy."

"The way I heard it, you negotiated the deal to abandon the planet and move the entire community to Flower."

"We abandoned the planet because the Horten landlord gave us our walking papers, and the only reason I was in charge of our last big product push was that Flower's representative in the matter was Dewey, an artificial person created on Bits. He chose to work with me because we'd been friends."

"Artificial intelligence nepotism?" one of the other members of the delegation asked.

Mouser sighed. "Look. I know you have a hard time believing this, but I'm perfectly happy with the idea of one of you replacing me as mayor. Work it out among yourselves however you want, and as long as the Zarents approve—"

"But that's just it, isn't it," the lawyer interrupted. "You're confident that the Zarents won't approve."

"I think you're all stuck on the title when the real job is running the department of complaints. And since I don't have any power, I can't do anything about the complaints, other than recommend that people take it up with the Zarents if they think it's that important, which they never do."

"That's exactly what's wrong about living on the Miklat," the first woman said. "We don't have any representation. If you elect me as mayor—"

"Save it for the stump, Mattie," the lawyer cut her off. "I joined the Miklat with the first batch of Colony One lottery winners," he continued, "so I've had a year to get a feel for how things work on board. Your friend Rayne assigns booths in the bazaar according to whim or favoritism and refuses to maintain a documentation trail or give me access to her correspondence related to my clients. Her husband, Hercules, runs the ship's renovation crews like some sort of Roman dictator, and you sit like a spider on that high stool pulling all of the threads of the web while protesting that the Zarents are the ones who are running the show. If there was a single court of law on board, I'd have you up before the judge."

Mouser set aside the coffee, which hadn't been hot when it arrived and was now cold, and regarded the lawyer in amusement. "I was born on Earth, but I left more than forty years ago, and I don't remember much about it," he said. "I can't tell you what to think, but I can state what I know to be facts. Every human on this ship is a guest of the Zarents. They could tell us all to get off at the next planet or insist that we all work sixteen hours a day swabbing the decks if we want to remain on board. Nobody is going to stop you from building a local human government if it makes you happy, but unless you feel you need the practice, I don't see the point."

"You're just afraid to debate," one of the delegation members said, and several of the others murmured their agreement.

"Fine," Mouser growled in frustration. "You want a debate, we'll have a debate." He held up his index finger. "One debate, not three. I don't care who you get to moderate as long as you choose an alien or an artificial intelligence. That way we won't have any arguments about loyalty to Colony One or Bits. In return, I don't want to hear about elections from any of you again, unless it's to tell me the date and time for the debate."

"We have to negotiate that," the lawyer said.

"I'm a big boy and I'm used to waking up at odd times. Whatever you choose is fine by me."

"And the audience," the delegation head said. "A third from Bits, two-thirds from Colony One, to mirror our populations?"

"This isn't going to end, is it," Mouser said in frustration. "Can I delegate somebody to negotiate with you?"

"If you'd done that two weeks ago when I first contacted you we wouldn't be having this conversation now," the lawyer said smugly. He produced a card and said, "Have your representative contact me, by the end of the week if you don't want another visit."

Mouser was still holding the card and muttering to himself when a scaly pair of hands with the claws retracted set a large glass box on the workbench in front of him. "Is this a bad time?" the Huktra asked in her growly English.

"Kyor," Mouser greeted her, brightening up immediately. "I'm glad you took the time to stop by and talk Game Theory. Did you just find the popcorn machine here in the bazaar? It looks like an antique."

"I bought it from a traveling salesman who guaranteed it would double my beer sales at Club Ucerin. An antique popcorn machine for an ancient species—I thought it would be a good fit. But the heat lamp barely came on, and my beer sign started to flicker, so I shut it down."

"Sounds like a voltage mismatch," Mouser told her, opening the glass door and sticking his head inside. "I don't smell any burnt insulation, so that's a good sign. When was this?"

"The last day we were stopped at Farling Four," Kyor said. "I found out from Kruik that the salesman left for the surface on the last shuttle out immediately after selling me the machine."

"He would have to be desperate to cheat a dragon variant, and the machine looks like it was cared for, though why anybody would be traveling with one is beyond me. I see an aluminum kettle with a built-in heating element, a stirrer, a heating deck, and an infrared light to keep the popped kernels warm. We had a similar model on Bits in the main gaming hall."

"I plugged it into the transformer that came with a neon 'Cold Draft' sign I bought on Earth when we stopped there. It had a spare outlet."

Mouser turned the machine around and checked the nameplate. "Sixteen-ounce popper, 230V—where did you buy the neon sign?"

"Manhattan," Kyor said. "At a gallery going-out-of-business sale."

"And this plug fit into the same transformer?"

"I had to modify it with paperclips."

"It's possible you damaged the transformer, but the popcorn machine should be okay, it was just trying to run on less power than it requires. This machine should be on its own circuit in any case, so I'll bring you a Dollnick transformer from my workshop later. I don't keep any here because it never comes up."

"With all of the legacy gaming electronics you repair?" Kyor asked.

"Almost all of that stuff has switching power supplies that automatically adapt to a decent range of input voltage," Mouser explained. "They still need a universal Dollnick transformer to plug into the ship's power grid because the frequency and the voltage are both higher."

"Good. That will save me having to hunt down the salesman next time we return to Farling Four."

"Was the machine that expensive that it would be worth your effort just to get a refund?"

Kyor bared her wicked-looking teeth. "Who said anything about a refund."

Mouser felt a sudden chill which had nothing to do with the temperature on the bazaar deck. "Were you just here for the repair, or do you have time to talk Game Theory?"

"I was killing two plump cattle with one stone, as Humans say," the Huktra replied. She crouched on her haunches in a sitting position, which brought her eyes closer to Mouser's level. "But before we begin, I need to clarify a language issue. I was reading up on Human science and I was struck by the number of prominent theories, which makes me wonder if we're using the word the same way. In Huktra, a theory is an experimentally backed system of ideas developed in response to a hypothesis for explaining some phenomena or state."

"That sounds about the same as what we mean."

"And once a theory is proven, it becomes a scientific law."

"I'm not sure that's always the case," Mouser said. "Maybe for a narrow set of equations that can be completely solved, but theories often address much larger systems where a complete proof isn't possible."

"At this level of your development," Kyor added.

"I suppose that's true, but Game Theory—"

"Game Law," the Huktra interrupted.

"Are you sure?" Mouser asked. "It gets into some pretty esoteric stuff, and I'm only familiar with the aspects that come up in games we play, as opposed to, say, evolutionary biology."

"I don't think that Game Law, or Game Theory in your case, is the best tool to examine evolutionary biology. My reading in your sciences to date indicates that your species attempts to overfit every new mathematical tool that comes along to problems where it doesn't apply. Or as my clutch-mate used to say, 'If the only tool you have is a rock, everything looks like a shellfish.'"

"We have that saying with a hammer and a nail."

"I wouldn't be surprised if Myort came up with it during one of his earlier visits to your planet," Kyor said. "Game Law is used to determine the best move when playing games where the players have imperfect information."

"Right," Mouser said. "And what's surprising is how often a player's dominant strategy turns out to lead to a worse outcome than would have been produced through cooperation."

"Why is that surprising to you? Cooperation always leads to the best outcome. It's one of the bedrock principles of the tunnel network."

"Now you're talking about a system with room for iterations where players can learn what's best over the long run. Game Theory only applies when—"

"What if you have a two-player game and what the first player does has no impact on the best response for the opponent?" Kyor cut him off.

"That's what we call the Nash Equilibrium," Mouser said. "It also comes up more frequently than you might expect."

The dragon variant snaked her head a little closer and looked directly into Mouser's eyes. "Did you ask Kruik to translate Huktra Game Law for you?"

"No, and I'm sure I wouldn't understand it if he did."

"What an amazing case of language echo," Kyor said. "Unless Myort was wandering around Earth a century or two ago and whispering about Game Law in the ears of some selected Humans. I can't explain it otherwise."

"Explain what?" Mouser asked.

"When a player's best move is independent of what his opponent does, the opponent gnashes his teeth. That's where the name comes from, Gnash Equilibrium."

"I'm pretty sure that in Game Theory, Nash is the name of the mathematician who discovered the rule. It sounds like you're talking about gnash with a silent 'G.'"

"Maybe your mathematician changed his name after the fact," Kyor countered. "With all the names that Humans have, who can keep track?"

"What do you call the Prisoner's Dilemma?" Mouser asked.

"Are they a music group?"

"We use it to describe a situation where there are two players who would attain the best outcome for both of them by cooperating, but lacking knowledge of each other's action, the safe move produces an inferior result."

"A failure to cooperate will always produce an inferior result, but what does it have to do with prisoners?" Kyor asked.

"Say that you and another Huktra were arrested on suspicion of being spies while visiting Farling Four, and G32FX locked you in separate cells."

"I register as an intelligence agent as soon as I land."

"You're a spy?" Mouser asked in surprise. "I don't think anybody told me."

"It's a side gig, and don't feel you have to spread it around," Kyor said.

"Well, say you and the other Huktra spy didn't register, and G32FX offered each of you a deal. Testify against the other and receive a short prison sentence. Now, if you kept your maws shut, the Farlings can't prove you're spies, and sooner or later they'll set you free. But if your partner agrees to testify against you first, they can execute you as a spy."

Kyor puffed out an angry ball of flame. "First," she said, "Huktra would never sell each other out, even for a profit.

Second, the Farlings don't have prisons. And most importantly, nobody executes spies during peacetime. We'd just pay a penalty and go on our way."

"Okay, okay, forget about Huktra and Farlings. Same deal, but it's humans on Earth, they're burglars, not spies, and execution is off the table. If they keep their mouths shut, they both get a one-year sentence, but if one of them breaks and informs on his partner, he'll walk free while the other guy gets five years. But if they both inform on each other, they'll each get three years, and—"

"Who makes up these scenarios?" Kyor demanded.

"They're not intended to be realistic," Mouser explained. "But the Prisoner's Dilemma is a useful tool for describing situations that come up in games where the players have imperfect information."

"I'm beginning to understand why it's just a theory."

Mouser took a deep breath and tried again. "So how would Huktra Game Law deal with the Prisoner's Dilemma?"

"It doesn't have to because it wouldn't come up," Kyor said. "A more realistic scenario would involve much larger numbers of players, all of whom would gain some sort of benefit by being the first to move against the others. But who would want to be a participant in a society that functioned that way? The fundamental equation of Game Law is that cooperation always leads to the best outcome for everyone."

"But you're completely ignoring the Reward Function for the individual!"

"Maybe that's why Human scientists apply Game Theory to your evolutionary biology," the Huktra mused. "You have selfish genes."

"That's just an expression, and competition in evolution is hardly unique to humans or Earth," Mouser protested. "Where do you think you got the compound wings, retractable talons, and flamethrower breath?"

"Who remembers back that far? The point is, we're an advanced species now, and members of advanced species understand that what benefits the group ultimately benefits the individual with a much bigger payoff than the individuals could hope to achieve on their own. That's how we all made the sacrifices necessary to develop interstellar drive. It takes a unified planet to make that kind of investment, you know."

"We sort of skipped that part. The Stryx let us on the tunnel network early."

"Sorry, I forgot."

Eight

"What's she doing?" Nigel whispered to Shadow as they watched their office manager, who was wearing a virtual reality headset and controllers on all four wrists and moving around the testing room in a flurry of motion.

"Beating my high score," Shadow said glumly. "Ulah thought it would be important to master *Rescue Dig* to understand what everybody was talking about. I helped her load the Dollnick version from the library so she could use all four hands. She's killing me."

"You have to admit that the office is running smoother than it did before we hired her."

"I've been thinking about that, and my high score is more important."

Nigel clucked his tongue in disapproval. "So much for you being the practical one in this partnership. I think Ulah is the perfect office manager, and now I won't have to worry about you running ReVisor based on your gut instincts when my cousin drags me off to Flower for a month to run a conference for the Human Empire about Galactic Historical Sites and Preserves."

"When is that going to be again?" Shadow asked.

"Vivian is still working on the date, but she said something about doing it when their school for government employees is out on vacation, so maybe next summer? It will be around when Katya is expecting, and her mother would probably like an excuse to spend some time around Human Empire headquarters on Flower."

"We should work up a special version of *Rescue Dig* for you to demonstrate at the conference. Maybe even give out free copies with virtual reality headsets if Flower will sell them to us cheap enough."

"I'm not sure that Vivian and Samuel would appreciate my mixing business with educating the future bureaucrats of the Human Empire about xenoarchaeology," Nigel said.

"That's where you're wrong," a whistle-y voice cut in, and the two men turned to see that Ulah had removed the visor, which she was holding out to Shadow. "One million and one," she continued. "I intended to stop on a million even, but sometimes my lower hands get ahead of my brain when I'm playing games."

"I can beat a million and one," Shadow said immediately. "I think."

"No altering the code," the Dollnick warned, her alien face taking on the now-recognizable expression it assumed when she was laying down the law to the human staff not cleaning up after themselves. "I finished scripting a configuration change control system and I'll know if you cheat. I still can't believe you've been shipping product for a year without having a system in place. How are the tech support people supposed to know what they're supporting?"

"Version numbers. We outsource all of that to Bits Away for a percentage, so it's not our problem."

Ulah let out a disappointed whistle. "That's the wrong attitude to take to anything, and your version numbers don't agree with the date codes. Until I started working here, a team would update a module they owned and push it out to customers without making sure that all the other teams installed it. You had programmers doing development on different versions of the software at the same time. I'd never seen anything so primitive."

"But it's all fixed now?" Nigel asked hopefully.

"Until the next time one of your hackers thinks they know better than I do and finds a workaround. I wouldn't have expected a bunch of gaming fanatics to have so much trouble following instructions."

"ReVisor is supposed to be a fun place to work," Shadow told her. "It's in our recruitment materials, and on the T-shirts that my friend Botan designed for us."

"You mean the humanoid figure with the little body and the huge head wearing a virtual reality visor?" Ulah asked. "I've filed for a tunnel network trademark on it."

"It's kind of unique to our products," Nigel said. "Do you think somebody would have copied it?"

The Dollnick began stripping off her wrist controllers with her upper right hand while taking out her tab from the belt pouch she wore on her left side and swiping it to life. She brought up a screen that was split into sixteen cells, all of them showing variations on a humanoid with a small body and a large head wearing some sort of gear or another.

Shadow felt his eyes bulge. "That many people have copied us already? Botan is going to be steamed."

"Not people," Ulah said. "And they haven't copied you, look closer." She handed over the tab and kept on talking. "Those are from the basic search I did before filing for the trademark. The most recent of them is the Drazen figure wearing the spectrometer visor that was a big hit with their miners around twenty thousand years ago, and the oldest one is a Verlock with what appears to be a personal planetarium viewer. All the trademarks have been allowed to expire because the products were eventually replaced with superior technology, but I think you get my point."

"It's tough to do anything original in a galaxy where sentients have been creating art for hundreds of millions of years," Nigel said, nodding in acknowledgment. "Thank you for filing the trademark, Ulah. We should have thought of it."

"It's my job as office manager to protect the assets of the business, and that includes its key employees. I'm concerned about your diets."

"Oh, no," Shadow said, backing away and making a cross with his index fingers as if to ward off a vampire. "Is this some sort of Dollnick thing, and now you're going to turn into Flower with all of the helpful health hints and the drill-sergeant approach to exercise? I already have a girlfriend and a mother. I don't need anybody else telling me how to live."

"I'm just pointing out that the consumption of soda and salty snacks in this office is almost triple what would be expected for the number of individuals working here," Ulah said. "If we just removed the free vending machines from the breakroom—"

"No," Shadow cut her off. "N. O. No. I'll be in my cubicle figuring out how to break a million and one points if you need me for anything." He handed Nigel the tab and stormed off, leaving his partner and the Dollnick office manager looking after him in surprise.

"I probably should have pretended it was harder to beat his score," Ulah eventually said.

"Don't worry about that," Nigel told her. "It's the vending machines comment that got him upset. All of the hackers from Bits are whacky about soda and chips. They claim it's part of their cultural heritage."

"It would explain quite a bit about your lack of longevity. Swipe down a screen."

Nigel advanced past the grid of former trademarked branding featuring small humanoids with big headgear and found himself looking at a detailed schedule for the Human Empire's xenoarchaeology conference. "Did my cousin send this to ReVisor?" he asked. "Vivian is usually more careful about security."

"It's not from the Human Empire," Ulah told him. "I made this up in my spare time. You can treat it as a template and modify any of the topics as you see fit."

"This is a lot better than anything I would have come up with," he said after taking a couple of minutes to carefully read through the schedule. "I thought you just got out of school. Where did you learn about how to organize a conference?"

"Kruik helped me. Dollnicks don't require as much sleep as Humans, and learning about how your people organize educational conferences gave me something to do in my spare time. There's an option on the next screen for awarding the participants with certificates if you think the Human Empire will go in for that sort of thing."

"What I'm not sure they'll go for is the three demonstration sessions you put in for ReVisor. The point of the conference is to educate our future bureaucrats and representatives from Earth and the sovereign human communities about our responsibilities and obligations should we ever colonize planets on our own."

"Shadow was right," Ulah said. "We're talking about the tunnel network, and it wouldn't exist without business. The sooner your bureaucrats understand that their primary job is to facilitate Human business, the better."

"Is that really how the Dollnicks see the galaxy?" Nigel asked.

"Do you think that we joined the tunnel network because we were lonely? The tunnel network is just a bigger and better version of your Conference of Sovereign Human Communities. Kruik told me that Humans have some fanciful ideas about running an empire, but he said I'd have to figure it out for myself. I think I'm beginning to see what he meant."

Nigel filed away that debate for another time and instead asked, "Where did you learn about Galactic Historical Sites and Preserves? This is as good a summary as I've seen."

"Oh, that's all part of our basic education," Ulah said. "We spent a few days going through the rules, and there were several holographic tours for students with an interest in digging deeper. I went through a xenoarchaeology phase before my crest grew in."

"And you remembered it all?" Nigel asked.

"What would be the point of putting in the time to study something and then forgetting it?" the Dollnick countered. "I didn't go to school to keep my teachers entertained."

A recent programming hire entered the test room with her head down studying something on her tab and almost ran into Nigel. "Good morning, Boss," she said to Nigel and then turned to the office manager. "Morning, Mom. Did my new jacket come in?"

"Yes, but the waist was too loose for you, so I had to take it in," Ulah said.

"You're the best, Mom. I should have listened to you and ordered the other one."

"Can you send me this, uh, template, so I can make a few changes and forward it to Human Empire headquarters?" Nigel asked the Dollnick.

"I already did," Ulah said. "You'll see the file in the top right corner when you activate your display desk."

Nigel handed back the tab and headed for his cubicle, acknowledging the greetings of a few more programmers who were straggling into the office at their usual time. Before he got a chance to access his display desk, somebody rapped on the frame of the cubicle panel at the entrance.

"Come in," Nigel said, looking up to see the head of the team working on the new product for the next-generation visors that Flower was now manufacturing based on the design that was still in use when the Stryx opened Earth. "Is there a problem with the resolution of the Verlock dig imagery I supplied?"

Caitlyn seemed taken aback by the question. "No, there's no problem, and I'm not even sure there's a resolution. That Verlock imagery is like fractals, the further you zoom in, the more you get. My holographic reconstruction guy, Klint, thinks it might go down to the atomic level."

"Wouldn't that require an infinite amount of storage space?"

"Not infinite, and the Verlocks are extremely good at data compression," Caitlyn said. "I just had a question about the life-like avatars. We were playing the prototype and it's really weird seeing the sweat dripping down the faces of the other players in virtual reality, but nobody ever wipes it off or gets stains in the armpits."

"I remember constantly drinking water on that dig, but not sweating much," Nigel told her. "The air was so dry that it would have evaporated right away. Are you taking humidity into account in the model?"

Caitlyn frowned. "That's the environmental team's rice bowl, I'll have to check with them. Then there's the whole bleeding thing."

"Do you mean like color bleeding in virtual reality? I don't know anything about the technology."

"Blood bleeding, like regular games. Didn't you ever scrape some skin off on a dig, or stab yourself with one of those little trowels?"

"I tried not to, but I suppose it can happen," Nigel said. "What's the question?"

"How copious do you want the blood to be?" Caitlyn asked. "A few of us worked together on a gladiator game before joining ReVisor, and we have some custom routines for different severities of wounds."

Nigel made a face. "I'd be more inclined to gloss over the bleeding, maybe give the person a virtual bandage. You should probably talk to Shadow. He has a better feel for gameplay issues than I do."

"He's sulking. I heard that Mom beat his high score."

"Is everybody calling Ulah that now? I never noticed before."

Caitlyn shrugged. "I guess it's a new thing, but she does take care of us. Maybe it's part of having four arms, but Mom's only been here a few weeks and she has a finger in every pie."

"Sounds like my mom," Katya said from the opening to Nigel's cubicle.

"We were talking about our new office manager," Nigel said, standing to greet his wife.

"How long?" Caitlyn asked Katya.

"Another six months, five days, three hours, and fourteen minutes, according to the Farling doctor on Flower," Katya said. "He offered me a countdown watch, but I didn't want to get obsessed with it."

"Didn't you say you were spending the day with that Drazen envoy we picked up at the last stop?" Nigel asked.

"He's waiting with his wife in the lobby. Sabina and I thought they'd be interested in touring the whole ship, but they're only interested in the business incubator. Rayne already had some visor teleconference scheduled so I brought them here to kill time."

"I see you've got your hands full, so I'll try Shadow on the blood thing," Caitlyn said and slipped out of the cubicle.

"The blood thing?" Katya asked her husband.

"Long story," he said. "No, it's not, now that I think about it. We have a lot of former action and adventure game programmers working for us and now and then they forget that we publish educational software."

"Come with me and tell the Drazens that. His name is Morp."

"How about the wife?" Nigel asked.

"Shinka. Drazen wives are all Shinka because we can't pronounce their real names. I'm not sure their husbands can either. Let's go."

The lobby was crowded with employees standing in a semi-circle. Nigel was about to scold the staff for staring at aliens when he noticed his favorite coffee mug arcing through the air behind an orange. Somebody's change purse flew back in the opposite direction, and what looked like a pastry in film wrap followed that, then he saw his coffee mug returning the same way and realized that there was some sort of game involving throwing going on. He followed Katya around the crowd to the right and came upon a Drazen female who was recording video on her tab. Nigel looked in the direction she was pointing just in time to see Morp snag the orange with his tentacle and toss it back to Ulah, who easily incorporated it into the arc of a dozen other items she was juggling.

"Give her a raise," Katya whispered to Nigel. "You can't afford to let that sort of talent walk out on you."

"But why are they juggling?"

"I asked Ulah to keep the guests amused and I guess she took me a little more literally than I intended. Still, she's a gem."

"That's all for now, folks," Morp said through an external translation pendant hung around his neck when he saw that Katya had returned.

The employees of ReVisor let out a collective sigh. Ulah began returning items to their owners with her lower set of arms while she kept the arc going with her upper two hands.

"Welcome to ReVisor," Nigel said, offering the Drazens each a handshake, so they'd get the complete human experience. "Katya tells me that you're interested in the business incubator. Any particular industry, or are you just looking for ideas?"

"We're stakeholders in a consortium that manufactures high-performance camping gear, everything from tents to backpacks, and we're interested in entering the Human market," Morp said. "Despite the similarities between our species in terms of height and mass, it turns out that your lack of opposing thumbs and a tentacle requires a complete rethink in product design."

"We have opposing thumbs," Nigel said, holding up his hand with the fingers spread.

"Not enough of them," the Drazen replied, displaying his own hands. "Your missing tentacle is an even bigger issue when it comes to erecting tents. I've been assigned to set up a research and development lab for the new line of Human-oriented products, and I heard about the business incubator on the Miklat through a young relative who attends the Open University on Union Station."

"Katya already showed us the living quarters intended for our species, which were very nice," Shinka said. "But there aren't any other Drazens living there yet."

"If you'd like to talk to members of an advanced species operating in the incubator, I was already planning to stop and see Dzar this morning," Nigel offered. "He's a Frunge chemist who had been building a lab to research new metallurgical coatings and he gave me an open invitation to drop by. Or we could stop in Horten Haptics, which is currently testing their existing product line with local gamers to get a baseline of the changes they'll need to make for our market."

The Drazens exchanged a look, and then Morp said, "I believe we'll start with the Frunge."

"Good. I'll just ping Dzar to make sure it's a convenient—" he interrupted himself when he saw Ulah motioning for him to get going with sweeping movements using both arms on her left side while giving him two thumbs up with her hands on the right. "It looks like my office manager arranged it while we were speaking."

"I'm impressed that you were able to hire a member of an advanced species to run your office," Shinka said as they began walking. "You must offer a highly competitive compensation package."

"We base our employee compensation on the model from Bits," Nigel explained. "Everybody gets profit sharing from the sales of the product they work on, and an office manager who puts in as many hours as Ulah could end up earning more than any of the other employees."

"You aren't worried that could cause resentment?"

"As of this morning, they're all calling her 'Mom', so I think she has it in hand."

Morp slowed to look in one of the shared equipment rooms they passed, and asked, "Is the gang holo-copier for everybody to use?"

"Yes," Katya said, that being one of the features of the business incubator she was familiar with. "You have to pay for the blank memories, but there's no charge to use any of the standard office equipment."

"And there's a gym facility with Drazen-specific apparatus," Nigel added. "We've started holding an open gaming night in the plaza every Tuesday, so the incubator members can get to know each other better."

"The promotional materials also say that the Zarents will provide technical support if asked," Morp said. "All of our consortium's manufacturing equipment is designed for the product line it produces, and some of the machines for our most in-demand backpacks and climbing harnesses haven't changed in thousands of years. We're planning on a small design unit here if we join, so support in prototyping production equipment will be essential."

"Are any of your products handmade?" Katya inquired. "I know that Flower employs thousands of people in her textiles division and most of them are working with treadle-powered sewing machines because that meets the tunnel network definition for handmade goods, though maybe it's second tier."

"An excellent question," Shinka said, glancing at her husband, which made Katya suspect that she'd stepped into an ongoing argument. "I'm strongly in favor of creating a handmade line of tents, backpacks, and safari wear, but my presentation to the consortium fell on tone-deaf ears. They used price points as an excuse, but if we could use low-cost alien labor..."

"There's Dzar," Nigel said as they came around a bend in the corridor. He waved at the waiting alien, who was puzzled by the gesture since in Frunge it would have meant a large carnivore was lurking in the grass. "If you come to game night, don't get in a game of battling tops with him."

Katya had met Dzar when he joined the incubator, so she handled the introductions. Then the alien entrepreneur brought them into his laboratory, where a half-dozen other Frunge wearing silvery lab coats with hoods that looked heat and flame resistant were attending vats of chemicals bubbling under fume hoods.

"It would have taken us at least another cycle to get the lab up and running without the help of the Zarents," Dzar answered a question from Morp. "First Chemist Miklat consulted on the design, and then he sent a team of apprentices to help install the equipment, some of which they fabricated for us in their labs."

"We saw some Zarents on the docking deck when our taxi from the elevator hub brought us to the Miklat," Shinka said. "They didn't look like they were capable of moving large loads."

Dzar produced a dry chuckle. "They have specially designed saddles that allow them to control four-armed robots with a degree of precision that's astounding," he said. "As apprentices, they each operated a single robot, but I understand that the adults can handle two robots simultaneously."

Nine

It took longer than Rayne expected to get the new bazaar merchant settled in, and when she checked her smartphone for the time, she swore out loud.

"Is there a problem?" Kruik asked through the device.

"I was supposed to pick Sarah up at her school ten minutes ago," Rayne said as she started for the lift tube. "Can you tell her that I'm running late?"

A few seconds passed in silence, and then Kruik replied, "She says she'll meet you at the restaurant, and she wants to know if you've forgotten how to send a text message."

"Very funny. Someday you'll have a teenage daughter and then—sorry, I forgot that you're an artificial intelligence."

"I hope to produce offspring one day in the distant future, though I could do without the teenage drama and mood swings. Flower has a theory that when Humans enter their rapid growth phase before maturity, it puts so much strain on their bodies that something else has to give."

"That something else being sanity," Rayne said. "Flower might be on to something there." She entered the lift tube and then hesitated. "Do you know where I'm meeting her?"

"Bindaal's Vegan Café," Kruik said. "It's the first time this month you let Sarah choose."

"I stopped letting her pick the restaurant every Friday because she always chose Vergallian Vegan. I want her to get a wider perspective on food so she doesn't end up being picky and waking up one day and finding that she's developed food allergies."

"Is that how it works?"

"I'm not sure," Rayne admitted, "but variety is always a good idea, and there wasn't a lot to choose from on Bits because all the food was imported. And I've come to respect how hard it is to get started in the restaurant business."

"I've noticed that you bring Sarah to lunch at the new stalls in the food court after you rent out the space," Kruik said. "I'm sure the owners appreciate the gesture."

"You know," Rayne said, leaning slightly against the wall of the capsule, "I feel a bit guilty when any of these people I'm renting space to, whether in the bazaar, the food court, or the business incubator, ask me for advice. I have plenty of experience with finance thanks to working as the treasurer for the Rules Committee back on Bits, but I've never started a business from scratch myself. I think everybody in Mouser's gaming group is an entrepreneur, other than me and Hercules."

"I provide Flower with data about the state of our economy, the bulk of which is given over to employment statistics. I would define your job as providing professional services."

"Not a rental agent?"

"You do much more than that," Kruik said as the lift tube doors opened. "And if you hurry, you can still get to Bindaal's Café before Sarah."

Rayne walked as quickly as she could without breaking stride, and just as the vegan café came into sight, she saw her daughter arriving from the opposite direction at a sprint, her long ponytail bouncing behind her. Rayne slowed so that Sarah wouldn't notice that she'd been hurrying, and watched as her daughter chatted with Bindaal, probably blaming her mother for not having eaten there in a month.

"You're late," Sarah said triumphantly when her mother arrived. "I was here minutes ago."

"Thirty-four seconds," Rayne countered. "I saw you arrive and checked my phone. How are you, Bindaal?"

"Business has been a bit slow lately," the Vergallian said. "I'm afraid that the subtle flavor profiles of my food aren't exciting enough for most Humans. I've noticed that restaurants selling heavy meals cooked with more salt than I use in a week are the ones that always have waiting lines."

"It's not healthy," Sarah said. "I would eat here every Friday, but mom likes to show me off to all the new food business owners she rents a space. It's embarrassing."

"I'm sorry that's how you feel," Rayne said, hoping to cut the latest drama off at the pass. "If you want to meet here every Friday, that's fine."

"You don't have to make any sacrifices for me," her daughter huffed and turned back to the café owner. "Guess what, Bindaal."

"You're getting married," the Vergallian said with a smile.

"Ick. No. I'm doing a trial apprenticeship for the Zarents on the ag deck, sort of, except it's only three afternoons a week, and we're actually working for Botan. He said that part of the experience of growing produce as a business is selling it, so we're going to have a farmstand when enough ripens. You have to come."

"Indeed I do. Please tell me when the farmstand is open."

"I will," Sarah said, shooting her mother a defiant look motivated by some inner thought process that Rayne could only guess at. "I know that our vegetables aren't the same as yours, even though some of them look similar or taste sort of the same, but maybe you could use them in the café."

"It's traditional for Vergallian chefs to use local produce as long as all of the tunnel network species can eat it without harm, and that applies to all of the produce from Earth," Bindaal said. "Now, what can I make for you?"

"Chef's Sampler for me."

"Make that two," Rayne said.

"You don't have to order the same thing as me," Sarah said as Bindaal retreated behind the counter to prepare their food.

"I know there's no right way to say this, but I don't make decisions for myself based on how I think you may react. Your grandmother tells me that I was so horrible at your age that she almost sold me to a pirate, so I thank my stars that you're turning out better than I did."

"Really? You don't think everything I do is wrong?"

"Of course not," Rayne said. "If you think that I'm judging you all the time, it's not intentional on my part."

"You make faces," Sarah said. "Or your shoulders get stiff and you start using bigger words than usual. I can pretty much always tell what you're thinking."

"Then that makes one of us. Can you tell what Hercules is thinking?"

"Sure, Herc is easy. I just ask him."

"Why don't you try that with me sometime?" Rayne asked.

"Because there's no point, I already know." Sarah thought for a moment and then giggled. "At least ninety percent of the time."

"Do you know what I'm thinking now?" Rayne asked.

"You're hoping that I won't bring up the fact that you're working too much and that Herc feels he has to stay home every evening to keep me company."

Rayne sighed. "The thought did cross my mind when I sat down. But Hercules supports my making a push to get the business incubator up and running, and as soon as—"

"You always say *as soon as*," Sarah interrupted. "You said it back on Bits when grandma was the one who always made me lunch, you said it on Flower when you were trying to figure out her finances, and you said it here when you took responsibility for the bazaar and the food court. Just when everything was starting to run smoothly, you started with the business incubator."

"The business incubator is important to the Zarents, and the financial incentives are important to the alien business startups they're trying to attract, so—"

"You're doing it again. The galaxy doesn't revolve around you, Mom. What am I supposed to think, other than that you're avoiding me because I remind you of my father."

Rayne felt the breath whoosh out of her lungs like she'd been punched in the gut. "Is that what you think?" she whispered. "That I work all the time because I'm avoiding you?"

"Occam's Razor," Sarah said. "I could look for a more complicated explanation, but that wouldn't make it right."

"I'm not trying to avoid you, Sarah. Having you is the best thing I've ever done. But you've always been so independent, and you used to get so annoyed if I interrupted while you were playing a game."

"Nobody wants to get interrupted while they're playing a game. That's how the games are designed."

"I don't miss your father," Rayne said slowly. "I know you miss him, and when we rendezvous with Flower, I expect you'll want to stay with him and your half-sister for a few days. But I don't see him when I look at you, and my relationship with Hercules is stronger than what I had with Gorgeous George. That was just an infatuation that I had a hard time growing out of."

"If you say so," Sarah said. "But if you aren't trying to avoid me, you're turning into a workaholic. First Educator Miklat substituted for our class a few weeks ago and she warned us that some humans try to make up for a lack of tentacles by working more hours."

"So now I have tentacle envy," Rayne said with a laugh. "Well, I guess I can live with that. And I'll try to schedule more of my visor conference calls during regular working hours, but you know how it is with time zones."

Bindaal silently materialized next to their table with a giant tray that looked like it included every item from the menu, and at the touch of a button, four legs telescoped out from the bottom of the tray so it could stand independently.

"It's too much," Sarah said in dismay. "We'll never eat all of that."

"I made extra because I hoped you'd invite me to join you," Bindaal said. "I don't have any take-out orders on the board, and you can see for yourselves how busy I am."

Both humans reflexively glanced around the seating area and saw that they were alone.

"Please join us, Bindaal," Rayne said. "I'll try to keep Sarah from quizzing you about every dish."

"I like explaining vegan food, but I'm sure that Sarah has already heard all of my lectures," Bindaal said with a quiet smile as she pulled a third chair over to the table to sit between the mother and daughter. "She's one of the few Humans on board who can pronounce the names of the Vergallian ingredients properly."

"I learned from Avisia on Flower," Sarah said proudly. "She used to visit school and teach us about Vergallian food whenever Flower ordered it."

The three of them fell to eating, as even Rayne knew that Vergallian vegan was best immediately after it was prepared, and the colorful contents of the tray disappeared faster than anyone would have thought possible. Then Bindaal insisted on performing a traditional tea ceremony, and Sara's eyes went wide at the first sniff. "It smells like chocolate!" she blurted out, even though the participants of the ceremony were supposed to remain silent until all the cups were poured.

Bindaal finished and said, "It's a new brew that I've been experimenting with to suit Belle's taste. You'll be the first Humans to try it."

Sarah blew over the rim of the cup a few times to try to cool the liquid, another faux pas in terms of Vergallian traditions, but the thirteen-year-old couldn't restrain herself. "It's brilliant. You're going to be rich!"

"It's not Earth chocolate," Bindaal told her. "I tried that first, but it didn't blend well with any of our teas. But it turns out that Keetle root, which we sometimes use in sweetened desserts, has a similar scent and flavor. The chemical structures of Keetle and chocolate have less in common than you might think, but they produce a similar scent. Belle says it's just not the same as chocolate, but she still prefers it to regular tea."

"I'll talk to her," Sarah said as if she thought that the clone needed straightening out.

"It is very good," Rayne said after venturing a sip. "Does it have the same caffeine level as chocolate?"

"No caffeine at all, not in the Keetle or the tea," Bindaal replied. "That's another reason I'm not convinced there would be any commercial demand among Humans. Your species is addicted to caffeine."

"Not me," Sarah said, and then checked her smartphone, which was trying to escape the table by vibrating itself toward the edge. She read the long text message, tapped out a response, and stood. "Botan is grafting fruit trees this afternoon, and he offered to teach us as a bonus, so I'm going to run. Thanks for lunch, Bindaal. I'll see you at home, Mom."

"She seems to be enjoying her work on the ag deck," Bindaal commented after the young teen disappeared. "Is she considering it for a career?"

"I think it's just a phase, but we'll see," Rayne said. "She's usually in a good mood after working on the ag deck. I suspect it takes her mind off worrying about my problems," she added with a laugh.

"Your daughter is worried about you? Is it anything serious?"

"She thinks that I'm working too hard at getting the business incubator established and that I still haven't gotten over her father. It's hard for children of divorced parents, especially at her age."

"And how about you?" Bindaal asked, pouring Rayne another cup of tea to replace the one that had been drained in three gulps as soon as it cooled enough to swallow.

"I'm fine, and I don't feel like I'm working hard because it's so much fun," Rayne said. "I never thought that I'd become one of those xenophiles, but the advanced species are all so interesting."

"Did I hear that the business incubator is planning a small food court next to the plaza as soon as occupancy reaches fifty percent? It might make sense for me to move my café there, especially if the rent is subsidized."

"I hadn't heard anything about that, but it's a good idea. We've been staging a get-to-know-your-neighbors event every time the incubator picks up a new tenant, but there aren't any food businesses on the deck, so everything is takeout."

"Why haven't you used a caterer?" Bindaal asked. "I've been doing parties and events as long as the client can guarantee ten customers."

"So far, most of the people, I mean, sentients who show up are from ReVisor. They mainly eat pizza and food like that. Takeout just works better."

"I understand. The manager of the research lab set up by Horten Haptics invited me to cater one of their events, but the Hortens were the only ones who ate my food. There must have been two dozen Human beta testers in attendance, but they all opted for pizza or Mexican food."

Rayne navigated to a map of the incubator on her phone, spread her fingers to zoom in on a section, and then passed the device to Bindaal. "That's the floorplan of the only place bordering the plaza that would make sense for a café. It has all the hookups, and there's room for a refrigerator and a counter, but not much else."

"Would I be able to set out tables in the plaza area?"

"Yes, I don't see why not. But it would probably be best to take them in whenever you're closed since it's officially a public area for all the incubator tenants. There are other open spaces bordering the plaza, but they're all too large, and I don't want to ask the Zarents to start subdividing. The reason I'm pretty sure you can have that space is it's too small for anything else."

"Because of the corridor and the lift tube." Bindaal nodded. "I'd have to see it, of course, but things can't get any slower than they are here."

"I'm sorry that I didn't notice you were struggling," Rayne said. "I would have dropped in more often and brought Sarah. But are you sure you want to have the only café on the incubator deck? My guess is that you'll have to start serving coffee and pastry if you want to make a go of it."

"I can sell coffee, and while I've never pushed vegan desserts at this location because I was trying to focus on full meals, I think I can offer an assortment that even Humans will find acceptable."

"I just don't associate vegan cuisine with desserts," Rayne said, fishing her programmable cred out of her purse.

"Put that away," Bindaal told her, standing and starting to clear the table. "You're going out of your way to help me and I'm not even paying you a commission. If the Zarents approve my moving to the incubator, you can come in for free Keetle tea any time."

"I'll send a text to First Engineer Miklat as soon as I get back to my office. I'm pretty sure he'll be agreeable, especially since you're an alien, I mean, a non-Human, and attracting non-Humans to the Miklat is the reason the Zarents set up the incubator in the first place."

Bindaal finished cleaning up, hung out the 'Closed' sign even though the luncheon crowd was still milling around the food court, and made her way to Club Ucerin, where Kyor was doing a booming business. Only a few patrons were standing at the bar sipping a lunch beer, but a line of people waited to buy popcorn for a cred a bag to take back to their offices for an afternoon snack.

"You look pleased," the Huktra said to Bindaal. "Just give me a minute to refill the kettle and I'll be with you."

"Why don't you make popcorn continuously?" the Vergallian asked. "I thought the heat lamp kept it warm."

"It's not as good that way, and in a few minutes, business will be deader than the Ucerins and not pick up again until people start drifting out of work early in a few hours."

"Then why make a new batch at all?"

"Strangely enough, I've come to like popcorn," Kyor said, pouring a few cups of kernels from a sack into the kettle. "That should do it. Good news from home?"

"I took your advice and Rayne agreed to ask the Zarents if I can move shop to the incubator," Bindaal said. She set a small device on the counter and powered it on, creating an audio suppression field around the two aliens so they could talk privately. "I've been opening later and closing early every day just so I could honestly tell her that business is terrible."

"Moving your café to the incubator makes sense for everybody. The Zarents get another attraction to bring in members of the advanced species, you get a location that will let you keep an eye on the incubator's tenants, and I get to move Club Ucerin into your space and expand my business."

"You didn't mention that last part when you pitched the idea."

"I didn't have to."

Bindaal smiled. "No, you're a bit more obvious than your illustrious relative. Has Belle stopped by today? I was going to offer to go down to the planet at our next stop since I don't have to keep the café open."

"We both owe her a dozen favors for doing all the leg work at stops," Kyor said. "What we need is to recruit some more independent agents."

"I don't know about independents, but according to my source on Flower, all of the other species are working to establish a presence on the Miklat now that the Zarents have made a success of the thing."

"If that's the case, it could explain the sudden influx of businesses to the incubator. Despite all the incentives, Rayne was having difficulty closing any deals until the floodgates finally opened."

"You're probably right," Bindaal said. "But neither of us is officially part of the arrangement that Belle has with the intelligence agents on Flower."

"It's newcomers from the Farling Empire that Myort wants me to watch for," Kyor said. "He's convinced that they're going to use the Miklat to start building new intelligence networks on the tunnel network."

"I can't imagine them getting anything past Kruik."

Ten

"Do you know what day it is today?" Sophie asked her husband as they took their seats on the shuttle.

"Since you're asking, it must be an anniversary," Mouser said. "Let's see. Last year was our fortieth, which I remember because G32FX came around to remind me and then claimed I owed him a favor, so that makes this our forty-first."

"It's strange to think that our marriage lasted longer than our community on Bits. When we all moved there from Earth, we were so sure it would be forever."

"Because none of us had the sense to read the planetary lease. I'm sure there's a lesson in there somewhere."

"Hello, Belle," Sophie greeted the correspondent for Gem Today. "Sit with us."

"Don't you usually take the first shuttle to the surface?" Mouser asked as the clone took the seat next to Sophie.

"I was reviewing the latest release of *Rescue Dig* to go with a story I'm writing about the business incubator and I'm embarrassed to say that I got so caught up in the gameplay that I wasn't paying attention to the time," Belle said. "The newer generation of virtual reality headsets that Flower is manufacturing based on the last generation of the technology that you abandoned when the Stryx opened Earth provide a near-immersive experience. It's inspiring what your engineers were able to accomplish without holograms."

"The headsets were already obsolete and forgotten when I started gaming. Horten holographic technology had already taken over the virtual reality market, and those of us who ended up moving to Bits rebelled by reverting to playing video games on flat screens."

"I never would have married him if he'd been walking around immersed in a virtual world all of the time," Sophie said. "Back when I was in university on Earth, there were quite a few students, and even some professors, who were experimenting with the augmented reality heads-up displays that the Hortens were selling for pocket change."

"Did they provide the same experience as implants?" Belle asked. "I thought I was familiar with all of the Horten holo-technology but I don't remember augmented reality projections. I'm having trouble imagining how it would even work without everybody else seeing..." she trailed off when Mouser's wife smiled and nodded.

"That's exactly how they worked," Sophie said. "I don't have an implant, but I understand that the heads-up display works by interfacing directly with the visual cortex, all of it inside your head. The Horten technology created a holographic overlay in front of your eyes, and it had to be far enough away from the user's face to prevent focusing problems. The result was people walking around with a holographic image at an arm's length, which meant it wasn't private. And if you can imagine trying to use it anywhere that people are milling around—let's just say that there's a reason the Hortens were unloading them cheap."

"I almost forgot about those," Mouser said. "There was so much alien entertainment technology flooding Earth in those days that the manufacturers on Earth gave up even trying. I remember a friend of mine, who didn't move to Bits with us, getting upset when he found out that the tunnel network species were all emptying their warehouses of stuff they couldn't sell back home because it was obsolete or simply unsuccessful, like the Horten augmented reality devices. He was sure the aliens were laughing at us."

"The Grenouthians certainly were," Sophie said.

"Are you going to see their clock?" Belle asked.

"On the planet? I thought the Grenouthians could all keep track of the time in their heads without technology. I read somewhere that advanced species all eventually evolve the ability."

"I hadn't heard that one, but Jipp is famous for its clock."

"Like an antique?" Mouser asked. "We heard about the gardens but nothing about a clock. Is it in a museum?"

"I've never been here before myself, but according to the tour guide I read, the clock is housed in a mountain, and the Grenouthians originally settled this world over two million years ago for the express purpose of constructing the clock. The Verlocks traded them the planet for one with active volcanoes."

"What I'm curious about is what sort of work the human contract workers here do for the Grenouthians," Mouser said. "I know that they hire our people to work in their immersive industry on that orbital where Flower stops—"

"Timble," Sophie interjected.

"—but other than that, I thought they didn't have much use for contract workers."

"You didn't know?" Belle asked in surprise. "Jipp is one of the worlds with a Human reenactment preserve. It was part of the deal that the Grenouthians made with EarthCent. In return for setting up reenactment preserves all over Earth for the alien tourist trade attracted by humorous documentaries about your recent history, the Grenouthians received the right to also create reenactment preserves on three other worlds, though they had to agree to hire Humans to staff them."

"Who could the bunnies have gotten to reenact our history other than us?" Mouser asked.

"Oh, plenty of humanoid species can pass for Humans in a pinch, and there are more unemployed actors in the galaxy than you might imagine."

"I hope the tourists coming to see the reenactment preserves don't all crowd into the gardens," Sophie said.

Belle smiled. "I don't think that will be a problem. I believe Jipp is a garden planet."

"The whole thing?"

"Except for the human reenactment preserves and residential warrens for the Grenouthians, though my understanding is they build vertically and underground to reduce their impact on the environment. According to the tour guide, the majority of the population work as gardeners."

"But the Grenouthians are one of the most advanced species on the tunnel network," Mouser objected. "I think the second most common occupation for human contract workers, after factory jobs, is agriculture."

"I don't know much about it," Belle admitted. "The leadership of our old empire frowned on gardening as a waste of productive time, and since we subsisted on a factory-made nutritional drink, we didn't require farms.

But I know several Humans who consider gardening and working with the soil to be a positive experience, including Botan."

The mention of a member of their *Speed Trader* group brought the conversation around to gaming, and Sophie let her husband and the Gem wander deep into the weeds of Game Theory while she read the brochure for Jipp that somebody had left in the pocket of the seatback in front of her. By the time they landed, she knew a hundred percent more about the planet than when they had boarded the shuttle.

"We have to go through customs," Sophie told Mouser. "Do you have anything to declare?"

"That after forty-one years, my love for you is—"

"Nice try," she cut him off. "I asked because I'm always finding tools and electronic components in your pockets when I do the laundry, and the Grenouthians discourage importation of high-tech to Jipp."

"It's a tech-ban world? I didn't know they had them."

"Not tech-ban," Belle told him as she stood up and stretched. "But as a garden world, they discourage anything that clashes with nature, and nobody wants to be bothered by beeps and ringtones."

"We should turn off our phones now," Sophie said, reaching in her purse. "If I had known, I wouldn't have brought mine."

When they reached the customs counter, a Grenouthian whose official banner made him look like an overgrown bunny from a fairytale regarded them through drooping eyelids. "Tourists or reenactors?" the customs agent demanded in oddly accented English.

"Tourists," Sophie replied. "We brought our smartphones by mistake but they're turned off."

The bunny produced a plastic box and placed it on the counter between them. "All electronics in the box. Take the claim number, and you can pick it up when you leave."

Sophie handed over their phones, and to the amusement of the Grenouthian, Mouser produced a random collection of components from his pockets. "I was working on a repair this morning," he explained.

"Exit to your left for the tube to the clock or to your right for the medieval Human reenactment preserve," the customs agent told them after placing the box on the conveyor belt that ran behind him. "I believe there's a jousting tournament scheduled to begin in twenty minutes."

"We're mainly interested in the gardens," Sophie said.

"And the clock," Mouser added.

"Go see the clock first because a sleep cycle is coming up soon," the Grenouthian said. "You can access the gardens by walking out any door. Try not to get lost."

"Do you think Belle would like to come with us?" Sophie asked Mouser as they exited to the left. "I didn't see her."

"She's probably registering as a foreign intelligence agent and doing spy stuff," Mouser said. "I think her main job on a planet like this would be visiting the reenactment preserve and seeing if she can recruit any of our people as sources. And you know, I've never heard an alien speak such good English. The Grenouthians must have special training."

"In lip-synching. You didn't notice?"

"No! I'm sure he was speaking English."

Sophie laughed. "I would have thought the same if I hadn't read the brochure, but the customs agents on Grenouthian garden worlds are famous for lip-synching ability. There are speaker beads on a necklace that's hidden by ruff fur."

"But the way translation pendants work, he'd have to talk out loud in his own language," Mouser protested. "Unless the bunnies are telepaths, and I don't think they are."

"I got close enough to the counter to peek over and he was moving his paws the whole time like he was playing an organ. It's a holographic controller for creating speech, almost like typing."

The tube proved to be a transparent glass cylinder with no visible tracks or mechanism, and they wouldn't have known where to wait if there hadn't been a yellow stripe on the platform with a warning in dozens of languages to stand behind it until the capsule arrived. Two minutes later, a glass capsule floated to a stop in front of them, and a section of the tube hinged up where they hadn't even spotted any seams.

"I guess it's just us," Sophie said as they entered and took a pair of empty seats. "Everybody else must have decided to start with the jousting tournament."

"Pneumatic, I think," Mouser said, answering a question his wife hadn't asked. "Must be using some sort of advanced field technology to make the seal since the capsule glass can't be in contact with the tube. I wonder if the tube ahead of us is evacuated and pressurized air blows from behind."

"I didn't even hear the door close, but I think it must have since we've started to move."

"Did your brochure say how far away this clock is?" Mouser asked.

"Yes, but I didn't recognize the units," Sophie said. "I remember it was over a thousand somethings."

"If it's a standard measure for traveling distance, we may be in for a long ride. The next time the capsule stops, we better make sure that we'll have time to get back to the spaceport before the Miklat leaves."

"I don't know. We still seem to be accelerating."

Mouser tried to make out any details of the scenery they were passing by, but it had all turned into a green blur. "If we are traveling in a vacuum, I suppose the capsule might be able to go supersonic, but—" he instinctively reached a protective arm around his wife's shoulder as their seats began to rotate, making it impossible to keep his arm in place. "Deceleration," he said.

"You mean the seats are turning so we'll be pressed back as the capsule slows." Sophie nodded. "That makes sense, and if we just reached the halfway point in the trip, the clock can't be far."

"I don't see any mountains on the horizon looking forward. It could be that the capsule has reached its top velocity and now we just travel looking backward until it's time to slow us down."

"Five minutes to Clock Mountain," announced a disembodied female voice that might have been copied from every electronics device manufactured on Earth in the last century. "Please remain in your seats until the capsule reaches a complete stop."

"It knew to speak to us in English," Sophie observed.

"There has to be a lot of technology on board that we can't even see," Mouser said. "Maybe it's under the seats."

"Or transparent."

"I hadn't thought of that, but an advanced species could probably make see-through circuitry if they wanted, or maybe it's hidden in plain sight inside a hologram. What did your brochure say about the clock."

"I think there was a presumption on the part of whoever wrote the brochure that the clock is so famous that it would be a waste of time to describe it or explain its purpose," Sophie said. "All I got out of it was the name, which is a translation from Grenouthian units, and came to twelve million years, with plenty of digits after the decimal point."

"Could be a doomsday thing," Mouser mused. "Maybe the Grenouthians believe that their civilization can hang on for another twelve million years and they're counting down.

"It's a translation," she reminded him. "The number in the Grenouthian name was a one with nine zeroes after it."

"A billion-year clock."

"Not years, some Grenouthian unit of time that translates to twelve-point-something million of our years."

Mouser shrugged. "They could still be counting down to doomsday."

"If they are, it's too far into the future for us to worry about," Sophie told him.

The capsule began to decelerate, but their weight remained within comfortable bounds, and a couple of minutes later, they were standing on a platform in an immense underground cavern.

A familiar figure wearing what could have been a British admiral's uniform from sailing ship days stood nearby sketching furiously on a pad of paper as she tried to capture the beehive of activity around what looked like a half-completed wooden structure in front of a towering machine that was also constructed entirely from wood. Giant wooden gears meshed together, turning so slowly that the motion would have been difficult to notice if each tooth hadn't been embellished with a large blue spot.

"Sabina?" Mouser ventured.

"Katya," the Zerakova twin said and looked up to see who'd arrived. "I'm glad you're here. You can be my witnesses because my sister is never going to believe this."

"I've never even imagined a scene where so many carpenters would all be working at the same time," Sophie said. "There must be hundreds of them."

"I counted five hundred before I gave up. Look at this," she continued, flipping back a few pages on her sketchpad. The drawing showed a pyramid of rounded figures with five levels, as the bunny at the top hammered a peg into place. "It's like watching a circus. They aren't using any machines beyond what the ancient Greeks might have had. And this," she said, flipping to another drawing.

"It looks like scaffolding. Is it around the other side?"

"They put it up in a matter of minutes, and took it down again as soon as they were finished placing that beam," the co-captain pointed with her pencil, "up there."

"But that must have been eight or nine levels of scaffolding," Mouser said. "It would be impossible to—"

"The Grenouthians can lash a connection in seconds, and undo it again just as fast," Katya said. "And they all stopped what they were doing to work at it, all five hundred plus of them. I think the scaffolding must be their version of bamboo, because it was light enough that they passed whole stages up, paw-over-paw, to bunnies who climbed each level."

"They don't seem to be rushing now, even though they're all working hard," Sophie observed. "They almost look like they're meditating, or worshipping."

"It's not a religious exercise unless you consider training for a government bureaucracy a religion," Katya said. "All of the Grenouthians you see have passed their civil service exams and are preparing to enter government service."

"By building a wood model of a clock?"

"It won't be a model when it's finished, it will keep time while they take down the old one. And they've been doing this for millions of years already."

"I'm sorry," Mouser said. "I can appreciate a certain beauty in the mechanism, and to create it with nothing but hand tools is a testament to their dedication, but there have to be better ways to keep the time and train the next generation of clerical workers."

Katya set aside her sketchpad and flexed her hand, which had cramped too much to hold the pencil any longer. "I've been drawing for three hours straight," she said as if apologizing for slacking off.

"Why don't you record what they're doing on your implant?"

"It's not allowed, I had to sign a pledge."

"I think it's brilliant," Sophie said slowly. "The government makes its new employees get together for a few months and work on a monumental project that requires a high degree of cooperation."

"Except it's not a few months, it's a few years," Katya said. "Of course, the Grenouthians live ten times as long as us, if not longer, so it's all relative."

"But why a clock?" Mouser asked.

"Jipp's Warren Mother brought me here for a special tour after I presented my credentials. She said that the clock symbolizes the frustration of government service and how difficult it is to change anything in a society that's had interstellar travel for over seven million years. Building the clock isn't just an educational tool, it's a screening process to weed out those Grenouthians who can't slow down enough to do the job the way it's supposed to be done."

"How well does it keep time?"

"Supposedly it's good to a few seconds a day, but that's not the point," Katya said. "Did you know that we have a giant mechanical clock in a mountain on Earth? It was made from the best parts our materials science could produce at the time."

"We as in humanity?" Sophie asked.

"EarthCent bought it from the original organization, which means the Human Empire will end up owning it. My mom went and saw it on one of her visits to Earth and she has a funny story about how it stopped just as the tour guide was telling her group how it was designed to keep the time for ten thousand years strictly through the mechanical movement. They started it a little before the Stryx opened Earth, so it only lasted a century in the end. I guess it's a tourist attraction now, but for the wrong reason."

"I thought Earth was broke when the Stryx came. Building a giant mechanical clock in a mountain seems like a frivolous waste of money."

"It wasn't government money, and it was supposed to serve as a symbol to remind people that our lives are short but our actions and our works extend far into the future, or something like that," Katya said. "Mom said she heard later that the Grenouthians were planning a funny documentary about humanity's ten-thousand-year clock. Now that I've seen their twelve-million-year clock, I get why we must look so ridiculous to them."

"Look, they just finished a beam," Mouser said, pointing to where a half-dozen of the furry aliens were hefting a long crooked timber from which the bark had been removed, but only the ends and a small section in the middle showed any chiseled flats and joinery. The rest had been left in its natural form.

"The Warren Mother explained that they use scribe-rule for all the framing. The way I understood her, it's a method that allows them to fit any timber into the frame as opposed to only working with pieces that can be milled into standard sizes. You'll never believe this, but she also said that they redesign the clock's motion with every iteration, not to make it run better, but to complete the job with the wood they have on hand."

Sophie and Mouser stared as the Grenouthians all put down their tools and swarmed over to a pile of long poles which proved to be the vertical members of the scaffolding. It was impossible to pick out who was in charge in the maelstrom of activity, but within minutes, staging seven stories high had been erected, and crude cranes powered by compound pulleys with teams of burly bunnies hauling on long ropes began raising the new timber to the top. Other Grenouthians wearing carpenter's belts climbed onto the beams of the existing structure that would serve as the new clock's frame, and they guided the beam into position and pegged it into place.

"You should go take a look at the old clock," Katya said as the aliens practically flowed back down the scaffolding, disassembling each successive stage as they descended. "If you look closely, you'll see that they remove all the pegs after assembly. The joinery is so tight that the pegs aren't needed once it's all together and gravity holds everything in place."

Mouser and Sophie skirted the large construction site as Katya returned to sketching, and as they approached the towering clock that had been completed by the previous draft of new government employees, Sophie squeezed her husband's hand and said, "I've never felt so small."

"It is a big clock," Mouser said, though he was pretty sure that's not what she meant.

"They're just so far ahead of us. We've lived on an alien world and two interstellar colony ships, but it took these Grenouthians working with tools and methods that humans might have used on Earth a thousand years ago to finally bring it home to me. It's not the technology that makes the difference, it's them. We have so far to go."

"Our grandchildren have so far to go. I'm practically retired."

"You know what I mean," Sophie said, wiping away a tear. "And maybe it's time you stepped up and did your part."

"What do you mean?" Mouser asked. "I'm a gamemaster and an electronics repair tech with a shaky soldering hand."

"You're the mayor of the human community on the Miklat. Didn't you learn anything from watching those Grenouthians work together? I don't want you stepping aside for some opportunist from the Colony One movement. If they're going to force an election, you have to win, because we both know that you have everyone's best interests at heart. Even the aliens."

Mouser stopped and took a step back from his wife so he could look her in the eyes. "Is seeing the Grenouthians building a Sisyphean clock really what makes you feel that way?"

Sophie let out a gentle snort. "All right, you got me. I've been working with some Oners and they told me that the lottery they've been using to select members to join the Miklat has a downside. None of their movement's leaders happened to win, and the people who have pushed themselves forward to fill the gap are the wrong sorts, but the Oners don't know how to get rid of them. Not everybody wants to go into politics."

"Including yours truly."

Eleven

"It's instant oatmeal," Shadow told Delphi. "I was wandering around the bazaar looking for a wedding present that would surprise my sister and there was a trader selling boxes of the stuff. I made two packages of maple syrup flavor and two packages of apple and cinnamon because the single servings didn't look like enough for a meal."

"Why are the bowls covered with plastic wrap?" she asked. "Is it to keep the oatmeal from getting cold?"

"I just took them out of the microwave and the plastic keeps the oatmeal from boiling over. The bowls are a little too small for two servings each."

"Is it supposed to look foamy like that?"

"I don't know," Shadow said. "My mom used to make oatmeal sometimes, but she cooked it in a pot, and you had to keep stirring or it got all lumpy. According to the instructions, I could have made this stuff just by adding boiling water to the bowl and letting it sit a couple of minutes, but I didn't want to risk it." He stripped off the plastic wrap, and the foamy mass at the top quickly collapsed. "That looks better."

Delphi took one of the high stools at what they called their breakfast counter and pulled a bowl toward herself. "You know, I think your sister would rather get a practical present. She was hinting at it when we went shopping together the other day."

"I almost bought her a cool Dollnick meat slicer, but I knew you would have said it was stupid."

"She's vegetarian!"

"That's why it would be a surprise," Shadow said. "You told me about her hints, and it was all stupid stuff like towels and cleaning supplies. I would have bought them a Verlock Sky, but nobody in the bazaar had one in stock."

"Those are for babies," Delphi said. "It's a little early to be buying them baby presents unless she told you something she hasn't told me."

"Like what?" Shadow asked, trying a spoon of the oatmeal, and then attempting to cool it by blowing when it was already on his tongue.

"Never mind. Just put wedding presents out of your head for now and we can go shopping together later."

"How about today? With Ulah running the office, I can skip out any time, and you're off today."

"I was off today, but I got some pings last night from traders in transit who want to see the consignment goods," Delphi said. "If I knew how much time I was going to have to spend playing shopgirl, I would have turned down G32FX's offer."

"Doubt it," Shadow said, and then blew vigorously on a fresh spoonful of oatmeal before quickly swallowing it. "You like that Farling, I can tell."

Delphi scraped a little oatmeal from the top of her serving, blew on it, and gave it a cautious try. "It's kind of sweet," she said. "Is it real maple syrup or artificial flavors?"

"Didn't check, don't want to know. So how long do you think you'll be playing Tetris in the hold?"

"My loadmaster station is on the docking deck, and I rarely go into the hold. It's just stacks of containers, and Kruik reminds me that we are on a moving ship and it's possible that some emergency maneuver could shift the cargo."

"He's probably hiding stuff down there," Shadow said. "I don't think a ship this big could change directions fast enough that we'd even notice. Imagine what would happen on the reservoir deck if Kruik tried."

"How is the new product coming?" Delphi asked. "You barely talk about work anymore unless it's to say what a great job Ulah is doing."

"That's because she's always putting out fires before they start. I used to think I was pretty good at listening to the employees—" he ignored his girlfriend's incredulous look, "—and preventing arguments from festering, but Ulah makes me look like an amateur. Sometimes I think she's hypnotizing people by moving her lower hands around while she's talking. Humans didn't evolve to have conversations with people who have four arms."

"Aliens who have four arms," she corrected him. "How's your oatmeal?"

"I can't taste it because the first spoonful burned my tongue," he admitted. "You don't think Lisa would like a stuffed alligator? There was a guy selling one that must have been twice as big as me. She loved stuffed animals when we were kids."

"Are you talking fifteen years old or five?"

Shadow thought for a moment. "Maybe she grew out of it."

"You know what would go good with this oatmeal?" Delphi asked, sliding off the stool and heading for the fridge. "Ice cream."

"You can't put ice cream in something hot. It will just melt."

"Don't you remember the food court vendor on Flower who sold fried ice cream in tortilla bowls?"

"That was different," Shadow said. "I watched him make those. He rolled a ball of ice cream around in a pan of crumbs, I think he said it was breakfast cereal and cinnamon, so it had a protective coating. Then he had a special basket for his deep fryer, and he stood right there so the ice cream didn't stay in long enough to melt."

"I'm not going to leave this ice cream in long enough to melt either," Delphi said, then frowned when she looked in the container. "There's not much left."

"Sorry. I got hungry when I was waiting for you to come home last night. You can finish it."

She used her spoon to free what was left of the ice cream from the container in a single chunk that barely displaced any oatmeal in her bowl. "Were you eating it out of the container again?"

"No," Shadow lied, and began rapidly spooning down his oatmeal so that his mouth would always be full if she asked follow-up questions.

Ten minutes later in the lift tube capsule on the way to the Miklat's core, Kruik asked Delphi, "Are you experiencing physical distress?"

"It's the ice cream I ate with my oatmeal," Delphi said and burped again. "I think I swallowed too much air. It will be fine."

"I've seen young parents burping babies and it seems to help. I could send a bot."

"To burp me? I don't think so. And see? It stopped."

Several seconds passed in silence, making Delphi suspicious that Kruik was listening to make sure she hadn't lied, and then the Dollnick AI said, "Your first customer arrived early and has been prowling around the loadmaster station, but the controls are locked out so he can't do any harm."

"Who is it?"

"A Grenouthian trader who came aboard at Jipp. Going by the amount of time he spent on his post-flight inspection after I parked his ship, I suspect that he's new to the business."

"The way Katya and Sabina have been sending me buyers, most of the good stuff is already gone," Delphi said. "I just wish I'd been able to get better prices, but this barter business is driving me crazy. How should I know how many Frunge Fascinations I should have asked for an Oosh Air Thickener? The only person I've ever seen use one is Shadow's sister, and she treats it like some kind of high-tech punching bag."

"That's exactly what Oosh Air Thickeners are designed for," Kruik told her. "They create adjustable resistance for shadow boxing. I think that technology will do quite well in dojos and gyms throughout the tunnel network and beyond."

The capsule doors opened, and Delphi continued the conversation over her implant as she started walking toward her loadmaster station. "I guess I don't understand the galactic economy. Okay, understatement of the year, but I specifically don't understand why all these advanced species don't already make everything they need. Dollnick scientists have mastered the retaining field technology that keeps the atmosphere of a ship's core from venting out into space. Are you telling me that they couldn't tweak it to do what an Oosh Air Thickener does?"

"Of course we can, I could show you old patents. Since nobody is manufacturing that technology at the moment, it's clear that our civilization didn't fall apart without it. Now that the same thing can be inexpensively sourced from the Oosh, why would we reinvent the wheel?"

"I bartered three of them to that trader yesterday for ten Frunge Fascinations. I don't know if that's cheap or expensive."

"Save one of the Fascinations for Lisa and Botan when they have a baby," Kruik said. "You might hold onto another for yourself."

Delphi didn't bother telling the Dollnick AI that he sounded more and more like Flower every day. Instead, she put on what she hoped was a non-threatening smile as she approached the Grenouthian who was studying the loadmaster's console. "It's locked out," she told him. "Besides, we'll be in the tunnel until tomorrow so you can't be in that much of a hurry."

The alien turned his large eyes on her, blinked, and then tapped a pendant hanging on a necklace. "Could you repeat that?" he said. "I didn't have my translation device turned on."

"You don't need it for my sake," Delphi told him. "I have an implant. And I thought all traders did."

"I'm new to the business and haven't decided if an implant is necessary yet."

"Is that your ship?" She pointed at the only ship in the parking area for traders that she didn't recognize. "I've seen the four-deckers your species builds, and also a few of the larger ships, but I've never seen the two-man version."

"One-Grenouthian version," he corrected her, and the lack of an echo from his translation pendant told her that he'd disabled the outgoing speech generation function.

"It's the smallest and least expensive ship we manufacture. For five creds I'll give you a tour."

"Sure," Delphi said, starting in the direction of the ship. "In English, we sometimes talk about giving people the five-cent tour, which is a way of saying that we aren't professional guides but we're happy to—are you coming?" she broke off.

"I'm waiting to see your five creds," the trader told her.

"Five creds? To look inside your ship? That's ridiculous. I can buy a good dinner out with a cheap bottle of wine for that."

"Three creds."

"How about no creds and I show you the merchandise I have on consignment this morning instead of deciding that the containers in the hold are due for a major rearrangement," Delphi said in the lowest register her voice could manage, attempting to match the Grenouthian's low-pitched speech.

"You drive a hard bargain," the trader said. "One cred to be the first alien life form who's ever seen the inside of my vessel."

"Only because you just got it yourself." Delphi hesitated, but she was curious to see what a one-Grenouthian ship looked like from the inside, so she dug out a cred and flipped it through the air to the bunny, who caught it in a furry paw. "Why did you decide to become a trader?"

The alien waved dismissively as he began hopping rapidly toward his ship, drawing Delphi into a jog to keep up. At some point, he triggered the ramp to descend, but it hadn't reached the deck yet when they arrived, and he unexpectedly said, "I planned a career in government service, but I was deemed unsuitable to join the imperial bureaucracy."

"Oh, that's—I'm sorry. Did you fail an entrance exam?"

He turned and fixed her with his giant black eyes. "I made the high score on the entrance exam for my cadre. But I got sick of working on that idiotic wooden clock and having to wash the sawdust out of my fur every rest period."

"I heard about that clock from one of our co-captains. She wants to see the Human Empire do something similar."

"I would advise against it," the Grenouthian said as he hopped up the ramp into his ship's small hold. "As you can see, I have a variety of forest products to barter, along with some rustic handicrafts," he pointed at a cargo net full of nested baskets, drinking gourds, and practice swords.

Delphi accepted one of the wooden swords that the trader pulled out of a bundle and passed to her. It had been shaped and smoothed with care, and the grip had been carved with a hatched pattern to prevent slippage, but she didn't think that G32FX would be pleased to have a load of them dumped on him.

"Don't you have any tech to trade?" she asked hopefully. "I realize you must have spent good creds to acquire such a cargo, but—"

"Made it all myself," the Grenouthian cut her off with a grimace. "Everything is carved or woven from materials recycled from the last clock. You're looking at almost two years of my life."

"You did all of this in your spare time after you finished your regular clock duty?"

The alien surprised her by letting out a groan and settling down on his haunches. "Do you want to hear the whole story?"

"Yes," Delphi said without hesitation. "I mean, I don't have hours because another trader will be here, but..."

"It won't take that long. At my exit interview from the clock project, I was given a list of my failings. Among them was a tendency to under-communicate that I was informed might be overcome with diligent practice, which is what I'm doing now. If you include my post-primary education, I'd been studying or interning in the government track for thirty-two years at that point, which just makes the disappointment to my family and clan that much harder to swallow. I took a job in a recycling facility to keep vegetables on the table, and then I began crafting an inventory for trading."

"But your ship must have cost more than—"

"Financed," he cut her off. "There's a special program for ex-government track employees. Perhaps failing at a career path that requires the highest degree of coordination with co-workers is seen as a qualification for the solitary life of a trader."

"Thirty-two years?" Delphi asked in horror. "You spent thirty-two years training for a job and then they cut you loose? That's a career for a human."

"We operate on different clocks," the Grenouthian said without a hint of irony. "And they were right to show me the exit. I had been unhappy and frustrated for years, but I faked making progress in the hope that once I had a real job without direct supervision, I could do things my way. But that's the whole point of the clock project, to winnow out those of us who aren't a good fit for the bureaucracy. When I was alone in my hut at night weaving those placemats or carving those salad bowls, I came to understand that they did me a favor by letting me go now. Imagine if I had put in three hundred years before finding out I'd started down the wrong career path. Half of my working life would have been wasted."

"You carved those salad bowls by hand? You didn't turn them on a lathe?"

"I built a pole lathe from scraps. My own design, though I'm sure it's been done a trillion times on a billion planets," he added. "Have I been successful in my attempt to fully communicate my position before we begin trading? You're the first human I've conversed with, and I suspect that the changing patterns in your facial wrinkles convey a meaning that I'm missing."

"I don't have wrinkles," Delphi protested, and she ran her hand around the inside of a bowl. "I'd like to see how smooth your skin is under all that fur."

The Grenouthian stood up again, then lifted one leg at a time, almost like a sumo wrestler preparing for a bout. "Do you want to see the bridge? I won't have you telling anybody that I shorted you on the tour."

"I wouldn't understand what I was looking at. The same goes for the engineering deck."

"That's in a crawl space under these deck plates and you wouldn't want to go down there. I don't fit myself unless I remove all the plates first."

"I can take some of the bowls and I want one for myself. I could gamble on a few practice swords for the dojo. What sort of merchandise are you interested in?"

"Anything from the Farling Empire. That's why I'm here meeting you rather than laying out my goods in the section of the bazaar set aside for traders."

"I'll bring up the containers of Farling goods I have on consignment, but I have to warn you that the pickings are a lot slimmer than they were a few months ago," Delphi said.

The Grenouthian took a giant pack down from the bulkhead and said, "Pick out the things you're willing to take and I'll bring them along. I don't have any real experience with bartering myself, but I understand that having the goods on the spot can simplify the accounting."

"Some traders do that, especially when they're trading with sign language. But let's see. I'll take eight of these bowls, four practice swords, a dozen baskets, and—ooh. Pan pipes."

"Do you play?"

"I'm more of a composer than a musician, but I can manage the human version of these," Delphi said.

The alien took the instrument from her and played a mournful tune that brought tears to Delphi's eyes.

"Sold," she said, and then corrected herself, "if we can come to a deal, that is. You should know that I'm working on a commission. The inventory doesn't belong to me."

It took another ten minutes to retrieve the two shipping containers into which Delphi had concentrated most of the remaining inventory of Farling goods with the help of a few bots supplied by Kruik. The Grenouthian waited impatiently for the gantry crane to roll up to the inspection area and set down the first container, and then he hopped right in as soon as one of the ends dropped open to form a ramp. Delphi waited until the second container was deposited next to the first, and then she went to join the trader.

"Take these," he said, thrusting two spools of narrow fabric at her that she hadn't even considered part of inventory because she thought they'd been included by mistake, perhaps from a repair kit. "I'll give you a bowl for the pair."

"Two bowls," she countered reflexively, even though she had no concept of the relative values of the items. "Uh, what is it?"

"Fancy material, though I won't know how it works for sashes until I sew one and try it on for comfort. What did you think it was?"

"Maybe repair tape, the kind you combine with stuff from a can, like fiberglass?"

The Grenouthian just made a grunting noise and returned to digging through the smaller items, though somehow, he managed not to make a mess. "This could be interesting," he said after studying the picture on the retail packaging for what appeared to be a kitchen appliance intended for use with tough root vegetables. "Do you have a translation of the text?"

"Let me see if my implant can make anything of it," Delphi said, setting down the narrow spools of fabric and taking the box. She stared blankly while invoking her heads-up display and navigating to the menu for image capture that combined a translation function. "Got it. You're looking at a heavy-duty juicer that's rated for—the word didn't translate—but works all day on a single charge, whatever their day is."

"I'll swap you two baskets."

"I think it's worth more than that. I've seen the Dollnick version of this selling in shops for twenty creds."

"How long do you think it takes me to weave a basket?" the Grenouthian demanded. "And keep in mind that I'm not working from pre-made materials, I start by making the strips."

"Oh." Delphi tried to remember what she knew about handmade goods and the premium they carried with aliens. "How about two baskets and a set of chopsticks? I saw a pair on the shelf."

"Those are my eating chopsticks. I had a snack in the hold this morning and didn't put them away, but I can whittle you up a similar set this afternoon."

"All right." She took the two spools of potential sash fabric and the juicer and went back out to where the Grenouthian had spread the items from his pack on the deck so they could keep the barters straight. As she paired the fabric with the four bowls she had traded it for, she noticed that in the brighter lighting outside the container, the variegated colors of the potential sash material seemed to be moving in slow motion, forming swirls and vertices. "Drat," Delphi muttered to herself. "This stuff is probably super expensive."

"I read the Grenouthian trader's manual, which condenses seven million years of intergalactic trading into a thousand easy-to-remember points," a voice said in her ear, causing her to jump. "Having no regrets about barter deals was at the very beginning of the first scroll."

"You don't use electronic books?"

"Not for anything truly important," the trader said, setting down a stack of the juicers. "I'm willing to take twenty units, and I don't have enough baskets to cover the deal. Will you take a practice sword for every three?"

"Did they really take you that long to make?" Delphi asked.

"I can show you a holographic recording of my labor, but it would take days."

She did the math in her head and realized that the alien, assuming he was speaking the truth, had been working for less than unskilled human contract workers.

"Two juicers per sword," she said half-heartedly, knowing that some negotiations were expected.

"Three and I'll throw in the scrolls," the Grenouthian said. "I won't tell you what I paid for them, but I have the information memorized, and I'm not sentimental about objects. In fact, that's one of the most important lessons the scrolls have for independent traders. You must be prepared to trade everything you own should the right deal come along, even your ship."

"I don't have a ship, but I'll make the deal, providing my implant can translate the scrolls," Delphi said. "I'm not sure if it does alien calligraphy."

"If you aren't satisfied with the scrolls, I'll let you return them the next time I'm on the Miklat. My plan is to alternate between front-running your route and parking on board so I can trade in the bazaar and save on my fuel pack. Besides, the Zarents grow good vegetables."

Twelve

Hercules ran the hot and cold water in the sink, flushed the toilet, and then tested that the temperature selector for the shower was working. "It all checks out," he told Darryl. "Congratulations. Your crew was the first to finish refitting their allotment of cabins. Ready for the next batch?"

"That's the prize?" Darryl said, trying to sound disappointed but unable to hide his grin. "I told the guys that the Zarents would probably spring for pizza."

"I'll spring for pizza," Hercules said. "That's about the limit of my authority when it comes to spending on anything other than building materials. How about Friday lunch?"

"Works for me. If—" Darryl interrupted himself, pulled out his smartphone, and shook his head in disgust. "I forgot that today is the primary."

"Primary what?"

"Election. Maybe we just got lucky the first time around because all this election nonsense didn't start until we picked up the new group of Colony One lottery winners. Hey, how about coming to the meeting?"

"Is it a support group thing?" Hercules asked suspiciously as he finished filling out the checklist on his tab.

"No, but sometimes I wish it was," Darryl told him. "It's instead of our regular Colony One gathering. Agreeing to attend community meetings was one of the conditions for participating in the lottery. The idea was that we would talk about our experiences so the secretary could record them to share with the millions of Colony One members who can't be here. Somehow the secretaries ended up setting a new agenda, and now it's all about organizing for political purposes."

"Is Colony One seeking separate recognition from the Conference of Sovereign Human Communities? We already have representation in the Human Empire through our co-captains, and they're right up near the top of the pecking order."

"Come along and you'll see," Darryl said, retrieving his toolbelt and slinging it over his shoulder. "The saving grace is that the meeting is limited to a half-hour by statute. One of the secretaries tried passing a motion to extend the time to an hour and he almost got himself lynched."

Hercules glanced at the smartphone he was wearing in a forearm bracer. "Let me just check in with Rayne and see if she has plans for me." He tapped out a message, read the reply that came back almost instantly, and said, "I'm good. Where do you hold these meetings?"

"This one is in Cafeteria Three. It can hold around two thousand people in a pinch."

"Without checking my tab, I would have guessed there were only six hundred chairs."

"Half an hour isn't that long to stand, and it helps keep everybody from falling asleep," Darryl said.

"Uh, maybe I should check with Rayne again, just to make sure," Hercules said. His smartphone buzzed with an incoming message, and swiping to the right, he found that Second Apprentice Miklat had come through with the promised dumbed-down translation of a technical manual describing electron remobilization techniques for renewing the tensile strength of structural elements. He grew absorbed in reading as Darryl led him into the cafeteria and didn't hear the greeting of the police chief.

The Miklat's chief of police didn't take offense when Hercules failed to acknowledge his greeting since he could see that the big man from Bits was lost in scrolling. Drake kept his back to the wall next to the door at the rear of the cafeteria where two thousand members of the Colony One movement were gathered to vote in the primary. "How many of these meetings do they have planned?" he subvoced.

"There are twenty-five such meetings scheduled over the next two weeks," Kruik replied over the chief's implant.

"They're very well-behaved."

"Practice makes perfect. Members of Colony One are expected to participate in a gathering of one type or another every other week."

The meeting started with the well-known theme music from a SciFi television show that had been groundbreaking when it first aired on Earth almost two centuries earlier, and the crowd chanted along with the voice-over labeling space as 'the final frontier.'

"Got everything under control?" a voice whispered in his ear, and he turned his head to see his wife, resplendent in her full uniform, including the hat.

"I thought you weren't coming," he replied.

"Their election committee asked me to speak and I couldn't think of a good excuse to turn them down," Sabina explained. "I also told them that I'm not doing this twenty-four more times, but they're welcome to record a hologram and replay that."

"Did you prepare a speech?" Drake asked.

"Nope. Either they can ask me questions, or I'll just stand there looking beautiful for a minute and leave."

"When do you go on?"

"I told them it has to be at the beginning because I have something scheduled at 16:30 and I want to get there early," Sabina said.

"Isn't that when you meet Katya to work out in the gym?" Drake asked.

"That counts too, and staying in shape so I can keep up with my duties as co-captain has to be a higher priority than whatever you call this."

"What do you call it?"

"I don't even know," Sabina said as a woman with copper-colored hair stepped up on the temporary podium that had been rolled out where the movable steamtable was usually positioned at meals. "I'm only here because I lost the coin flip with Katya."

The quiet conversations in the cafeteria died out before Mattie, the head of the election committee, had a chance to call for silence. Drake couldn't see any evidence of a microphone, but when she began to speak, her voice came out of the public address system at the perfect volume, so he assumed that Kruik was handling the sound engineering.

"My fellow Colony One members," Mattie began. "We've come a long way together, over a hundred thousand light years if my math is correct, but this afternoon is truly different from all other afternoons because it's the first time you'll be asked to cast your vote. I know that some of you think that it's silly to elect somebody to represent you when, as I was informed so eloquently by the Miklat's current mayor, we're merely guests of the Zarents on this ship and we have no rights, not even the right to ask for rights."

"That doesn't sound like something Mouser would say," Drake whispered to Sabina as the crowd murmured during the pause.

"Not the exact words, but I wouldn't be surprised if he expressed that feeling to get Mattie to go away. She and her committee are tiringly persistent."

"I could have put myself forward as the Colony One candidate for a mayoral election," Mattie said, "and I don't think any of you would have objected—"

"Because we don't care," somebody called out, before being hushed by his neighbors.

"—but our movement is founded on the principle of one man, one vote, and I think it's important to go through the exercise of holding a primary even if the outcome is in no doubt."

"Nobody can accuse her of lacking self-confidence," Sabina whispered to her husband.

"The ship's artificial intelligence has offered to handle the mechanics of the election for us, which will be by a simple show of hands after each candidate speaks," Mattie continued. "Kruik has assured me that his thermal imaging in the cafeteria is of sufficiently high resolution to count raised hands and not be fooled if somebody should feel the need to put up both of their arms."

There was a sprinkling of laughter, accompanied by scattered remarks urging the speaker to get on with it so they could go home and do something meaningful. Mattie looked out over the crowd and easily spotted Sabina thanks to her distinctive uniform hat.

"Before the candidates speak, our ship's co-captain has a few words for us," Mattie concluded, leaving the audience to think that their election had drawn attention from the highest levels.

"Thank you," Sabina said to the round of applause that greeted her ascent to the podium. "I'd like to welcome those of you who only joined the Miklat recently, and if you have any questions, I'll be happy to answer them."

Mattie frowned and made a slicing gesture under her throat, perhaps a signal to tell Kruik to stop amplifying her voice, but if it was pre-arranged, the artificial intelligence must have missed it, because the whole audience heard her ask, "You don't have a speech?"

"We have a saying in the Human Empire that talk is cheap," Sabina said, and looking out over the crowd, pointed at a raised hand. "Yes?"

"Is it true that the Zarents have the final say about any changes on board?" the woman with her hand raised called out, and again, her voice was picked up and amplified for everyone to hear.

"The Zarents are at the top of the pyramid, followed by Kruik, who as the resident artificial intelligence, is responsible for the safety of the ship and the inhabitants."

"Where do you fit in?" somebody else called out without waiting to be recognized. "I thought that captains were the final authority on ships."

"If you want to get married, I have the legal authority to tie the knot for you, but as an official representative of the Human Empire, my job is focused on representing humanity to the aliens," Sabina explained. "If you're wondering how the Zarents arrived at the rules governing the conduct of humans on board, they were copied, with certain redactions, from Flower, who has almost a decade of experience hosting a much larger community of humans."

"What redactions?"

"Flower enforces an exercise regime for everyone on board her ship, and there are requirements for playing a team sport and volunteering as well. Yes," she said, pointing at a raised hand closer to the podium.

"What if we want to change one of the ship's rules?" a young woman asked. "Can we vote on it?"

"Nobody will object to your voting, but the outcome won't change the rules. You could petition the Zarents, but I suspect they would want to see a supermajority of the humans on board requesting a change to take it under consideration. Yes?"

The young man near Drake who Sabina had just pointed to put down his hand and asked, "How do we go about joining the ship's crew?"

"Do you have a job?" she asked in reply.

"I work construction, renovating cabins."

"It sounds like you're already part of the crew."

"I mean real crew, you know, uh..." the young man struggled and failed to come up with an example of what he meant.

Sabina thought for a moment. "All right, I don't want to put words in your mouth, so stop me if I get this wrong. You're thinking crew like in a navy, or a ship without artificial intelligence."

"Yes."

"The Zarents are the crew, though Kruik handles many of the functions that are well suited to artificial intelligence. All of you whose jobs involve maintenance or renovation are working as contract crew members if you want to look at it that way. But for the Zarents, being the crew of a ship is their whole identity. That's why they have names like First Engineer Miklat or Fourth Administration Apprentice Miklat. Their jobs are their lives. Yes?"

"What's the point of our voting on anything if—"

"Thank you, but we're out of time," Mattie interrupted the man who had begun asking the question. "And thank you, Co-captain Zerakova. I'll report the primary results to you as we discussed."

Sabina didn't bother contradicting her, in part because the applause would have drowned her out, and in part because the burgeoning politician probably had said something about reporting to her, which might meet the legal definition of a discussion. While Mattie introduced the first candidate, Sabina made her way back through the crowd to where her husband was standing.

"I didn't know I'd married such an effective public speaker," Drake said, straightening her hat, which had begun tilting to one side. "Are you going to stay for the speeches?"

"I really do have to meet Katya for our workout. She keeps finding new pregnancy exercises that require two people. Are you staying?"

"One of the speakers may be my next boss," Drake said with a grin. "I just have to hope that they're as easy to work for as you and Mouser."

"—and together we can move forward to our dream," the lackluster candidate finished reading off his tab as Sabina slipped out of the cafeteria. "Was that sixty seconds?"

"Yes, you did fine, Bryan," Mattie said. "I wish we had more time, but Colony One meetings are limited to a half-hour unless I can get a majority vote to—"

"No!" two thousand voices thundered in unanimous dissent.

"I was just kidding. Next up is our committee's lawyer, Ephriam Snell. Ephriam?"

A tall, thin man mounted the podium and launched into his speech without preliminary comments.

"I've studied the legal precedent of sovereign human communities on alien open worlds, and I see no reason that the Zarents wouldn't grant us a similar level of sovereignty if we can show them that we're capable of governing ourselves. I am withdrawing my name from contention for mayor to offer myself as a candidate for the president of a city council that will work hand-in-hand with Mattie, or whoever you elect, to carry out the business of the Colony One members on board."

"What about the thirty-five percent of the people on board who aren't Colony One members," somebody called out.

"As you just pointed out, we are in the majority. I will notify the appropriate community leaders of our expanding the planned election to include a city council, and they can present their own slate of candidates."

"What a good idea, Ephriam," Mattie said in poorly feigned surprise. "I've had the feeling since my first conversation with Mayor Mouser that he finds the job overwhelming, and a city council would also provide a backup for if your elected mayor is incapacitated." She gestured at the next individual in line to speak, who was also a member of the election committee. The new woman announced her own conversion experience, stating that she was running for a seat on the city council and throwing her support behind Mattie.

Drake kept expecting somebody to object to the political charade, but as his eyes searched the crowd for signs of revolt, what he saw was a sea of people ignoring the candidates in favor of looking at their smartphones. Within ten minutes, it was all over, with the audience responding mechanically to requests for a show of hands, and Kruik announcing the results. Mattie was chosen as Colony One's candidate for mayor, the secretary of the election committee was chosen to stand for president of the as-of-yet non-existent city council, and the other election committee members filled out the slate. When the victorious candidates crowded onto the podium to take a bow, the crowd was already streaming for the doors.

"Hey," Hercules said, stopping in front of the police chief who was still standing against the wall. "When did you get here?"

"Before you," Drake said. "I tried to catch your attention, but you walked right past me reading something from your phone with your lips moving. Is your wife sending you love texts?"

Hercules laughed. "I'll have to tell her that one. Rayne's idea of a romantic text is a shopping list."

"What did you make of the speeches?"

"Speeches? I guess I wasn't paying attention. One of the Zarent apprentices has been translating technical materials into plain English for me, without the math or the chemical formulas."

"Is it useful in your work?" Drake asked.

"Nobody is going to put me in charge of an electron remobilization team, but I get enough out of it to fake that I have a clue if somebody asks me," Hercules said. "Speaking of which, Rayne will probably want to know what the speakers had to say since she knows that I came to the meeting. Anything stick in your mind?"

"Sabina answered questions for the crowd, but the rest of it reminded me of theatre. The candidates had obviously made a backroom deal, and the crowd didn't seem to care one way or the other."

"One of the corridor foremen, Darryl," Hercules looked around for the tall man and then shrugged, "told me that the politicians are almost all from the recent Colony One lottery winners who we picked up at Earth a few months ago. He's the one who invited me, but I guess we got separated in the crowd."

"That happens if you never look up from your smartphone," Drake said.

"Speak of the devil." Hercules glanced at the phone for the incoming message. "Snap wants to see us."

"First Engineer Miklat? And he asked for both of us?"

"He's waiting in the corridor that one of the new crews finished today. I hope it's not a problem that I missed during the inspection."

"It must be about the meeting," Drake said. "He wouldn't want to see me to talk about quality control."

"Good point," Hercules said. "Let's go out through the kitchen to avoid the crowd. I'm pretty sure there's a freight lift tube the next spoke back, and it beats waiting for the log jam to clear."

When the two men emerged from the freight lift tube capsule on the latest deck tackled by the construction crews, the lights were bright, and a furry little alien who resembled an octopus emerged from a cabin on his unicycle and changed course in their direction.

"Perfectly adequate work," First Engineer Miklat spoke through his transceiver. "The new kitchen layout should work for humanoids as long as they aren't too wide or too short. Is it standard on Earth, or did Darryl's crew come up with the design themselves?"

"I don't know," Hercules said. "I haven't spent any time on Earth."

"Thank you for coming as well, Chief. You have probably guessed that I'm interested in what you thought of the meeting. I've listened to the audio, and I was left puzzled by the proceedings."

"I was just telling Hercules that it was a bit of theatre," Drake said. "Some aspiring politicians playing at democracy."

The unicycle leaned a bit toward Hercules as if posing a question on behalf of its rider.

"I wasn't paying attention," Hercules admitted. "But the corridor foreman who handled this group of cabins told me that most of the political types are from the second group who got their places through the Colony One lottery."

"It is unfortunate," Snap said. "Third Mathematician Miklat analyzed the lottery data and she believes that the results were manipulated."

"Was it widespread, or are you talking about the individuals who offered themselves as candidates today?" Drake asked.

"The candidates and a couple dozen others. In a group of twenty-five thousand Humans operating on the honor system, one would expect a much higher rate of cheating. The drawing was run by the contractor who handles the Chicago city-state lotteries, and Flower tells me that there's a long tradition of corruption in that municipality."

"I thought Flower arranged the lottery."

The unicycle leaned from one side to another, almost as if Snap was trying to make up for his lack of ability to perform a headshake. "Colony One handled all the arrangements. Third Mathematician further reported that it's statistically unlikely that none of the elected officers of the Colony One movement won the lottery. She suspects that they were excluded to clear the path for the individuals who are now pushing to become humanity's government on the Miklat."

"Will you cancel the elections?" Hercules asked.

"We haven't agreed to be bound by the results, though the current mayor suggested that we do," Snap said. "It's unfortunate because I find Mouser to be very reasonable for a Human."

"He's a good guy," Drake said. "If you allow the elections to go ahead and he loses, I think he'd refuse if you reappointed him."

"That's my analysis as well. But I'm concerned about these self-appointed leaders of the Colony One movement. No good comes of putting ambitious sentients in positions of power."

"You can withhold it."

"But what about Human morale?" Snap asked. "While your wife's description of the Miklat's command structure was accurate, it would come as a blow to us if all of you packed up and left. There are few things more depressing than a colony ship without a colony."

"You wouldn't lose anybody from Bits by banning elections, and from what Corridor Foreman Darryl tells me, the Colony One members from the first lottery aren't very happy with some of the newcomers. It's possible that nobody would go anywhere."

"But it would be a bad look," Drake said. "The committee has already announced the upcoming election in the electronic newspaper that Colony One publishes for their membership, and I wouldn't be surprised if they rush out a story describing the results of the first primary caucus."

"The slate of candidates and the offices they're running for was published within minutes of the meeting's conclusion."

"They probably wrote the story beforehand and just waited a couple of minutes to throw off suspicion."

"It included a few heavily edited quotes from Co-Captain Zerakova's question-and-answer session," Snap said. "That may have delayed them."

"Do you want me to do a little investigating?" Drake asked. "Between the statistical anomalies you mentioned and what Hercules told me, I can't help wondering if there's an outside force interfering."

"If you can do so quietly. Don't take any chances of letting your curiosity turn into a weapon for the Colony One candidates to claim that they're being persecuted."

Thirteen

Mouser slipped on the fingerless glove, picked up his soldering iron, and activated the Verlock motion suppressor. The tiny magnetic coils sewn into the glove were caught in the projected field and moving his hand was like trying to stir concrete. He dialed down the field strength by an order of magnitude, and when his hand remained steady, continued backing off until the tremor began. Then he turned it up a notch, picked up the roll of fine solder, and began the repair. He had just replaced the last capacitor when he heard the door slide open.

"Kyor," he greeted the Huktra. "Are you bringing me another repair?"

"I hope not," Kyor replied as she set the large stainless-steel and glass appliance on the floor next to the coffee table around which the players would gather. "I just bought this for my new location, and I want to try it out on some real Humans. But first I need to figure out how it works."

Mouser turned off the Verlock motion suppressor, removed the glove, and joined the alien in studying her latest acquisition. "Okay," he said. "What's it supposed to do?"

"I'm not sure exactly, but the salesman said that every Human bar on Earth has one."

"Let me guess. Did you meet the salesman on the docking deck as he was leaving the Miklat?"

"It's the best way to find bargains," Kyor insisted. "Nobody likes paying extra for oversized luggage, and he was transferring to a passenger liner back to Earth. I got it for the wholesale price."

"Do you know why Club Ucerin is such a success?" Mouser asked her.

"Because I run the only craft brewery on board and my prices are reasonable."

"It's because you're so good at sales, but that makes you vulnerable to every other sales pitch you hear."

"I don't follow your logic," Kyor said, taking a hasty step back as something inside the device began to move in response to her having touched the control pad. "Selling beer to Humans doesn't take a marketing genius, and I only buy things that I need."

"What does this do again?" Mouser asked.

"If everybody waited until they had complete knowledge of a product before making a purchase, nobody would ever buy anything and the galactic economy would grind to a halt. It's enough to know that all the bars on Earth have one."

"What if he was lying?"

Kyor's leather lips pulled back, revealing a double row of daggerlike teeth. "It's one of the advantages of being a dragon variant. Mammals don't lie to us."

"Are you sure he said that every bar on Earth has one, as opposed to, say, every bar on Earth wishes they had one?" Mouser asked.

"Aren't they equivalent? Desire to purchase an object is a better indicator of its utility than ownership. If everybody in the business wants one, that's proof that it's good."

"Whatever it is."

"Some sort of food preparation device, I assume," Kyor said. "I can hear it getting ready to cook something."

"There's no power cord on the back and running an oven on battery power doesn't make a lot of sense," Mouser said. He moved around it to where he could see the dark glass that started about halfway up the front of the appliance and began to curve, almost like a rolltop desk. "You know, this reminds me of an old offline data archive we had in the museum on Bits. What was it called?"

The Huktra and the human both jumped back when the machine suddenly lit up and sound began blaring from hidden speakers while holographic text was projected from the top section.

"Is that coded instructions to turn the noise off?" Kyor asked, her ear flaps flattening against her head to protect her auditory canals as if she were flying in a thunderstorm. "Why is he talking about getting a 'Nine' and taking over the hood? It makes no sense."

"The hologram is displaying lyrics," Mouser told her. "You're now the proud owner of a karaoke machine, and now I remember what we called that offline storage. It was an optical disc jukebox."

"Don't karaoke machines play music?"

"Humans have been arguing over what is and isn't music for centuries and the definition changes with every generation. Let me see the control pad." Mouser stepped in front of Kyor, who was happy to keep her distance from the booming bass, and he saw that it was protected by a peel-away strip of dark plastic. Once that was pulled off, the display area lit up with a menu. "Pick a decade," he said. "I wonder why they don't have anything later than 2011?"

"Just make it stop and I'll tell you," Kyor said, and let out a sigh of relief when the thumping bass and the explicit lyrics were extinguished. "Myort collects old Human recordings. He made a killing selling lost over-the-air broadcasts from the early twentieth century that were picked up by radio-frequency monitoring equipment Huktra Intelligence had installed on Earth's moon. Intellectual property laws on Earth are written to protect investors in the backlists of dead artists and authors, and the expiration dates for more recent works are often extended."

"So everything recorded before 2011 is in the public domain?"

"I doubt it, but I'll bet that a lot of businesses and heirs stopped renewing copyright registrations after the Stryx opened Earth. However popular a recording is in its era, a century or more later, the commercial value is usually gone."

Mouser continued poking at the menus and grunted. "I found the voice control actuator and the volume. I can't imagine why they made this karaoke machine so big, though. The speakers are using Dollnick airwave technology, so there's no reason the whole thing wouldn't fit in a device the size of a translation pendant."

"Maybe it makes salty snacks," Kyor said hopefully. "Salty snacks sell beer."

"I kind of doubt—well, look at that."

"Does it roast peanuts?"

"No, but it recharges its battery with heat scavenged from anything you put in the main compartment," Mouser said.

"I bought a sing-a-long refrigerator?" The Huktra considered her options. "Maybe I'll start selling canned soda for the lunch crowd."

"You've started serving lunch?"

"Soda and popcorn."

"Well, I can start you off with your first case of soda," Mouser offered. "The warm cans are in the cases on the back table."

While Kyor was picking out a starter collection of warm cans of soda to recharge her karaoke machine batteries through heat transfer, the other members of the gaming group began trickling in, starting with Rayne and Hercules, who arrived together. Lisa and Botan came in a minute later, the latter carrying a large hand-carved bowl filled with a fresh mixed salad, followed by Shadow, who brought an imported bag of pretzels. Belle arrived and made the usual contribution of chocolate, and Delphi rushed in just a minute before the official starting time.

"Sorry I'm almost late," Delphi said, watching hungrily as Lisa passed Botan a small salad bowl to fill for her. "I had a last-minute appointment to show some consignment goods to a Fillinduck trio that the co-captains sent over."

"You should be killing us at this game with all of the real trading experience you're getting," Rayne said. "What's your running total."

"I forget. Mouser?"

The gamemaster looked at the Grenouthian thin tab that included the relevant data for the eight players. "You're in third place behind Kyor and Belle."

"That makes you the top human," Shadow said.

The Huktra returned to the gaming area with an armful of soda cans and began stocking them in her karaoke machine. "These are still warm, but you can have one when I'm done with them," she cut off Shadow's unspoken question. "I need the heat."

"Sure. I'll just get a can from the fridge in the meantime. Does anybody else want one?"

"Here," Hercules said. "Rayne?"

"I quit soda," Rayne said. "It's not worth the calories and the dental work."

"Is that a common perception?" Kyor asked, the concern clear in her guttural English.

"Only with people who aren't any fun," Shadow said as he returned with the sodas. "What are you doing with warm soda, anyway?"

"Cooling it with advanced karaoke technology."

"I've heard of thermoacoustic cooling," Hercules said. "The Zarents use it to scavenge the energy from noisy equipment. They don't like using Dollnick acoustic suppression fields because those take power rather than making it."

"This is different," Kyor said. "It's a direct energy conversion process used to charge a battery. The music comes afterward."

"Seems like a waste of alien technology to me," Shadow said. "Earth had refrigeration long before the Stryx came."

"Did you ever think that may be why the Stryx came? Earth was probably the only planet in the galaxy where people thought that adding heat to a room to cool the inside of an insulated box was a smart idea. Everybody is playing the same game when it comes to heat, and you can't win or break even."

"Doesn't that mean that everybody always loses?"

Kyor opened the door of her karaoke machine again and checked the temperature of a soda can by touch. "Everybody else cheats," she said. "This one is ready."

"I'll take it," Mouser said. "And since you're all having a late lunch, I'll start with a recap of where we left off. It's the second day of the fair on Huravia, and the monks have exhausted their stock of trade items. You all engaged in a late-night session of trading with each other, and Kyor participated in every deal that included more than two parties."

"It's like playing poker with somebody who bluffs every hand," Rayne grumbled.

"Nobody's stopping you from trying," the Huktra said complacently and reached into a leather shoulder bag. "Does anybody want some mutton jerky? No? More for me."

"Belle continues to ration out her initial cargo of Earth chocolate, and has concentrated her trades in the secondary market, taking in items that other players have traded for versus their original inventory." Mouser looked up from his gamemaster's thin-tab. "Is your strategy original, Belle, or have you played it in a Gem trading game?"

"It seems to me that humans value their inventory according to what they paid for it, which in the case of this game, was their starting capital," Belle said. "As soon as that value conception is once-removed, your trading becomes sloppy, from a mathematical perspective."

"It's because my short-term memory is bad," Rayne said. "I can't remember how many alien whatsits I traded for a widget, especially when I don't have a clue what they're for."

"Then why make the trade?" Hercules asked.

"Because if you just sit on your starting inventory, you're sure to lose in this game," she told him. "Why do you think you're in second to last place?"

"Who am I beating?"

Shadow raised a hand. "I tried following Kyor's strategy, but I'm running out of stuff, so I guess I've made some bad deals. It's not my kind of game."

Mouser cleared his throat and continued. "Delphi has made the two biggest trades so far, including one multi-party deal in which she turned over nearly her entire inventory. Botan is concentrated on art and artifacts, so he has built up a small cargo that packs a large punch."

"It wasn't planned," Botan said. "I'm just trading for the items that attract me."

"I better not find another woman in your inventory," Lisa growled.

"Rayne is building a cargo of industrial supplies, even if she doesn't have a particular application in mind, and Lisa, to nobody's surprise, has been concentrating on sporting equipment, especially protective gear for martial arts training."

"That's why I haven't been trading," Hercules said. "Lisa keeps jumping in and grabbing the stuff I want."

"The name of the game is *Speed Trader*," Lisa reminded him. "And you should be an expert in construction supplies by now."

"Nobody put construction supplies in their starting inventory, and they're too bulky for our hold space in any case."

"Hercules is still sitting on most of his starting inventory, some of which remains private unless he chooses to reveal it," Mouser continued, "while Shadow is behind only Delphi in turning over his inventory."

"Turning it over to Kyor and Belle," Shadow griped. "If I find out that either of you can read minds, I'm going to declare a forfeit."

"Gem have some telepathic abilities from cloning, but only with our sisters," Belle said.

"You're an easy read," Kyor added. "Think of a number. Two. Was I right?"

"How did you do that?" Shadow demanded.

"Human males always think of two the first time. Think of another number. Ten."

"Damnit! You are a mind reader."

"I've served hundreds of kegs of beer to Humans in the last year, and my biggest demographic is males your age," the Huktra said. "I add at least twenty percent to my gross revenue by wagering with customers."

"You guess what number they're thinking?" Mouser asked. "What if they lie?"

"Refer to our earlier conversation. They'd have to be drunk to lie to a dragon variant, and I don't serve drunks, or gamble with them. And I'd get bored guessing numbers all night, so I've been doing an informal investigation of Human psychology by going double-or-nothing on bar tabs."

"Are we that simple?" Rayne asked.

"Guys his age are," Kyor said, pointing at Shadow with a talon. "I can always rake it in by guessing that they're thinking about sex. Even if they aren't, they're too embarrassed to admit it, so I still win. Human females are much tougher."

"What do we think about?" Lisa asked.

"Sex, but you don't like admitting it in public, so I usually guess food."

"But men eat more than we do. I swear that Botan eats twice as much as me, but we weigh the same, and I work twice as hard."

"You work out twice as hard," Botan said. "It's not the same thing."

"That's what's so amusing about Human psychology. Your thoughts are almost entirely unrelated to your everyday lives and goals," Kyor said. "If you put as much effort into thinking about your trades as you do thinking about your bodily needs—I'd still be in first place, but the gap would be narrower."

"Let's just start so I can lose the rest of my stuff and win the low," Shadow said. "We did agree to play Hi-Lo, didn't we?"

Delphi threw a pillow at her boyfriend, which he allowed to bounce off his face so he wouldn't spill his soda trying to block it.

Mouser fooled around with his thin tab for a moment, and then said, "You awake to a red dawn, your ships arranged in a rough octagon on the trading grounds. Kyor emerges first and takes a quick flight around the fairgrounds to stretch her wings, and then Belle starts a small campfire to make hot chocolate. The smell of the chocolate brings Delphi, Rayne, and Lisa out of their ships. Rayne, this is your chance to engage in a trade without Kyor horning in."

"I could return," the Huktra said. "I have excellent vision."

"I'm ready to trade," Delphi said. "I believe I saw you take a Huravian automaton in exchange for some bar chocolate and a bundle of blank Horten holographic scrolls, Belle. I want that automaton and a cup of your hot chocolate, and I'm willing to let you have a bolt of spider silk from the Farling Empire. The strands are stronger than carbon fiber, and the silk changes color with your body temperature."

"It's not spider silk," Belle told her. "It's a synthetic thread made by the L'meuf, and it's called that because they look like giant spiders."

"They don't, uh, excrete it from their abdomens? Then the description was wrong in the original inventory listing."

"You don't have any original inventory," Shadow reminded her.

"But I use the guide to look up items whenever—" she interrupted herself and glared at Mouser. "The guide isn't accurate?"

"The Grenouthians believe we live in an imperfect galaxy with imperfect information," the gamemaster told her. "One of your goals as a trader is to fill your knowledge gaps. Think of it as a journey of discovery."

"Can I come back yet?" Kyor asked. "I have a customer for a Huravian automaton."

"Me," Delphi said. "But I'd rather buy direct and cut out the middle-dragon. How about some Verlock heat stones," she offered Belle. "You can trade those anywhere. They're like children's shoes."

"I could use those in an improvised sauna," Lisa said. "What do you want for them?"

"An automaton."

"How many Verlock heat stones?" Belle asked.

"These are the big ones that retail for twenty creds each," Delphi said, doubling the first number that came to mind. "How much could a crude automaton made by monks be worth? A hundred creds? It probably doesn't even work."

"As a collector's item, I imagine it's worth a thousand creds, so let's call it fifty heat stones."

"I can't go that high! I don't have the stones."

"Can I *pleeeease* swoop in for a landing," Kyor pleaded with Mouser. "I can get this deal done and everybody will come out a winner."

"I could trade you a gross of boxing gloves for the automaton," Lisa offered. "But you have to agree to give me enough heat stones for a sauna first," she added to Delphi.

"Rayne?" Belle asked.

"I don't know if you'd want anything I have, but you can look at my whole inventory," Rayne offered.

"That's it, I'm landing," Kyor declared, and leaned forward toward the clone. "Swiss Chocolate. A metric short ton."

"Done," Belle said without hesitation. "Where did you get it?"

"From me," Delphi said mournfully. "I traded my entire inventory of Alt musical instruments for it when that NPC trader from Earth was in the game a few weeks ago. I knew you'd eventually have something I wanted, but then Kyor offered me the Tyrellian synthesizer, and I'm a sucker for alien music tech."

The Huktra chuckled. "And now you can have the automaton for all your heat stones plus that L'meuf silk and a hundred creds at the final cash out. Yes or no."

Delphi grimaced and studied her inventory sheet. "Without the hundred creds—"

"Done," Kyor interrupted, and spun on Lisa. "I doubt you need two large heat stones to get a sauna boiling, but I'm in a good mood so I'll give you three for your collection of Frunge cutlery."

"I don't have any Frunge cutlery," Lisa protested. "Just a few axe heads and two long swords, one with a damaged pommel."

"I'll take them." Kyor made the note on her Grenouthian sheet with one carefully extended claw. "What's my score now, Mouser?"

"Let's just say that you increased your lead by more than Shadow is worth."

"You went too fast for me," Rayne complained.

"*Speed Trader,*" Kyor reminded her.

"You know, I've been trading with aliens for three months now and it's nothing like this," Delphi said as she adjusted her inventory. "They all make deliberate decisions. The one Grenouthian trader took the time to tell me his life story, though he was new at it, and I did pay a cred to see his ship."

"Maybe *Speed Trader* is like wearing ankle weights," Lisa suggested. "A training game that makes Grenouthian traders better when they have time to think. How did you make out on the trades?"

"Who knows? I don't have a starting value for any of the consignment inventory from Farling Four so I'm trading in the dark."

"When are the boys going to get here?" Kyor asked Mouser. "Botan was looking for some heat stones, Hercules has to start trading or he'll just sink lower and lower, and Shadow will go for anything I offer."

"I'm sitting right here," Shadow said.

"Only in the real world," Delphi reminded him. "According to the gamemaster, you're sleeping late."

"I'm fine just watching and learning," Botan said. "I need to be able to fake that I know something about business when I set up the farm stand with the school kids I'm teaching."

"You own a pickle company in real life," Kyor said. "It sounds to me like you know exactly what you're doing."

"We—" he gestured at Lisa, "own a pickle brand, but I haven't had my hands in brine for almost a year. The actual pickling takes place on Flower or back on Earth. We licensed my family's story in return for royalties and Drazen Foods buying all the pickles my family in Japan can produce."

"I still say you made the right decision," Rayne told them. "If you turned down Flower's offer, she would have found somebody else to front a pickle brand for her, or just gone with her own labeling. She jumps on anything that allows her to extend the shelf-life of food while creating value. If you could figure out a way to preserve avocados without freeze-drying, you could write your own ticket."

"Why without freeze-drying?" Botan asked.

"Flower already does that."

Mouser cleared his throat again, and said, "Hercules emerges from his ship carrying a large trader pack stuffed with items he's decided he has to move, and approaches Belle's small campfire just as the hot chocolate is ready to serve."

"What have you got there, Hercules?" Rayne asked. "How about giving me the first look."

"Just dump it all out on the ground," Kyor suggested. "You know you want to."

"She's right," Hercules said. "I empty my pack onto the ground and you see canned food, hand tools, and blankets."

"Were you planning on visiting a tech ban world?" Rayne asked.

"I thought that if I focused on commodity inventory I'd be able to trade anywhere. And I could have, but nobody wants to pay what it's worth."

"Maybe not us, but why didn't you unload your stock on the Non-Player Characters that Mouser voices?"

Hercules shrugged. "What can I say? It's not my game."

"You're ahead of me," Shadow pointed out.

"Botan arrives at the campfire and—"

"Heat stones," Kyor interrupted. "I want that silkscreen of a gryphon that you got from a Human trader."

"It's not an original," Botan said. "The NPC told me that he bought it from a mail-order catalog back on Earth, along with a whole bunch of art reproductions."

"Don't talk down your goods," Lisa hissed at him.

"I know it's not an original," Kyor said. "I also know the gryphon. She used to hang out with Myort and drive me crazy with all her talk about how they're better fliers than dragon variants."

"Are they?" Mouser asked, seeing this as an important bit of information for a gamemaster.

"We're better in a vacuum."

"How can you fly in a vacuum?" Shadow demanded. "There's no air for your wings."

"We cheat," Kyor reminded him. "Everybody cheats, but dragon variants have been at it longer than mammals."

"Aren't gryphons more bird than mammal?" Mouser asked. "I have them listed as birds."

"They nurse their young. The terms are only rough translations when you're talking about life from anywhere other than Earth or Alt. And you all owe me a cred, except Belle."

"Why?" Delphi asked.

"If a Grenouthian can charge you a cred to see his ship, I should be able to charge a cred for all of these gems of wisdom I'm imparting, no pun intended, Belle."

Fourteen

"—so you see," Ulah concluded as she handed Nigel an espresso and steamed milk, complete with latte art depicting a partial skeleton of an alien species just as it might have been unearthed at a xenoarchaeological dig, "*Rescue Dig* makes a perfect platform to expand into other game spaces involving patient detective work."

Nigel stood there for a moment with his mouth hanging open. He was about to ask the young Dollnick if she ever slept, or if her species went through a phase of manic productivity that lasted for months, but at the last second, he changed the question to, "Where did you learn how to do latte art?"

"I've been watching Grenouthian documentaries about Earth, just to get up to speed. I thought it might help with office morale if I learned to make coffee drinks. I've been practicing in the morning before anybody comes in."

"You're overqualified to be working as our office manager. Maybe the job title translates to something else in Dollnick, but—are you okay?" he broke off as she let out an involuntary whistle like a punctured tire.

"I did it again, didn't I? You're going to fire me because I'm overstepping my bounds."

Nigel set down his latte and took the Dollnick's lower hands in his own. "No, I was trying to give you a compliment," he said. "I'm counting on you to help Shadow keep the business running while I'm away on Flower with Katya."

"Are you sure you don't mind my bringing up new business opportunities?" she asked, shyly averting her gaze.

"I'll always be willing to listen to anything you have to say."

"Good," she said, her posture and poise returning to normal. "I've prepared a presentation and I asked Shadow to come in early so we could go through it before the employees begin to arrive. It shouldn't take more than an hour."

The latte took the sting out of the prospect of spending an hour getting lectured about missed business opportunities by their new office manager, and Nigel texted his wife to let her know that he'd confirmed their reservations for an early lunch. Then Shadow arrived, received a latte embellished with a foam assassin character from his favorite fantasy game, and the two men allowed themselves to be herded by their four-armed shepherdess into the test area that doubled as a conference room.

"I've sent your tabs my plan for expanding the *Rescue Dig* platform into new educational gaming areas," Ulah began. "Let's all take as much time as we need to read it, and then I'll make my presentation and we can have an informed discussion."

"Why didn't you send it to me last night?" Shadow asked.

"You wouldn't have read it. I've attended enough Human meetings to notice that the presenter is often interrupted with objections or questions that would have been addressed in due course. If you read through my plan first, everything I'm going to say will be reviewed, and the meeting will be more efficient for all involved."

"Can I ask if I have a question while I'm reading?"

"After you finish," Ulah told him sternly. "As with a verbal presentation, it's likely that your question is already addressed in the next paragraph."

Nigel finished reading almost five minutes before Shadow, and he found the arguments presented by their office manager so compelling that he went back through it a second time. Ulah was in and out as she watered all the plants in the office, emptied the smaller recycling bins into the larger ones in the lobby that were picked up mid-morning, and employed an ionic broom to clean the corners which the disc-shaped robotic vacuum that prowled the office couldn't reach. She returned to the conference room just as Shadow finished.

"Are there any questions before I begin?" Ulah asked, the thumb of her lower left hand just above the power button for the holographic projector's remote control.

"We used to have new product pitches on Bits all of the time, and kids who were old enough to play the proposed game were always welcome," Shadow said. "I didn't always read the whole package, but this," he gave the tab a shake, "would have gotten funded, even if it meant abandoning some other work in progress. I've never seen such a compelling business argument. I don't think we need to hear the oral presentation, do we, Nigel?"

"She convinced me on the first read-through," Nigel said.

"But I practiced it all night, and you've never seen me give a formal presentation," Ulah said, clearly distressed by the possibility that they would approve her plan without further discussion. "And then you have to grade me."

"Like in school?"

"Dollnicks always grade presenters at meetings. Constructive feedback is key to improvement."

"I only read it once," Shadow said with a glance at his business partner, "so I can listen to it again."

"It's still sinking in with me," Nigel agreed. "I'd like to see you present, and we can grade you afterward."

"Thank you," the Dollnick said with a whistle of relief. She powered on the projector, and a hologram appeared showing somebody working with a paintbrush to remove the dirt from a partially buried skull. "What do you see?" she asked.

"It looks like a cranium," Nigel said.

"From a dig on a planet that was populated with humanoids," Shadow added.

"Are you sure the hologram is from a xenoarchaeological dig?" Ulah asked.

"They used some sort of plastic tape instead of string lines," Nigel said, turning his attention to the details of the hologram. "And now that you mention it, they aren't excavating to level."

"It's a crime scene, isn't it?" Shadow asked.

"From a training hologram for coroners on Earth," Ulah said. "Police Chief Drake was kind enough to loan it to me. And this?" she advanced to the next hologram.

"Ground penetrating radar, from the planning stages of a dig," Nigel said confidently. "I can see the outlines of a circular tower, maybe a buried granary, and—"

"Those are missile silos," Shadow interrupted. "Is it an ancient asteroid defense installation?"

"These holograms are from a training collection that Kruik retained from his time in the Dollnick military," Ulah explained. "You can see how the game engine from *Rescue Dig* could be adapted for training to spot hidden weapons systems. The process on a planetary scale is similar to a xenoarchaeological survey from space."

"Reusing that platform for training systems makes sense, but when it comes to gameplay, you need to come up with storylines, or something that will keep the players engaged. I think your idea with detective work should be our first target, and it will have a market advantage over *Rescue Dig*, where there's no opponent, other than time."

Nigel suppressed a groan. "You want to do a cops and robbers game?"

"An educational game, but one that keeps the players involved by adding the elements of loss and danger," Shadow said. "Think of how much more interesting *Rescue Dig* would be if the skeletal remains that are excavated could reanimate to defend their homes."

"Next hologram," Ulah announced, putting an end to the old argument before it could get going in earnest. "Describe the action."

"The player is examining a rock for fossilized remains," Nigel replied immediately. "The stone has weathered away from the cliff exposing an inner layer that may have been underground for hundreds of millions of years."

"I think she's looking down into the valley," Shadow said. "Her head is turned away from the cliff, and that doesn't look like a camera she's holding. And what's with the puffs of smoke in the distance? It almost looks like somebody was blowing something up."

"Those are the dust plumes from explosive charges set off in shot holes for a seismic survey," Ulah explained. "It's a technique that still has value for imaging deep inside a planet's crust using soundwaves. Our engineers always perform seismic surveys before digging deep wells to ensure that they don't accidentally tap into underground fields of petroleum or natural gas, which can be quite dangerous."

"Earth's economy ran for more than a century on hydrocarbons," Nigel told her. "Geologists were trained to find oil and gas, not to avoid it."

"Yes, the Grenouthians made a whole series of documentaries on the topic. It would have been funny if not for all the wars and pollution that ensued."

"I saw where you talked about geological surveys in the reading, but I don't get the game potential," Shadow said. "Going back to the crime idea, rather than making the game about searching for evidence and forensics, we could expand it to the whole detective squad, and maybe there could be players who take the part of the criminals and try to get away. It's all coming together now in my mind's eye, and Delphi loves doing soundtracks for suspense, or she will when I tell her about it."

Nigel put a restraining hand on his partner's arm since it looked like Shadow was about to jump up and run back to his office to start programming the new game. "I don't think that's what Ulah is presenting here, Shadow, and we should give her a chance to finish explaining since she put so much work into preparing. If the two of you decide to go ahead with a violent action game, I won't get in your way, but leave me out of it."

Ulah clicked the remote to bring up a new hologram, this one showing a man with a trowel who was using the tip to make a groove in a plot of land surrounded by a string line. "Final hologram," she announced. "Please discuss."

"If he's excavating something, he's never heard of best practices," Nigel said. "I can just imagine that trowel leaving a long scratch in a pristine mosaic."

"And why is the dig site surrounded with grass on three sides?" Shadow asked. "Was somebody building an addition on their house, but the contractor found archaeological remains and had to call for a rescue dig? Or," he became more animated, "is it another police investigation where they're digging up evidence from the killer's backyard?"

"I borrowed this hologram from Alfred, one of our recent hires," Ulah said. "He was using it as the default image for his display desk, and that's his father getting ready to plant seeds in his garden."

"You want to use *Rescue Dig* as the basis of an educational gardening game? Our platform would handle all the dirt-work aspects, but we'd have to buy a library with plant-growing routines and imagery, and there are already a ton of farming games on the market."

"For visors?" Nigel asked. "Don't forget that we have an exclusive deal with Flower to get our demos shipped with every new virtual reality headset she sells."

"Constraint equals creativity," Ulah contributed. "I agree that ReVisor should be concentrating on the visor market where we have both expertise and a competitive moat."

"Is that it?" Shadow asked as the Dollnick turned off the holographic projector. "I thought you were going to go through everything we read."

"That would be a very inefficient use of our time. The point of having a meeting is to engage in ideas, not to listen to somebody give a speech. My presentation was intended to get the two of you thinking about the possibilities of the *Rescue Dig* platform, but I wouldn't presume to be able to predict what would make for a successful educational game in the Human market."

"And for Dollnicks?"

The office manager didn't reply, and suddenly found something interesting about the back of her upper-right hand to study.

"Ulah?" Shadow followed up. "I know that your species isn't our top tunnel network demographic, but I'm pretty sure we've sold Dollnicks a few hundred copies of *Rescue Dig* with modified virtual reality headsets."

"It could be the humorous juxtaposition," Ulah finally replied. "Archaic technology to run an educational game about exploring the remains of extinct civilizations."

Nigel face-palmed. "Why didn't we ever think of that? I wondered why we were getting so many orders from Verlock academy worlds where they have all the same digs available on advanced holographic systems."

"Doesn't matter," Shadow said. "I know enough about business to take sales where I can find them, and I'm going to start roughing out a detective game with a forensics option. Thank you for the presentation, Ulah. We should run all our meetings like this."

The Dollnick waited a few seconds after Shadow left, and then she said, "That didn't go exactly how I expected."

"If working on a new game keeps him busy while I'm gone, I suppose it's worth it," Nigel said. "I keep expecting him to suggest that we sell the business to the employees and try something new. I gather there were a lot of serial entrepreneurs on Bits."

"I know that you're more interested in the educational aspects of the technology than gameplay," Ulah said apologetically. "But Shadow does know more about that market than either of us, and it's dangerous for a business like this to be overly reliant on the revenue from a single product. If we can leverage the *Rescue Dig* platform to build market share in another vertical, I'll consider it a success."

"Someday you can explain to me where you learned so much about business, but not today because I have to meet my wife and the in-laws for an early lunch at Bindaal's. Would you like to join us?"

"Oh, I couldn't. Humans have a saying that two's company and three's a crowd. The Dollnick equivalent is that four's the perfect number."

"And?"

"That's it. Four's the perfect number."

"I'll keep it in mind," Nigel said. As he exited the room, he realized that several employees had been waiting to get in to do some beta testing and mumbled an apology. With perfect timing, his phone vibrated with an incoming text from Katya informing him that she'd arrived. She was waiting in the reception area with one hand on her baby bump, chatting with her twin about something.

"Where's Drake?" Nigel asked his sister-in-law after kissing Katya on the cheek. "I thought he was coming."

"He'll meet us there," Sabina said. "Drake pinged me a few minutes ago to say that there was a problem at a Colony One meeting in one of the cafeterias and the manager wanted everybody out so the staff could get ready to serve lunch."

"A problem?"

"That was his word. It could mean anything from littering to a riot. Drake can be very laconic when he's in a hurry."

"You used another Human Empire civil service exam word," Katya tweaked her sister as they headed for the business incubator's shared plaza. "That's the third time this week."

"Laconic?" Sabina asked. "That's a normal word. People use it all the time."

"You referee, Nigel."

"I can't go against my pregnant wife," he said. "I know what it means, but I don't think I've ever heard it in conversation before."

"That's because you spent a decade on a Verlock academy world and they're all laconic," Sabina said.

"Only if you don't have the patience to listen," Nigel said. "When they get to know you and find that you're interested in what they have to say, they can talk for hours."

"To convey dialogue that should have taken twenty minutes."

"True, but that just makes them slow speakers. They aren't naturally terse—"

"Laconic," Sabina interjected.

"—but they cut down on the number of words they would normally use when they're talking to humans."

"Plus, they dumb down the vocabulary," Katya said as the trio emerged from a passage into the plaza where a few dozen aliens who were sticking with their own clocks were taking meal breaks, though which one was anybody's guess.

"Hey, Bindaal," Sabina greeted the Vergallian proprietor of the only restaurant on the plaza. "How's business?"

"There's nothing like a good monopoly," Bindaal said without looking up as she diced an alien root vegetable that looked like an oversized parsnip. "Kyor was right, I'm going to make a killing down here. Can I get you some drinks?"

"Have you expanded the menu since moving?"

"Still no alcohol, if that's what you're asking, but I have some coffee drinks, hot or cold, and I bought a new heavy-duty juicer that I swear could turn furniture wood into a smoothie." She gestured at the juicer with a quick flip of her hand without looking up.

"Isn't that one of the machines G32FX is trying to export?" Katya asked her sister. "Where did you buy that, Bindaal?"

"A Grenouthian trader sold it to me for cash and then spent a good chunk of the proceeds on a vegan banquet for one," the Vergallian said with a chuckle. "The poor bunny must not have eaten for weeks."

"Can they go that long without food?" Nigel asked.

"Grenouthians and Verlocks are both extremophiles in their own ways. Any species that's had interstellar travel for more than five or six million years tends to evolve a lot of flexibility around regular eating and sleeping." She scraped all the chopped vegetables into a glass bowl with the side of her chef's knife and finally looked up. "Do you know what you're having?"

"We'll start with coffee and give Drake a chance to get here," Sabina said.

"No coffee for me," Katya corrected her. "M793qK said one cup a day max, and I already had it. I'll try whatever juice you want to whip up."

"The same for me," Nigel said loyally.

"It's a good thing you're both leaving in a month since I'll be the only one sufficiently caffeinated to get any work done," Sabina said. "Does the coffee ban extend to nursing?"

"He said two small cups with several hours in between," Katya said mournfully. "Oh, well. I suspect the baby will keep us up."

"Why?" Nigel asked. "I thought babies sleep all of the time."

"You haven't given him the book Mom sent?" Sabina asked her sister.

"I've been putting it off," Katya said. "I don't want to make him nervous."

"What are the two of you talking about?" Nigel asked, and he noticed that Bindaal had one ear turned in their direction while she made the drinks.

"I'll give it to you when we get home. It's just that you're an only child brought up in space by your mother and you never spent much time around other children, let alone babies. It's not all cuddling and talking in high voices."

"I'm glad I missed the beginning of that conversation," Drake said as he entered the vegan restaurant. "It's amazing how fast you got set up, Bindaal. This space was empty a week ago."

"And I've been open for five days," the Vergallian told him. "Not having to deal with interior decoration was a big savings. There's only room for the one table that I reserved for you, and everybody else takes their food and eats at tables in the plaza."

"How was the riot?" Sabina asked her husband. "Break any heads?"

"You laugh, but it was a close thing," Drake told her. "If Frankie and Josh hadn't been on standby when I called for help, the candidates in this rolling primary that Colony One is holding may have gotten themselves tarred and feathered. Or maybe covered with syrup and muffin crumbs, since they were still serving late breakfast when the meeting began."

Nigel accepted a glass of pale blue vegetable juice from Bindaal and gave it an experimental sip. His eyes popped open wide. "It *tastes* blue! I've never tasted a color before."

"I'm sitting in case it comes as a surprise," Katya said, slipping past the others and taking the far seat at the table for four. She tried the drink and her nose crinkled. "It's good, but I'm not getting a color."

"I guess I have to try one now," Drake said. "I drank enough coffee listening to the same speeches for the eighteenth time."

"Why do you keep going to those meetings?" Sabina asked, taking her coffee to the table as Bindaal turned back to the juicer.

"Because my instincts tell me that something fishy is going on."

"All politics is fishy. How bad it stinks is just a question of how long the politicians have been rotting."

"Well, today they exceeded their expiration date," Drake said, accepting his drink from Bindaal and joining the others at the table. "What are we having?"

"Whatever the chef thinks is best today," Katya said. "Did you hear that, Bindaal?"

"Chef's Choice for four. It will be a while because I'll need to boil the Flenches."

"We're not in a hurry as long as you don't need the table for another reservation."

The Vergallian laughed musically. "No, I don't run that tight a schedule."

Nigel finished his drink and looked mournfully at the glass. "I'd order another one, but my mother told me that too much of a good thing isn't good."

"Including mothers," Sabina said before Katya could beat her to the punch, and then resumed the conversation with her husband. "So, what was the particular rottenness that almost caused a riot."

"Salaries. Colony One's mayoral candidate and the seven people standing for the city council suggested that they were willing to sacrifice their current careers to dedicate themselves to their fellow citizens, who couldn't begrudge them a living wage."

"They begrudged," Katya surmised.

"The city council members are expecting a salary that's three times what I'm getting paid as chief of police, and better benefits. Mattie, the woman who has the mayoral nomination locked up, let the council members talk her into accepting six thousand creds a month to uphold the honor of the position."

"That's more than me and Katya put together, with your salary thrown in for a kicker," Sabina said angrily.

"That was the view taken by the voters, bringing about my daring rescue mission during which the candidates fled through the kitchen while me and the boys held off the mob with ice cream," Drake said.

"You threatened to throw ice cream at them?"

"No, we offered free servings. The supplier had just dropped off a whole case of those big containers, so we gave everybody a scoop. My elbow is killing me, and I told the cafeteria manager he could charge the ice cream to the ship."

Fifteen

"Why does our farm stand smell like pickles?" Sarah asked.

"That's where I got the wooden barrels," Botan explained. "I used them to make our first couple batches of pickles before outsourcing that part of the business to Flower and—well, I guess I kind of outsourced every part of the business. But that's an important lesson to learn too, kids. You can't be good at everything, and you have to set priorities in life."

"The Zarents are good at everything."

"But not every Zarent is good at *every* thing. They specialize."

"They also cross-train," Davu said confidently. "Third Educator Miklat substituted for our regular teacher last week and explained that the Zarents are always learning. She said that First Engineer Miklat and the other Firsts can cover for every job on the ship."

"And even though they're so small, they aren't physically weak, and they operate robots through servo-thingies to do jobs that require more strength," Mio said. "I wish I could ride around on a robot. I'd make myself taller than Greta."

"Being tall isn't that great," Greta told the petite girl. "I'm taller than any of the boys in our class and they're always saying stuff about it. Everybody thinks that you're pretty."

"She is pretty," Davu said and then realized he wasn't helping. "I mean, you're pretty too. So is Sarah."

"Thanks for getting around to me," Sarah said sarcastically and then pointed. "What's under the blanket?"

"I'll get to that in a minute," Botan said. "Your farm stand opens in a little over an hour. I know that a couple of pickle barrels topped with composite planks that the Zarents make from natural fibers don't look like much, but marketing is trickier than growing vegetables. Do any of you know what you'll be selling today?"

"That's what we forgot! We have to pick stuff."

"There's still time for picking, and the reason I set up the stand right at the edge of your field is so two of you can pick while the other two work the farmstand. People will be willing to pay a premium in return for seeing you pick vegetables while they wait because the freshness is guaranteed."

"You weren't talking about the vegetables when you asked if we knew what we'd be selling today," Greta said slowly, figuring it out as she spoke. "You're saying that we'll be selling a story, just like you and your pickles."

"Exactly. And what's the story you're selling?"

"That we're four orphans who live in that little shack," Davu improvised while pointing at the tool shed. "If we don't sell all of the produce we've grown, we'll be beaten."

"I don't want to be beaten," Mio said. "Can't we have a story where we don't get beaten?"

Botan let his shoulders slump and sighed. "You aren't writing Manga, Davu, though you might have a talent for it, but we can talk about that later. You're selling a story of freshness, of wholesome organic food straight from the farm. That gives you more pricing power than if your selling proposition was that you have a bunch of ripe tomatoes that are going to go soft in a few days if nobody buys them."

"I like soft tomatoes," Sarah said. "They're sweeter than the hard ones."

"Did any of you remember to check out produce pricing in the markets on the bazaar deck?"

Three of the kids stared at Botan blankly, but Greta pulled out her tab and said, "I did. I went to four different places. The least expensive one was the Ag Deck Outlet, but when I asked the fat guy running it—"

"Hank, and he's not that fat," Botan put in.

"—he said they sell the leftover produce that the stores don't want because it's too ripe. But the weird thing is that there was also a section for ugly vegetables, like crooked carrots and lopsided eggplants, and those sold for more than the regular ones."

"Because they have a story to tell. When people see a display of nearly identical carrots, they can't help wondering if they were grown in a factory, using hydroponics. But a crooked carrot with a little dirt still clinging to the skin? It tells its own story."

"But how will we know whether our carrots are crooked before we pick them?" Davu asked. "The whole thing is underground."

"I was just giving an example of why ugly vegetables can sell for more than perfect ones," Botan said. "Greta is in charge of pricing today. Now, before you start picking, I have a surprise for you." He dramatically whisked away the blanket to expose two stacks of nested baskets woven from wood strips, all of them handmade. The kids immediately took possession of several baskets each.

"Ouch," Davu said. "Something sticking out of the basket poked me."

"The weave isn't entirely straight, but I guess that's because the strips aren't all the same width," Mio said. "Do you want us to use these for picking?"

"Yes, and even more importantly, for display," Botan said. "Now you'll have a farmstand with old pickle barrels, planks made from recycled fibers, and handwoven baskets."

"The handles fold up," Sarah said, experimenting with one of the strap handles on her basket. "That's clever. Are these from Earth?"

"Believe it or not, they were made by a Grenouthian, and according to my friend Delphi, the wood strips come from a giant clock that's always being rebuilt."

"Why would anybody rebuild the same thing over and over again?"

"Back in Japan, where my family comes from, there are temples and shrines constructed from wood that are rebuilt every twenty years," Botan told her. "It's based on *tokowaka,* which involves renewing objects with an eye to eternity. It's also a way to pass on building skills from generation to generation."

"I'm picking carrots, and I'm going to find a crooked one," Davu said.

"I dibs tomatoes," Sarah declared to the surprise of no one.

"Everybody should take turns picking everything since you all helped do the planting, but just one kind of vegetable per basket, because that's how they're going to be displayed," Botan said. "We want two full baskets of each vegetable, or fruit, in the case of Sarah's tomatoes."

"So when the first one is empty, we swap the second basket in, and the two of us who aren't working the stand refill it," Greta surmised.

"Close. Another trick is that you never want the display basket to look empty. The two of you working the stand should constantly refill the display basket from the spare."

The four young teenagers spent the next hour harvesting under Botan's watchful eye, and when the opening time arrived, there were twelve baskets full of produce displayed on the planks that constituted the farm stand. Davu announced the countdown and everybody looked in the direction of the nearest lift tube as if they expected the doors to open when he reached zero.

"Three," Davu said, slowing as he reached the end of the countdown. "Two." The kids all shifted nervously. "One?" The lift tube doors remained stubbornly closed. "A half."

"You can't count down in fractions," Sarah told him. "The arrow will never reach the wall."

"What?"

"A non-player character in a game from Bits told me that. If you shoot an arrow at a wall, first it has to fly halfway. Then it has to travel halfway of what's left, and half of that, again and again forever. It proves that the arrow never reaches the wall."

"That's stupid," Davu said.

"Is not," Sarah countered. "If you agree with the NPC, you get the suspension-of-disbelief skill, and it gives you as much protection from projectiles as plate armor."

"Where is everybody?" Mio asked. "My parents promised to come."

"And my mother," Greta said.

"We told everybody at school," Davu added.

"You can't expect them all to show up the second you open," Botan told them. "I told my friends that you were in school in the morning so they should come in the afternoon."

"But it's afternoon now," Sarah protested and got out her smartphone. "I'm texting Hercules."

"Yeah, he's huge," Davu said. "He must eat a ton."

The lift tube doors slid open and a Vergallian towing a two-wheeled shopping cart appeared, accompanied by a Gem with a backpack slung from one shoulder by both straps.

"It's Bindaal and Belle," Sarah said excitedly. "They're both mine."

"Do we have to keep track of who gets the most customers?" Greta asked Botan, her hand hovering over her student tab. "I don't have a column for that in my spreadsheet."

"It's not important," Botan said and then corrected himself. "If this was a large established business, then sales and marketing would be specialized jobs, and the management would certainly track who was attracting customers and how much they spent. But that's a bit much for a farmstand, and I didn't say anything ahead of time, so, no."

The two aliens walked up to the farmstand, and the four teens practically stood at attention. "Everything is super fresh," Sarah told her favorite chef. "We picked it all ourselves just now."

"I'm impressed by the dirt on the carrots," Bindaal said. "Very organic." She picked up a tomato, squeezed it slightly, and nodded. "I think I'll be running a special on tomato juice."

"Do you have any spinach or kale?" Belle asked.

Sarah drooped. "Botan wouldn't let us."

"They do better if you plant the seeds in the cold and we went with fast-growing early summer crops or transplants," Botan told the Gem. "Are they your favorite Earth vegetables?"

"Spinach and chocolate make a good smoothie, and kale is my backup," the clone said. "For some reason, chocolate doesn't pair well with a lot of vegetables."

"Have you tried it with beets?" Mio spoke up. "We have beets, and my dad brought home a chocolate beet cake once."

"I'd need to see a recipe before trying something like that."

"Those string beans look like they have plenty of fiber," Bindaal said as she moved along the front of the stand. "Are you selling everything by weight, or are the prices displayed for a whole basketful?"

"I knew I forgot something," Botan said. "Just a minute." He went back over to where the baskets had been, and from under the crumpled blanket he produced a large copper dish bolted to a copper rod with a notch cut in the middle and an iron ball at the end. With his other hand, he picked up a triangular wedge of what might have been glass, and a dark disc with a hole through it which he fit over his thumb to carry.

"There's no room left on the planks for a scale," Greta said. "Should we take some baskets down and make room?"

"There's space on the barrel. This is what I was thinking of when I turned the middle one upside down."

"Is that a balance beam?" Bindaal asked. "Unless that disc is a moving counterweight or there are more parts, and I don't see how the disc can slide on with the ball at one end and the dish at the other."

"It's made by one of the species in the Farling Empire, I forgot the name," Botan said. "My friend Delphi has been trading some of their goods, and she loaned it to me with the baskets she bought." He set the copper plate with the rod on the barrel, put the triangular wedge next to the notch in the rod, and after a bit of twisting, got the disc off his thumb and placed it as far from the wedge as there was room. "Now, if I remember how this works…" He held onto the rod while loosely fitting the narrow tip of the wedge in the much wider notch, turned the whole assembly until the ball was above the disc, and let go. The copper dish bobbed a few times, trembled, and then stabilized, looking perfectly level.

"So how does it work?" Mio asked, slipping under the planks to come up on the customer side of the stand for a closer view. "How will it stay balanced when you put any vegetables in the dish?"

Bindaal obliged by moving a handful of string beans to the copper plate which didn't even dip. But glowing numbers appeared on parallel sides of the glass wedge so that one number could be read by the customer and the other by whoever was working the counter.

"The disc must act like a magnet to pull down the ball and keep the scale balanced, but how does it figure out the weight?" Mio asked.

"Calibration would be my guess," Belle said. "The wedge must have a processor that monitors the current creating an electromagnetic field in the disc, and by weighing a few known masses, it can calibrate the scale for any environment. Did you do the setup, Botan?"

"Delphi did, but Kruik sent a bot to help her so it must be accurate," Botan said. "The scale and the baskets are all for sale, but you'd have to ask Delphi about the scale's price. She said she'd take anything reasonable for the baskets, but cash, not barter."

"Do we get a commission?" Greta asked.

"We didn't discuss it, but I think she'd agree to, uh, fifteen percent?"

"That's clever. The higher the price we negotiate, the more we get."

"I'd like to buy one of these scales for my new place," Bindaal said. "Some of the Hortens are maniacal about their diets, and they don't trust my ability to weigh by eye, even though I'm certified to be ninety-eight percent accurate."

"Does that mean you can tell the weight within two percent, or that you're way off two percent of the time?" Mio asked.

"I still struggle with expressing math in Humanese," the Vergallian said. "My estimate is within two percent of the true weight over ninety-nine percent of the time, and I was never off by more than five percent during the testing."

"I'd like to buy one of those baskets," Belle said from the end of the stand where she seemed to be searching for something. "No bananas?"

"We can't grow bananas in three months," Sarah said. "You're just teasing us."

"Fill a basket with those beets for me, and I'll try roasting them and adding a bit of chocolate sauce. Are the greens edible?"

"Everything is edible," Botan said. "It's hard to say which parts of Earth vegetables other species will like. The Verlocks eat the parts that would break our teeth."

"The Verlocks also chew pebbles, or so the rumor goes," Bindaal said. She added a single small string bean to the scale and said, "There. I got it exactly."

"We can't let green beans go for that," Davu said in dismay after checking the weight against the price that Greta had written on the front and back of the slat stuck in the string bean basket. "I thought we'd sell them for a cred each."

"Your parents couldn't afford to feed you if string beans each cost a cred," Botan told him with a laugh. "That's enough to buy a sandwich in the food court."

A few more shoppers arrived before the Vergallian finished picking out enough produce to fill her cart with the net bags the Zarents had contributed, and for the next two hours, the kids took turns serving people who they mainly knew, or picking fresh vegetables to refill the dwindling supply. When there was only an hour left on the selling day, they began to let the stock run out so it wouldn't have to sit overnight. The tomatoes were the only item to be completely exhausted, but there was also a run on bell peppers and cucumbers as people planned their dinner salads.

"How much did we make?" Davu asked Greta as they began loading an autonomous floater cart with the leftovers for the Cafeteria Two manager who had offered half price for anything that didn't sell.

"One hundred and sixteen creds and a few odd centees," the tall girl replied after totaling a column on her tab. "That comes to twenty-nine creds each."

"We're rich," Mio said. "And we still have three-quarters of the vegetables left in the field to sell, as long as people keep coming."

"But we've been working for three months," Davu pointed out. "That's less than forty creds each per month. Even if we sell the rest at the same prices, that's still only a hundred and twenty creds each."

"We made forty creds a month for working part-time?" Sarah asked in disbelief. "That's enough to by a unicycle."

"How many hours did we work a month?" the boy persisted. "Three afternoons, four hours an afternoon."

"Twelve hours a week, forty-eight hours every four weeks," Mio said. "Months aren't exact, so add another week, and it's—"

"A hundred and fifty-six hours," Greta announced, looking up from her tab. "We'll earn less than a cred an hour." They all turned to Botan, who just smiled.

"What?" Sarah demanded.

"Have you forgotten the point of this educational exercise?" he asked them. "What has it taught you about farming?"

"That we'll never get rich," Davu said grumpily.

"Or that we'd need to grow and sell a lot more," Greta said. "And none of us had any experience when we started, so I bet we could get a lot faster."

"We didn't spend all of the time working our field," Mio pointed out. "Now that I think about it, I bet that more than half of those hours were helping on other sections of the ag decks, like when we were grafting trees."

"Are you going to pay us for that?" Davu asked Botan.

"Do you get paid for going to school?" Botan countered.

"Can we?" Sarah asked, her eyes going round.

"That's above my pay grade, but I'm going to guess you're out of luck there."

The nearby lift tube doors whooshed open, disgorging Rayne and Hercules.

"Sorry we're late," Rayne began explaining when they were still five steps away. "I got caught up with a group of Verlocks looking at space in the business incubator and you know how slowly they talk. I pinged Hercules to come, but he was giving a safety seminar to a new renovation crew."

"You can't have sold out on your first day," Hercules added as he surveyed the empty planks.

"One of the cafeteria managers buys all of the leftovers at a discount," Botan told them apologetically. "The floater cart just left."

"I could pick some tomatoes," Sarah offered.

"The Zarents might not like it. You're all students and you've worked the maximum hours you're allowed for a school afternoon."

"Could we pick our own?" Hercules asked.

Greta shook her head. "We can't allow customers into the vegetable field. It's one of the rules."

"You can come back tomorrow," Mio offered helpfully.

"How about the baskets?" Rayne asked. "I can picture one of them filled with dried flowers on the shelf over the gaming console."

The kids all looked to Botan, who said, "They are for sale, but we need them for the next few days, so you'll have to wait."

"Sorry, Mom," Sarah said. "But I earned twenty-nine creds, so I can treat you both to dinner at Bindaal's. She was our first customer, so they'll be the same tomatoes."

"We agreed not to distribute the money until the last day," Greta reminded her.

"Dinner is on me," Hercules said, putting an arm around Rayne's shoulders and turning her toward the lift tube. "If any of your friends want to come, Sarah, they're welcome. You too, Botan."

"Mio's mom already invited us all to dinner," Sarah told him. "I texted."

Rayne checked her phone and groaned. "I had notifications on mute so the Verlocks wouldn't be offended."

"And I start the safety training by explaining about the dangers of getting distracted while working with power tools," Hercules said. "I started by powering off my phone."

Sixteen

"What is that?" Mouser asked Hercules.

"Your birthday present." Hercules maneuvered the floating mini-forklift around the back of the leather couch, but the path to the work area of the lab was blocked by an old overstuffed armchair. "Should I set it down next to your bench?"

"It's not my birthday, and I'd still like my question answered," Mouser said, but he pushed the chair to the side and walked ahead of the forklift moving other items out of its path. "Where did you get it?"

"Third Engineering Apprentice Miklat said it's either an exercise robot or," Hercules paused dramatically, "a gaming robot. It was abandoned in a cabin that the rehab crews just reached. Untouched by any hands for thousands of years."

"Then the battery will be toast and it may be impossible to find a replacement." Mouser waited for Hercules to set down the pallet with a roughly humanoid robot that was in a sitting position with its knees up and its arms wrapped around its lower legs in what was likely its most compact form for shipping or long-term storage. "It's been a while since I've seen an alien-made robot with all its workings exposed. They usually skin them over with something to keep out the dust if nothing else. I'm surprised it's as clean as it is."

"The cabin was sealed." Hercules dismounted from the improvised human-sized driver's saddle on the mini-fork and came around to stand behind Mouser as the older man crouched to examine the robot. "Third Apprentice was going to take it to their recycling facility, but it looked so sad to me, sitting on the floor like that. Even if it's trash, I thought you might want the opportunity to take it apart and see what makes it tick."

"Help me spin it around. There isn't enough room between the pallet and the bench to get at the back side."

The two men tried to turn the robot, but it wasn't light, and the parts resting on the pallet kept getting stuck in the safety grooves. Hercules started rocking the robot from side to side and then spun it around as the projecting parts came free.

"If you could get Shadow to come by, the two of us could probably lift it onto your bench," Hercules offered.

"Are you implying that I'm too old to pick up a robot?" Mouser asked, studying the access panel on the back of its torso. "You were rocking it yourself, there. How much do you think it weighs?"

"More than you. And Sophie will kill me if I let you throw your back out again. She's still mad at me from two years ago when we set up your lab in here and you decided to move the soda fridge yourself without taking out all the soda first."

"Hold on, I have an idea." Mouser got out his smartphone, enabled the camera function, and focused on the robot. "Kruik?"

"Yes, Mayor," the ship's artificial intelligence responded through the speakers of the entertainment system on the other side of the room.

"Can you see through my phone's camera?"

"You have to start a conference call with me first."

"I haven't done this in so long that I forgot," Mouser said, snorting in amusement. He swiped the camera closed, navigated to the messaging app, and placed a videocall to Kruik. Then he navigated back to the camera, swiped it open again, and hit the sharing icon. "How's that."

"You look the same as when I saw you through the corridor camera roughly an hour ago."

"Oops." Mouser touched the icon to switch to the front-facing camera. "I also forgot that conferencing chooses the rear-facing camera by default."

"Very interesting," Kruik said. "It's one of ours, but the specifications are missing from my standard—got it."

"I didn't know that Dollnicks manufactured any two-armed robots," Hercules said. "Is it something for the export market?"

A dry creaking sound came from the front of the robot, which was now shielded from view due to the way it was turned, and both men reflexively moved back a step.

"Almost have it," Kruik said, his artificially generated voice sounding completely human with its tone of anticipation. "Almost. Almost. There!"

"Nothing happening," Mouser said.

"I'm running its self-diagnostic. When the robot was shut down, somebody put it in sleep mode rather than doing a full power off. That led to the complete exhaustion of the fuel pack, which will have to be rebuilt or replaced."

"But I heard it move a moment ago."

"It can also operate on the ship's internal power carrier transmission, like all of our bots," Kruik said. "I had to break the encryption to access the command module since I'm not the owner."

"But wouldn't it have Dollnick encryption?" Mouser asked.

"Commercial grade, not military grade, and I know a few tricks."

"You figured out who the bot belonged to and tried his birthday," Hercules guessed.

"The serial number from the nameplate that I saw in the Mouser's phone video," Kruik admitted. "That was the default password for this series of bots."

"It looks more like something we build than a robot from any of the advanced species," Mouser said. "Was it for the export market like Hercules guessed? Maybe a butler bot?"

"I don't want to spoil the surprise, but it's older than you'd think, and—"

A whistle from the robot cut off the artificial intelligence's words, and then Kruik said, "Diagnostic complete. I'm going to proceed to full power up, but you should move to a safe distance in case one of the actuators experiences a catastrophic failure after being unused for over ten thousand years. We build robots to last, but even in a sealed cabin, self-welding can take place over that length of time as what you would call atoms inadvertently share electrons with their neighbors."

Hercules hopped back on the mini-fork and backed it up as close to the exit as he could get it without blocking the door, and Mouser took the opportunity to visit the soda fridge and help himself to a can of diet cola. "Can I get you anything, Herc?"

The big man's answer was lost in a cacophony of creaks, shrieks, and snapping sounds as the robot released its death grip on its lower legs and moved its arms back to its sides.

"Sorry about the noise," Kruik said. "I'm giving it a minute to cool down again. The degree of self-welding was less than I'd feared because the actuators and joints were sufficiently worn for the tolerances to have increased. Had the robot been new or lightly used, it would have required careful disassembly and polishing of all the bearing parts."

"I'll admit I'm dying of curiosity, but you don't have to rush on our behalf," Mouser said. "Would it be better to hot-tank the robot in a cleaning solution, or to freeze it?"

"Dollnick robotic designs allow for long periods of inactivity. Imagine sending explorer bots on missions to uncharted areas of the galaxy where they may be expected to remain in a quiescent state until the mother ship locates a candidate planet worth investigating."

"Any orange juice left in there?" Hercules asked, coming over to where Mouser was standing next to the small refrigerator. He accepted the bottle of 'Flower's Orchards,' and was twisting off the top as the robot sprang to its feet in one convulsive movement. "Holy—! I hope it's friendly."

"It's not sentient," Kruik assured them. "I'm controlling all its actions. While it has the ability to perform certain preset routines based on default programming, and that's probably how it was used by its last owner, this type was designed specifically for use in games involving martial arts combat."

"Punching that thing looks like a good way to break a hand."

"It shipped with full-body padded suits that allowed it to emulate opponents of different species."

"It's pretty skinny, so I guess the right padding material would keep it from getting too bulky," Hercules said. "I suppose it could work for training, but it would be hard to suspend your disbelief fighting it in a game unless the story called for an attack by heavily padded robots."

"The kinetic damping materials developed by Dollnick science for sporting purposes would surprise you," Kruik said. "And you're forgetting about the hologram."

The robot turned in the direction of the two men and a blue-ish haze surrounded its body before solidifying into the shape of an ogre that could have been ripped directly from a Live Action Role Playing studio. The ogre extended an arm toward Hercules, the hand turned palm up, and made a 'come here' curling gesture with its index finger.

"No chance," Hercules said. "There's no padding under that hologram."

"That's a phenomenal wrap job," Mouser said. "I'm beginning to understand why the kids on Flower were so crazy about LARPing."

"I should go back to the cabin and see if there's a padded suit around somewhere. Are you sure that thing won't attack Mouser, Kruik?"

"It has no ability to initiate actions on its own," the ship's AI assured him. "I'm going to put it through a standard calibration routine to make sure that the sensors are all within tolerance."

The robot stepped off the pallet, moved into an open area of the floor, and began working through a complicated series of movements.

"That reminds me of watching Shadow's sister doing the Cayl warmup exercises," Mouser said. "I'm going to text Lisa and see if she's free. She might want the robot for her dojo."

"Regifting?" Hercules asked as he picked up the pallet and walked it over to the mini-fork.

Mouser looked up from his phone. "I'll tell her it's from you. Sophie already bought a wedding present to give them."

"Something tells me that Rayne won't agree to make our wedding present to Lisa and Botan an old exercise bot that I found abandoned, even if it's worth—what is something like that worth, Kruik?"

"A collector would pay several thousand creds for a training bot in that condition," Kruik replied. "But first you'd have to replace the fuel pack, which would cost almost the same amount since it would require customization."

"Dollnicks don't manufacture these anymore?"

"It was a fad, and we probably stopped manufacturing them long before this one was sold. Robots have long shelf lives."

Hercules climbed back into the saddle and said, "I'll let you know if I find the padding," as he eased the mini-fork out of the lab.

Mouser's phone vibrated and he glanced down to see a message from Lisa that she was on her way. "How long will the robot be doing calisthenics?" he asked out loud. "Lisa is coming right over, and her text sounded excited."

"Almost done, and how can a text message sound exciting?" Kruik asked.

"Four exclamation points. I'm a bit surprised that the Wanderers never sold the bot off, or that the Zarents didn't reprogram it for use in maintenance."

"Perhaps the Wanderers didn't know it was there or found that they couldn't easily sell it without the password or a new fuel pack. Powering robots via direct broadcast is only practical inside ships."

"And the Zarents?" Mouser asked.

"What would they do with a two-armed robot without any built-in floater technology?" Kruik countered with a question of his own. "I'm also unsure how long it would have taken for them to break the encryption. I'll have to ask Snap."

"I'd be curious to hear what he says."

"Are you also curious to know how Colony One's primary elections concluded?"

"No," Mouser said. "But I have a feeling you're going to tell me anyway."

"You are the mayor of the Human community, and you did ask me to serve as your intermediary for any election negotiations," Kruik reminded him. "Now that Mattie has officially won the primary, she's pushing me to set a date."

"Do what you have to. The co-captains have been keeping me in the loop more than I'd like, and they said that the Oners have a whole slate of candidates ready to run for our non-existent city council."

"Mattie came up with the idea to eliminate her opposition by giving them all the chance to win political posts that they view as a sure thing. Unfortunately for those candidates, she did so without first checking with the Zarents."

Mouser laughed. "That sounds like the best news I've heard in a while. No city council?"

"The Colony One movement is free to elect their own leaders, of course, but only as an internal affair," Kruik said. "They won't have any budget or authority that isn't explicitly given to them by the people who want their leadership."

"You mean they can form a private club, but they can't extend their nonsense to anybody living on board who doesn't join."

"Exactly. The Zarents recognize the position of mayor, as you know, but only as a sort of spokesperson for Humans."

"If I had any authority, I would have noticed by now," Mouser said. "That's why I can't understand why the Oners are going to so much work trying to get themselves elected."

"Hope springs eternal," Kruik said. "They believe that symbolic power can be converted to real power and that they can tax their community to pay themselves salaries."

"Would the Zarents allow that?"

"As long as it's voluntary, I don't see a problem with the people who work supporting the people who don't work. Maybe it's the Human version of a post-industrial society."

"What do the Dollnicks do with citizens who don't want to work?" Mouser asked.

There was a pause, and then Kruik replied, "I suppose they join the Wanderers. There's no place in Dollnick society for idle hands. Maybe that's why we ended up with four of them when most species are limited to two, or two with a tentacle or prehensile tail."

The door slid open and Lisa entered, her red cheeks testifying that she'd run the whole distance from her dojo even though her breathing appeared even. "Where's the—ooh."

"Pretty impressive for a robot that's been sitting on the floor with its arms around its legs since Rome was at the peak of its power," Mouser said. "I couldn't move like that even when I was a kid."

Shadow's sister slowly lifted one foot in front of her, the knee bent, and raised her arms in imitation of the robot's stance. Then they both brought their arms down while launching into a high kick.

"It's good," Lisa said. "I've worked with sparring robots, but most of them are floating platforms that offer padded targets and blocking arms rather than mimicking humanoids."

"Kruik says that it would have shipped with a padded suit to match the species of the buyer, and Hercules went back to the cabin to see if it's still there. Do you want it?"

"Want it?" Lisa's eyes shone. "Can it be programmed with different styles of martial arts?"

"According to Kruik, it comes with limited programming for exercise modes, but it was designed to be controlled by an artificial intelligence in gaming mode," Mouser said.

"Kruik? Do you charge a lot for that sort of thing?"

"It would be my pleasure," the Dollnick artificial intelligence replied. "I helped Flower with her LARPing studio while I was hosted in her infrastructure, and I found something very satisfying about filling the role of non-player characters."

"How are you on martial arts?" Lisa asked.

"Don't forget that I was in the military. In addition to being able to simulate our fighting styles, I can control a bot with the appropriate appendages to perform the martial arts of all the tunnel network species and a few dozen besides."

Lisa moved past Mouser to take a closer look at the bot and it suddenly stopped moving. "Did it just fail?" she asked in disappointment.

"It's completed the calibration routine," Kruik told her. "I can now control the bot with complete confidence. Watch this."

The robot came to life again and walked over to where Hercules had set his empty orange juice bottle on top of a parts cabinet. Without warning or any apparent preparation, it spun into a roundhouse kick, its metal foot stopping so close to the bottle that Mouser and Lisa were astonished it didn't make contact.

"And a combination," Kruik said. The bot lowered its leg and then began throwing a flurry of punches at the bottle, all of them coming within a hair-width.

"But can it recycle?" Mouser asked playfully.

The bot snatched the bottle with one hand, turned so that its binocular cameras could measure the distance to the mixed recycling barrel, and tossed a hook shot in a perfect form that would have made a professional basketball player jealous. The bottle barely contacted the far edge of the barrel before bouncing off the floor and rolling under a table.

"Remind me not to let the robot throw knives at me," Lisa muttered.

"How embarrassing," Kruik said. "I haven't done this in a while and I chose my own inertial reference frame rather than that of the robot. I hope we don't need to mention this to Flower."

"Your secret is safe with us," Mouser said. "I'm just happy that when I drop something it falls on the floor rather than shooting across the room."

"If you guys are going to start discussing radial acceleration, I'm taking my robot and leaving," Lisa said. "What's its name?"

"Whatever name its previous owner called it by was lost when the fuel pack completely discharged," Kruik said. "I've talked it over with Snap and the Zarents are willing to rebuild the fuel pack for the cost of materials. It will make an interesting project for the apprentices."

"Does that mean I can't play with it today?"

"Not at all. I'll walk the robot back to the dojo with you, and if you want to put on boxing gloves and do some light sparring, I can have it wield a practice target."

"I'll text Hercules and tell him that you're taking it so he can bring you any padding he finds," Mouser told Lisa.

"Thanks," Lisa said. "I've got a student coming in two minutes so I have to run back. Can the robot keep up Kruik?"

"It could carry you and get there faster than you will on your own," the Dollnick artificial intelligence replied confidently. A few seconds after Lisa and the bot set off, he added, "Trouble coming your way."

"Don't tell me," Mouser said. "My honorable opponent from Colony One."

"And her entourage."

"As my official intermediary, you stay and talk to them. It's a shame Lisa took the bot or you could have pretended it was your physical manifestation."

"I could send a maintenance bot if you think it would help," Kruik said. "Where are you going?"

"Anywhere other than here," Mouser said as he waved open the door. "Tell me when they're—Hello, Mattie."

"Mayor Mouser," the woman at the head of the delegation said grimly. "I have a bone to pick with you."

"I was just on my way to, uh…" he trailed off as she stalked past him into the lab and her followers crowded in after her. "I can give you five minutes, but, uh…"

"Oh, stop it," Mattie said, and her face showed a bit of humor for the first time in Mouser's memory. "You're a terrible liar. You wouldn't last two seconds in politics anywhere that matters."

"That's what I was just saying to Kruik. Why do you want to be mayor? The job amounts to making announcements when we enter or exit tunnels and I just repeat what I'm told. You strike me as more ambitious than that."

"Your shortcomings are your own. When I'm elected, the Zarents and your artificial intelligence friend will find themselves dealing with another thing altogether."

"And us," the lawyer running for president of a new city council chipped in. "We're all on the same page."

"Do any of you have a legitimate source of income?" Mouser asked. "I heard from our chief of police that there was nearly a riot when you suggested to your constituency that you take salaries."

"Sticker shock," Mattie said. "They'll come around. If I've learned one thing about political power it's that the squeaky wheel gets the oil, and you're looking at the squeakiest wheels in the Colony One movement."

"Is that the sort of thing you want to say in public?"

"Who would believe you?"

"It's not me you have to worry about, it's Kruik," Mouser said. "He hears every word that's spoken on this ship, though he chooses to ignore most of it."

"We have rights," the lawyer said. "Conversations recorded by omnipresent technology aren't admissible in courts of law, and I'll sue if you publish one word of what any of us say here."

Mouser stared at the Oners, unable to hide his bewilderment. "Do you think that you're on Earth?" he finally asked. "Sit down. Please. We seriously need to talk."

"You've already given us your helpless humans lecture," Mattie said, even as she availed herself of the gamemaster's armchair. "We don't need to hear it again."

"Maybe I wasn't blunt enough," Mouser said as the other members of the delegation settled on the two couches.

"Have any of you lived on alien worlds or orbitals, or is the Miklat your first experience with living in space?"

"I worked on the moon," a woman replied.

"What moon?"

"*The* moon. How many moons are there?"

"Look," Mouser said. "I'm beginning to suspect that you think I do what Kruik tells me because I'm weak. And maybe you look at the Zarents riding around on their little unicycles and think that all they lack is human leadership. But they're superior intelligences, superior lifeforms."

"Kruik is just software," Mattie said.

"Kruik is an artificial lifeform, with more rights than us."

"Don't you mean the same?" the lawyer demanded.

"More. The Dollnicks are full members of the galactic tunnel network, Earth is still a probationary member. And colony ship artificial intelligences are their own class of life in Dollnick law. You've heard of Flower?"

"We know that the Miklat's sister ship run by the Human Empire is named Flower, but we all came aboard after your last rendezvous."

Mouser thought about giving up but decided to make one last effort. "Flower isn't run by the Human Empire, if anything, the opposite is closer to the truth. I brought her up to drive home my point. When Flower had a difference of opinion with Dollnicks who built her, they abandoned ship, not the other way around. If the artificial intelligence running a colony ship doesn't listen to the legal owners, what chance do you think there is that it would listen to you?"

"I thought the Zarents owned the Miklat," the lawyer said stubbornly, though the rest of the Oners looked thoughtful for a change.

"The Zarents aren't going to listen to you either," Mouser said tiredly.

Seventeen

"You don't know if you're having a boy or a girl?" Belle asked in surprise. "But you're as big as a house."

"Size doesn't have anything to do with it," Katya told the clone. "I told the imaging technician at the clinic I didn't want to know. Can the Gem who have started having babies the natural way tell the sex of their child before it's born?"

"Of course. All of the advanced species can." Belle realized what she'd said and tried to backpedal, but the Miklat's co-captain just laughed.

"We know that we're playing catchup," Katya said. "And having a clearer idea of what's going on inside of our bodies might be the next step. But Nigel and I talked it over and we want to let mother nature surprise us. Right, Nigel?" She sighed and poked her husband's shoulder, and his expression when he looked up from whatever he was reading on his tab made it clear he hadn't been following the conversation.

"Have we landed?" Nigel asked.

"In a few minutes," Belle told him. "Your wife was just telling me that you'll be happy whether she has a girl or a boy."

"Both would be fine too, but the imaging tech at the clinic would have mentioned twins."

"What were you reading about that's so interesting you can't hear your pregnant wife talking when she's sitting right next to you?" Katya asked pointedly.

"The catacombs," Nigel said. "They're open to tourists now and G32FX sent me the brochure. I could be the first human xenoarchaeologist to set eyes on Farling ruins from before they became a space-faring species."

"Isn't the planet named Farling Four because it was the fourth world they colonized?" Belle asked. "Or maybe the third, if Farling One is their homeworld."

"They could have started counting at zero," Katya said.

Nigel's face expressed tragic disappointment. "I didn't think of that. The ruins will be from whatever civilization went extinct before the Farlings arrived."

"The Farlings were never signatories to the tunnel network treaty. They may have conquered this world."

"Or, they could have been slow-boaters, like us," Belle said. "Years ago, I attended a lecture about species that began interstellar exploration without jump drives, like the original Wanderers. The speaker had a theory that the Farling empire began with slow interstellar ships carrying colonists in suspended animation, or embryos that were frozen and later brought to maturity by robot attendants."

"Now that you mention it, I remember a Verlock lecturer visiting from another academy world mentioning that theory," Nigel said, growing excited again. "Maybe G32FX can tell us."

"What do you have to offer him in return?" Katya asked.

"I can't believe the Farlings would treat their origins like trade goods. Why would they open the catacombs to tourists if they're trying to protect their privacy?"

"I assume there's an admission fee."

"The brochure said it's to cover the expenses," Nigel said, but he sounded a little less certain of himself now. "The price was in the Farling currency, so I'm not sure if it was cheap or expensive."

"The Dibel is roughly equivalent to the Stryx cred," Belle told him.

"But that means it's a week's pay for most people!"

"I wasn't very excited about wandering around some dusty catacombs anyway," Katya told him. "Why don't you go directly from the spaceport, and I'll wait for you in Humantown after I get the visit with G32FX out of the way. We'll save half the cost of admission for two, and you'll be able to spend longer staring at scratches on rocks and wondering if they were made by tools."

"Are you sure?" Nigel asked. "We were going to spend the whole day together."

"We spend every night together. It will be fine."

After the shuttle landed, Belle explained to Nigel how to catch the maglev into town, and then she and Katya went in the opposite direction to the waiting limo. They got in the back, but the Oosh chauffeur didn't make any move to close the door. Katya shot him a questioning look, the meaning of which the alien must have guessed, because he said, "There's another coming."

"My husband decided to go directly to the Farling catacombs," she told him.

"Then you must have married into money, but my instructions were to pick up three female humanoids. I see the third coming now."

"Sorry if I held you up," Delphi said, struggling out of the straps of a large backpack. "I had to put my oversized carry-on in one of the storage cabinets at the back of the shuttle and it got buried under other people's stuff."

"You're taking this trader business seriously," Katya said. "Are you planning on going to the fair later?"

"G32FX asked me to bring him a few small items so he could make a better assessment of my trading acumen. I'm a bit worried that he's going to think that I went out of my way to cost him a lot of Dibels."

"If that's the case, then Sabina and I share the blame because we sent you most of your counterparties."

The limo began moving, and soon the scenery was flashing by so fast that it was a blur. "Did you hitch a ride?" Delphi asked Belle.

"I have to register as an alien intelligence agent, and G32FX is a bit of a micromanager," the clone explained. "I think he tries to make all of the decisions for the governing of the planet rather than delegating."

"That doesn't sound healthy," Katya said.

The Gem shrugged. "Farlings are a high-capacity species in many ways. I'm not sure if concepts like stress or overwork mean anything to them. I only have our visits to this planet and a few meetings with M793qK on Flower to go by, but I suspect that the older members of the species are generalists, or maybe it would be better to say that they specialize in everything."

"I'll believe it for M793qK. I just didn't realize that G32FX was anywhere near his level."

"He's a full letter short," Delphi said as she got a small bottle of water out of the minibar. "I wouldn't want to meet a seven-letter Farling."

"If there are any, talking to outsiders is below their dignity," Katya said. She gazed into the blurry distance and added, "I hope Nigel finds the catacombs without a problem."

"Your husband may be the smartest Human on the Miklat," Belle said. "Plus, he has an implant, so all he has to do is show somebody the brochure and listen to their instructions."

"I've come to realize that he's a bit gullible. I think it has to do with growing up an only child and then spending a decade on a Verlock academy world."

"But why would anybody intentionally mislead him?" Delphi asked.

Katya smiled to soften the blow. "I think you're a little gullible too. Don't take it the wrong way, but you grew up in a closed community where everybody had a shared interest in seeing each other succeed because you all contributed and drew from the tithe."

"It was super competitive. Some product groups even got caught spying on others, and there was always a trickle of people leaving because they didn't fit in and made everybody around them miserable."

"I didn't know that. Maybe it's just something I picked up from my mother, but it seems to me that none of you are very paranoid."

"Isn't that a good thing?" Belle asked. "Part of my training for this job was filtering out potential threats that are supported by little or no evidence. There are plenty of legitimate problems in the galaxy without letting your imagination invent new ones."

"Part of leadership is recognizing potential problems before they become obvious," Katya said. "A friend gave me some of the materials that Vergallian princesses study in their royal training, and it's a wonder that they don't all end up in rubber rooms. They have a Theory of Threat Assessment that stipulates everything and everyone can become a threat if circumstances change. That includes close family, pets, the palace you live in—"

"Palace?" Delphi interrupted.

"Earthquakes. Imagine a giant chandelier falling on your head."

"I meant, do they really live in palaces?"

"They're princesses," Katya said. "Where else should they live?"

"I recognize that tower," Belle said as the limo started to slow. "We're almost there."

The three passengers turned their attention to the windows now that the scenery was no longer blurring by, and they were enchanted by the gardens on the roof of every structure they passed.

"I wouldn't have guessed that the Farlings would be such avid gardeners," Delphi said. "They look more like the burrowing types."

"You're extrapolating from Earth's beetles," Katya said. "Don't let an alien's resemblance to fauna from our homeworld fool you. The Grenouthians aren't super-sized bunnies, and Huktra aren't flying lizards."

The limo slowed further as it rapidly shed altitude, and it was down to street level just as the gate slid open to admit it to the courtyard of the administrative complex where G32FX lived. The Oosh held the door as they exited, and then retrieved Delphi's pack from the storage compartment where he'd placed it. Katya tried to slip the alien a tip, but he simply turned his back and waited for them to move into the garden.

"It's just as well," Belle told her. "My experience has been that you can't buy information from Farlings or the member species of their empire. Some of them will take your money, but that's where it stops."

"Were you trying to bribe G32FX's chauffeur?" Delphi asked in surprise.

Katya shrugged. "Not bribe-bribe, but a little acorn can grow into a giant oak."

"Not if a Huktra eats it first," Belle said and sniffed a large orange blossom. Her head jerked back. "Smells like poison."

"It is poison," G32FX rubbed out on his speaking legs as he entered the grove and made a sweeping gesture with one of his upper limbs. "All of the plants in the garden are poisonous to Farlings. It's a bit of a game with us."

"So that your guests don't ask for refreshments?" Katya asked.

"Exactly wrong. Metabolizing poisons is one of the ways that we demonstrate our maturity, but we can go into that another day when you have something to offer in return. And thank you for coming, Belle. I'm sure that your sources in Human Town will wait."

"They're all at work this time of morning," the Gem said. "Thank you for not deporting any of them."

"What would the point of that be?" G32FX rubbed out. "For starters, you'd just find new sources and we'd have to start the counterintelligence process all over again. Besides, haven't you heard that all publicity is good publicity?"

"If that's the case, you could let me into your archives."

"It wouldn't help since you don't read Farling. But I wanted a journalist, even if it's just your cover job, to be present for this meeting."

"I thought that the trading I was doing on your account was private," Delphi said.

"It would be difficult to build a customer base if you traded in secrecy," G32FX observed as he led them to the table and reclined against a Farling couch to take the weight off his carapace. "Don't you tell your friends about the merchandise I consigned to the Miklat and the deals that you make?"

"I guess I do, but that's not the same thing as reporting about it in the news."

"No. A widely circulated news story would be better. Now let's see what you brought me."

Delphi began emptying items from her backpack, and the Farling seized on one of the carved bowls she'd received in barter from the Grenouthian.

"What did you trade for this?" G32FX asked.

"It was a throw-in with a bunch of other things," Delphi said defensively. "He wanted some heavy-duty juicers and that fabric tape stuff that kept changing colors which he was going to try to sew into a sash. I don't even know where to start when it comes to valuing handcrafted goods, but you said that the important thing for this trip was to make trades, so I did."

"Katya?"

"My sister and I took turns visiting the planets, and every time we brought up that we had access to a few containers of goods from the worlds of the Farling Empire, we got a bite," Katya said.

"I kept track of all the trades in a spreadsheet," Delphi said, offering the Farling her tab. "You can transfer it off to something, or I can ask Kruik to send you the file after we return."

G32FX employed one of his middle limbs to page through the spreadsheet, occasionally rubbing out a comment about one of the entries. The sound of clattering came from somewhere behind the shrubbery, and a human rounded the corner pushing a wheeled catering cart that looked like it had been copied from something belonging to a nineteenth-century Earth ocean liner. The silverware hadn't been wrapped in cloth napkins and was responsible for most of the noise.

"Ah, Marcel," G32FX rubbed out. "We're you able to find a little something for my guests?"

"Oui, Monsieur," Marcel replied and adjusted the white towel hung over his left forearm. "We are speaking the English?"

"Yes, please," Katya said. "And we are hungry because we are eating for two."

"I see." He started by moving a silver bowl of fruit to the table, then opened the lower compartment of the cart and began bringing out baked goods of every shape and size, most of them desserts. "There is here somewhere a healthy—"

"I'm good with dessert for breakfast," Katya interrupted as she reached for a wedge of the layer cake that had been cut out and left artistically on the tray like a pâtissier might prepare for an advertising shoot. "I'll make up for it at lunch."

"The chocolate gâteau," Marcel said. "An excellent choice."

Belle appeared to be overwhelmed by the chocolate-infused choices on display and waited for Delphi, who took a croissant. Finally, the Gem reached for a Plié au Chocolat and seemed almost surprised when Marcel offered her a spoon for the custard.

"Very good," G32FX said, handing the tab back to Delphi. "I'm quadrupling the number of containers consigned to the Miklat, and they're already in orbit. Marcel. I will join the guests for coffee."

Marcel raised one eyebrow, but filled a white cup from the urn, placed it on a small saucer, and handed it to his employer. "Ladies?"

"Is it strong?" Katya asked. "I'm watching my caffeine."

"I also have mint tea in the small pot," he said, picking it up and assuming an expression that reminded the co-captain of an adult trying to tempt a child into trying something healthy.

"I'll take it," she said.

Delphi and Belle opted for the coffee, and then G32FX said, "I think you can leave the cart and return for it later, Marcel. Thank you."

"Thank you, Sir," Marcel said, bowing from the waist, and then backing three steps along the path before he turned and left.

"If your baker ever quits, send him to me," Katya told the Farling.

"His wife is the baker, a husband-and-wife team that M793qK forwarded to me," G32FX said. "A bit of a sad story. They trained for years to work on passenger liners, but it turns out that they're both so sensitive to tunnel transitions and jumps that they couldn't stand constant travel. Here they get to experience an alien culture and high standards without moving."

"Should I have Kruik send you the spreadsheet file?" Delphi asked.

"I already read it. Do you have any questions?"

"I have a million questions, but let's start with whether or not I'm making any money."

"You're in for a percentage," G32FX reminded her. "Do you need for me to recite our contract?"

"A percentage of a gain or a loss?" she asked cautiously.

"The only way you could generate a loss trading goods with no cost basis is if you get sued. Did you hit somebody with a L'meuf scale?"

"No. I loaned one to Shadow's friend Botan when he was helping students run a farmstand and a lot of people commented on it. I sold it to Bindaal for cash."

"I saw that in the spreadsheet, an excellent piece of business."

"Did I get more than it's worth?" Delphi asked.

"If you're talking in terms of Stryx creds, and do the conversion based on comparisons since the L'meuf have never exported scales in the past, I lost a little under a hundred creds on the transaction," G32FX rubbed out while taking a sip from his coffee, a trick that always made Delphi feel like she was talking with a ventriloquist. "My rough estimate for all of the goods on the spreadsheet puts my loss at over twenty thousand Stryx creds, but maybe you'll get better prices than I'm projecting for some of the goods you took in barter. Oh, dear," he added and began thumping Delphi on the back with a middle limb as the girl choked on her croissant. "Do I need to call Marcel to perform the Heimlich Maneuver?"

"Twenty thousand creds?" she wheezed. "I thought I was falling short of the true value, but that's more than I earn in a year as loadmaster."

"Fortunately for you, your compensation doesn't take into account the cost of goods, only what you get for them."

"What kind of business operates like that?" Katya asked, though she was loathe to break the rhythm she'd established of forking tiny off-cuts of layer cake into her mouth.

"You tell me," G32FX said.

Katya froze, the fork halfway between the plate and her mouth. "It's not a business at all."

"What do you mean?" Delphi asked.

"He's using us." She took a sip of tea to buy time while she thought about the implications of what the alien had just told her. "We're running a low-cost trade delegation for the Farling Empire," she concluded. "To establish Farling Four as a bridge between their empire and the tunnel network, M793qK needs to build up trade as quickly as possible."

"We're giving away free samples?"

"Not free, or your commission will come to zero," G32FX rubbed out complacently. "But Katya has the basic concept."

"You're putting a lot of faith in humans, and in the wrong circles, you may be drawing a target on our backs," Katya said.

"In for a Zylot, in for a Zylotee, as the saying goes. We wouldn't have a tunnel network connection without the implicit support of the twenty million of your people who agreed to come here and live. If the other species want to be angry at humanity for letting itself be used by the Farling Empire, that's the peg they'll hang their cloaks on. Not the loadmaster of the Miklat acting as a casual trade rep."

Belle came up for air and pointed at the Farling with her spoon. "And you want me to write a story about this for Gem Today? How will that help anyone?"

"It won't," G32FX rubbed out cheerfully. "But if you're willing to accept my explanation, you can ignore the part about my fortunes being joined at a lower limb socket with humanity and focus on the trade issues, which aren't getting as much attention as we'd like. After all, the Stryx never would have gone for M793qK's plan if it wasn't their own as well."

The two women and the Gem stopped and stared at the Farling. "You're saying that we're all working for the Stryx?" Delphi asked in a small voice.

"Not directly. I've never, well, very infrequently, had any direct contact with the masterminds of the tunnel network. But it's not difficult to figure out that they see closer integration between major empires in the galaxy as a step toward the best possible outcome. As a Farling who hasn't yet earned a place in the hierarchy, I'm just playing the cards I'm dealt."

Belle nodded. "Business all the way down."

G32FX reached behind himself, plucked a sickly green blossom from a plant, and added it to his coffee. "Deadly to ninety percent of Farlings," he informed them as he took a sip. "It's a shame we can't practice nepotism like the rest of the advanced species, but our lack of family structures makes it impossible."

"There you go dropping hints again," Katya said. "How do you breed? Did you abandon natural selection for the laboratory so many millions of years ago that nobody can remember?"

The Farling's wings peeked out of his carapace in amusement and then settled. "Nothing so dramatic. We don't fall into the standard models practiced by any other species I'm aware of and let's leave it at that."

"I don't understand what's so great about nepotism," Delphi said. "Humans try to avoid it."

"Not really," G32FX told her. "You just talk about avoiding it. Humans who don't accept nepotism die out. It's just a question of degree."

"What do you mean?"

"During the long and dreary years I spent on Earth, I had a Human friend who was an idealist of sorts. I met him through his environmental work, and thanks to M793qK's connections, I was able to help him start the reintroduction of some extinct species that were preserved on Alt when the Stryx moved starter populations from your homeworld. He purported to have equal love for all of humanity, across all geographic and ethnic boundaries, and would insist that the future of the children of people on the other side of the globe who he'd never met was just as important to him as the future of his son."

"If they were all clones, maybe," Belle said.

"That's the opposite of nepotism," Delphi said.

"It was also an obvious case of self-deception," G32FX said. "He was saving money for his son to attend university and buy a home. I pointed out that if the future of a child on the other side of the planet was as important to him as his son's happiness, I would be willing to act as an intermediary and deliver money."

"I take it he declined, but maybe it was because he didn't trust you."

"He declined because he favored his offspring above somebody else's, and in my experience, the same would be true even if the son had been adopted. It's hard-wired into your genes, into the genes of most biologicals who raise families. I've seen some funny computer models of what would happen if you didn't practice nepotism."

"Are you sure you aren't confusing nepotism with parental love?" Katya asked, a hand on her swollen abdomen.

G32FX plucked another poisonous blossom and popped it directly into his mouth. "It's you who are confused," he simultaneously rubbed out on his speaking legs.

Eighteen

"It's normal to be nervous before a wedding."

"For the bride and the groom, it's normal," Delphi told Shadow. "There's something deeply wrong with you."

"I'm nervous for both sides," he protested. "Lisa is my sister, Botan is my best friend, and I'm the one who set them up. What if they don't get along?"

"You didn't set them up, and they've been living together as long as we have. I think running your own business is turning you into a drama queen."

"I need a drink," Shadow said decisively. "Just to break in the tux. Who ever heard of renting clothes?"

"It's an Earth thing, or maybe an alien thing," Delphi said. "And we're out of beer. I needed the space in the fridge for the cake. Don't you remember taking out the shelves so we could fit it?"

"I can't just sit here waiting for the clock to strike midnight. This is driving me nuts. And why midnight? Lisa never would have become a witch when we were sharing an apartment. Maybe Botan is neglecting her."

"Lisa isn't a witch. She hired a wedding planner and midnight on the ag deck is the plan. You can wait another half hour."

Shadow groaned out loud and went over to open the fridge. "How did we ever get it in there? I should take it out now and bring it to—"

"No!" Delphi almost tripped over the skirts of the rental gown as she raced over to stop him. "You're too nervous. You'll drop it or run into something. I just pinged Kruik to send a bot."

"Now you're saying I'm useless."

"Go to Kyor's and have a beer before you start crying. In all the years we've known each other, I've never suspected you could turn into such a mess. What are you going to be like if I ever agree to marry you?"

"That's different," Shadow said seriously. "You're not my sister or my best friend."

"Kyor's. Go. One beer," Delph rattled off the commands. "I'll see you on the ag deck at five minutes to midnight. And don't lose the ring."

"What ring?"

"The wedding ring, you goof," she said, before noticing the grin on his face. "Go."

On his way to the lift tube, Shadow removed the clip-on bowtie and undid the top button of the dress shirt that made him feel like he was choking. "Food court," he told Kruik. "Did you send a bot for the cake?"

"I'm waiting until it's needed," the Dollnick artificial intelligence replied. "A multi-tiered wedding cake is a magnet for accidents."

"I've never been a best man before," Shadow confided. "I guess I'm a little nervous. Where do we get these stupid traditions anyway?"

"The original role of the best man in Human history was to help kidnap the bride from her family and then guard her so she couldn't escape."

"You're making it up."

"I have it on the best authority possible," Kruik said.

"A Grenouthian documentary?" Shadow asked suspiciously.

"Documentaries are true by definition."

"You may want to talk that one over with Flower. Thanks for the ride." Shadow wound his way through the food court to the former location of Bindaal's restaurant. Even if he hadn't known where Kyor had moved Club Ucerin, he could have found the brewpub, as the Huktra now styled her establishment, by following his nose to the popcorn.

"Have you become a member of the interstellar intelligence community?" Kyor inquired when Shadow walked up to the standing bar.

"Not unless I get a free draft for joining," Shadow said. "Why do you ask?"

"You're dressed like the most famous Human spy of all time."

Shadow looked down at his tux. "Everybody on Earth must have been badly overdressed if he could blend in wearing one of these monkey suits."

"It's on the house," Kyor said, setting a draft on the bar. "Bond didn't blend in, he stood out. His modus operandi was to show up at some luxurious location, pick up the most beautiful woman, and wait for the villains to kill her to draw them into the open. And you can help finish off the popcorn."

"He sounds like a jerk, and it's not even midnight. Why are you closing so early?"

"I have a wedding to attend and early is on time."

Shadow swallowed and let out an appreciative belch. "Your last batch is the best yet. Have you changed the recipe?"

"It's a work in progress. I thought this batch turned out a bit hoppy."

"I like hoppy." He drained another quarter of the mug. "Have you ever been to a wedding before?"

"Hundreds," the Huktra said. "I'm older than you think."

"I meant a human wedding."

"I stood next to you at Katya and Nigel's wedding. You asked me the same thing then."

"I guess I'm nervous," Shadow said. "My sister is marrying my best friend. It's like the end of an era. Before you know it, they'll be asking me to babysit."

"Humans have short eras," Kyor observed as she held up a half-full glass pitcher that she used to capture the foam from the recently tapped keg. "I should have let the beer settle longer before tapping, but I was in a hurry."

"Did you get them anything?"

"I consulted with my colleagues and purchased a present of appropriate value given our relationship. Participating in Mouser's weekly game with the happy couple drove up the cost."

"You're killing us all, even Belle," Shadow said. "Tell me the truth. Have you played *Speed Trader* before?"

"For the seventh time, no, but I'll tell you a secret," Kyor said, and leaned forward so her snout with its exposed front fangs almost touched Shadow's ear. "In trading games, you have to—Hello, Bindaal."

"Kyor. Shadow," the Vergallian said, placing a gift-wrapped package on the bar. "Should the best man be drinking before the wedding?"

"Nerves," Kyor said. "Can I get you anything?"

"I'm saving space for the buffet. The last time I went to one of these midnight weddings there was dancing all night. I still remember sneaking out to check the Grenouthian news and hearing that the Stryx had granted Earth probationary membership on the tunnel network."

"That was a century ago," Shadow protested.

"And there are elements within the Empire of a Hundred Worlds that still haven't gotten over it," Bindaal said. "They were gearing up to invade, you know."

"Myort wouldn't have let you," Kyor said confidently. "He's a Humanophile."

Shadow finished gulping down his beer and looked hopefully at the empty mug. "What are you guys talking about? It's like you think the people on Earth wouldn't have a say in anything."

"Nobody heard you saying anything when the Stryx connected your planet to the tunnel network and announced that governments wouldn't be allowed to interfere with emigration." She took Shadow's mug and filled it about a third of the way. "Brace up. You can get drunk after the ceremony."

"That's different. It was the Stryx. At the same time they made their announcement, all of Earth's weapons of mass destruction went missing, and everybody's naval ships were instantaneously moved to their home ports. People say that any leaders who tried to protest were disintegrated on the spot."

"The Stryx moved them to Earth Two where they either worked on the Container Prince's terraforming job or starved," Bindaal said. "The colonists have found a few grave markers for the ones who worked."

"They didn't have any children?" Shadow asked.

"Too old, and mostly men."

"We should get going," Kyor said. The Huktra reached down and came up with what looked like a giant piñata with a bow tied around the neck. "Guess what it is?"

"Did you wrap that yourself?" Bindaal asked instead.

"What? Did I do it wrong?"

"The wrapping paper is supposed to come off easily so they can reuse it. I'm recycling this paper from a grand opening present that Belle gave me."

"Stuffed dragon variants cost more than you'd expect, and it was the only one I could find on board," Kyor said. "I wrapped it in plastic first to protect it from the papier mâché."

"It's the thought that counts," Shadow said. "I got them a vintage copy of *Alien Demon Slayer*. It's the only cool game I know that requires two players and doesn't support any more than that."

"Very romantic," Bindaal said, picking up her present. "Shall we?"

Most of the invited guests had already arrived when Shadow and the two aliens exited the lift tube on the ag deck. A young Frunge was running around frantically giving instructions to the caterers, and Sabina was waiting with her despised hat in the crook of her arm, staring into space with her lips moving as she tried to memorize the wedding ceremony text on her heads-up display. Four flowering cherry trees in giant pots that had been brought specially from Flower formed a sort of canopy, and the immediate area had been decorated with green clippings that must have been pruned from the orchard that day.

"Midnight," Kruik announced over the public address system.

As the wedding procession began to play, Botan pulled Shadow under the canopy, buttoned his soon-to-be brother-in-law's collar, and pantomimed tying a bow tie. Shadow remembered the clip-on in his pocket and pulled it out, not noticing the box with the wedding ring dropping to the deck at the same time.

"Shadow," Delphi hissed from her place under the canopy next to the spot where Lisa would stand. "You dropped something."

Botan figured it out first, picked up the box, and pressed it in his friend's hand. "Just hold onto it," he said. "Lisa is coming."

Shadow looked up to see his sister's face floating down the aisle, the rest of her being camouflaged by clouds of green lace that blended in with the background. "A green dress?"

"Fonzil helped her pick it out. Don't say anything to Lisa. She loves it."

"I still don't get why Mouser gets to give her away. I'm the brother."

"You're my best man and you can't do both," Botan said, not adding that Lisa had worried that Shadow would get inadvertently tangled in her gown's train or be so nervous that he practically ran her up the aisle.

When Lisa reached the canopy of cherry tree flowers, her eyes were shining so brightly that Shadow wondered if she had gotten an implant and it was malfunctioning. Mouser returned to stand with his wife Sophie at the front of the crowd, and Sabina, her hat now on her head, came forward and stood at the back of the canopy, so she could face both the couple and the audience.

"Friends and family," the co-captain began. "We are gathered here at the stroke of midnight to celebrate the grafting of two healthy young trees who in the due course of time will bless our community with a new fruit all their own. They have chosen to be married with a modified version of the Frunge liturgy suggested by Fonzil, their wedding planner, in part because the original version takes seven hours and requires the participation of ancestors from both sides, and in part because I don't speak Frunge."

Fonzil, who was standing to the side where she could keep an eye on the caterers while watching the ceremony, began pantomiming something with both hands brushing back her hair vines.

"Right," Sabina said, turning to Botan. "Do you have the trellis?"

Botan grinned and reached inside his tux to produce a silvery framework that opened on a hinge. He stepped closer to Lisa, who flipped her veil back so her hair was exposed, and in a series of deft movements that had been practiced, he placed the trellis on her head and wove Lisa's French braid through the framework to produce an elegant updo with the leftover braid hanging to the back.

"The ring," Sabina said to Shadow, who was standing with his mouth open and didn't respond.

Botan nudged his friend and muttered "Ring."

Shadow handed the box to Botan, who removed the ring and handed it to Sabina, who placed it on Lisa's palm. Then Lisa took Botan's left hand and slipped the ring onto his fourth finger.

"Now, if all present will repeat the Marriage Affirmation after me," Sabina said. "We, the friends and family of Lisa and Botan…"

"We, the friends and family of Lisa and Botan," everybody repeated faithfully.

"undertake the sacred duty of gardeners…"

"undertake the sacred duty of gardeners…"

"and will strive to keep their relationship weeded and watered..."

"and will strive to keep their relationship weeded and watered..."

"until petrification sets in and it no longer matters."

"until petrification sets in and it no longer matters."

Sabina paused, mouthed, "Don't repeat this part," then continued with, "I now pronounce you grafted for life. You may share a public kiss."

Botan and Lisa didn't waste any time taking advantage of the invitation, and Fonzil, dabbing her eyes with a handkerchief, slipped around the knot of well-wishers who crowded the couple and whispered to the co-captain.

Sabina began to say something that was lost in the rapidly increasing volume of conversation, pointed at her ear, and then her voice came over the public address system. "Everybody is expected to take part in the traditional chiseling of the marriage contract. My husband will be watching to make sure you keep the chisel between the lines, so don't try anything funny. Those of you who plan to drink should do their chiseling now, and this means you, Shadow. The bride and groom will receive your well wishes after you carve your intentions in stone."

Shadow, who had already removed his clip-on bowtie and opened the collar button on his shirt again, stopped edging toward the table where he'd seen Kyor help set up a barrel of her draft and instead headed for where Drake was standing at parade rest, dressed in his best uniform.

"What do I do?" Shadow asked the Miklat's police chief.

"Pick a chisel and a mallet and start chipping away on the black lines. Fonzil said that it's not important if the engraving gets finished tonight, and it would be better if it's not since she can neaten it up as long as we don't go too deep or wide."

"It looks like Elvish from a game," Shadow complained as he chose one of the identical chisels from the tray, took a mallet, and began carefully tapping at the calligraphed stone under Drake's watchful eye.

"It's Frunge. And it's not a race," Drake added as Shadow began getting into a rhythm. "The point is for everybody to participate."

A line began to form behind Shadow, so he put down the chisel and the mallet and moved in the direction the police chief was pointing, which brought him face-to-face with his sister and brother-in-law.

"Uh, hey," Shadow said awkwardly. "Why Frunge?"

"Shut up," Lisa told him. "And don't get drunk and start crying."

"Here," Botan said, handing Shadow an envelope. "It's traditional to give something to the best man."

"You didn't have to do that," Shadow said. "I almost screwed up my only job." He glanced behind himself to make sure he wasn't holding anybody up and then opened the envelope and pulled out a card that Botan had illustrated himself. "It's me at my desk with some kids standing behind me and watching what I'm doing."

"The school is looking for more volunteers next year to offer afternoon apprenticeships to students," Botan told him. "I put your name in."

"I already signed up," Lisa told him.

"My present is that you volunteered me?" Shadow asked. "Don't I get a choice in this?"

"Nope," Botan told him. "It's a Frunge wedding tradition. You have to do whatever the married couple asks. I think it's pretty cool."

"And stay away from the cake until everybody else sees it," Lisa called after her brother as he moved off. "Watch him," she added to Botan under her breath.

The sound of tentative chiseling continued intermittently for an hour before Drake crossed the last name off the checklist on his implant and took a turn of his own. Then Fonzil claimed the stone and put it in a special carrier that she kept strapped to her back for the rest of the night. Even though everybody had napped in preparation for the late wedding, by two in the morning, most of the guests over the age of thirty had made their apologies and headed home.

"It was a beautiful ceremony," Delphi told Lisa, slipping into the chair that Botan had just vacated behind the departure table. "I was worried that following a slimmed-down version of Frunge traditions might be a little weird, but it was so much more meaningful than I expected."

"They've had millions of years to work out a good way to get hitched," Lisa said. "The only thing I tried to get Fonzil to change was this part, but I'm glad she didn't let me talk her out of it."

"It does seem funny for the guests to have to watch you open their presents before they leave, but I guess it cuts down on returns and gag gifts. You're going to need a baseball bat to unwrap the stuffed dragon that Kyor gave you."

"I got a waiver for that one since you can see what it is through the papier-mâché. Did you see what First Agronomist Miklat gave us?"

"A silver watering can?" Delphi teased.

"They're too practical for that sort of thing." Lisa pulled a small stainless-steel appliance out of the collection of unwrapped gifts and showed it to her friend. "It's a plasma vegetable peeler."

"Really? How does something like that work?"

The new bride shrugged. "I don't even know how smartphones work and this is Zarent technology. First Agronomist Miklat said that it uses multiple imaging technologies to determine the thickness of the peel or the rind, and then it vaporizes it with plasma."

"What happens to the stuff?" Delphi asked. "Do you end up breathing it?"

"The Zarents don't waste matter like that." Lisa opened a compartment on the side of the device and pointed out a little jar with a clear hose leading to the top. "When the jar fills up, I'm supposed to empty it into a recycling chute."

"Do they manufacture these in volume? It seems like the sort of thing the aliens I've been trading with might be interested in."

"Who would have thought you'd go from moving cargo containers to moving inventory," Botan said as he returned to the table. "Your boyfriend is asleep on the other side of that hedge. I think he had too much to drink."

"Poor guy," Delphi said, getting back to her feet. "I'll get some coffee and wake him up. He'll be mad at himself if he sleeps through the rest of the reception."

"Here comes a sleeper-walker now," Lisa murmured to Botan. Hercules and Rayne approached the table with Sarah supported between them.

"Checking out," Hercules said. "Your wedding planner told us we can't leave until you open our gift."

"It's a Frunge tradition," Lisa said, rapidly sorting through the diminishing pile to find the box with Rayne's card. "We've been perfectly happy with everything, and I couldn't even imagine—Oh."

"Oh?" Sarah asked sleepily.

"The juicer from the Farling Empire is perfect, I've used the one in Bindaal's restaurant. But…"

"But?" Rayne asked, her eyes narrowing.

"It's what Mouser and Sophie gave us," Lisa said.

"Okay, we should have coordinated with Mouser, but there's no point in our bringing it back to Delphi and picking out something else you might already have. Keep it, and you barter with her for what you want. I hear that G32FX dropped six full-sized Dollnick shipping containers on her."

"You're right, and thank you," Botan said as Lisa vacillated. "Don't worry," he added in an aside to his wife. "Fonzil never has to know."

"You're right," Lisa said, rapidly using some discarded wrapping to strategically disguise the retail box. "It's funny that out of all the things G32FX could choose to try to build an export trade, he's focused on household appliances."

"Huge market, lots of demand," Rayne told her. "I'm sure they'd rather be doing business with high-value scientific equipment and luxury goods, but there's probably a limit to how much of a loss G32FX can absorb with Delphi trading for handmade crafts and whatever else is on offer."

Belle arrived just as Hercules and Rayne frog-walked the snoozing Sarah toward the lift tube. Lisa easily located and unwrapped the present, which turned out to be an abstract sculpture constructed of glass or crystal tubes that were closed on one end. Then Belle said, "Gem light," and the nano-luminescent element created a warm glow. "It's voice adjustable," she continued. "I set the default words to 'Gem light,' "Gem dark,' 'Gem up,' and "Gem down," so

Kruik wouldn't think you were talking to him, but you could ask him to control it directly as well."

"It's lovely," Lisa said and turned to Botan. "This would make the perfect light for the table next to our bed."

"That's what it's intended for. They're being marketed back home as a fertility token for new Gem couples pursuing natural procreation. I hear it's an inexact science."

"It's not a science at all," Botan said. "That's kind of the point."

"Are all of these glass tubes recycled test tubes?" Lisa asked, her voice sounding a bit flat.

"Yes, but not from our cloning program," Belle told her with a smile. "We handled all of that with nanobots. The test tubes are just symbolic."

Bindaal followed immediately after the clone, and Lisa found her present almost immediately. "The wrapping paper is lovely," she said as she carefully removed it. "You won't be offended if I reuse it?"

"Not at all," Bindaal said. "And before you ask, it's not a Vergallian chef's knife.

"But it's pretty cool," Botan said, looking over Lisa's shoulder as she opened the box. "Is that a horn handle?"

"According to the maker, it's sustainably harvested elk horn. It's an Ulu knife with a walnut cutting board, though where the indigenous peoples of the Arctic would have gotten the wood is beyond me."

"Maybe they harvested it from wrecked sailing ships. Is the curved blade used for skinning?"

"It's an all-purpose food preparation knife, and it works well for chopping vegetables," Bindaal assured him as Lisa grew wan at the concept of skinning. "This one was hand forged by an Inuit smith who was doing a guest appearance in Colonial Jeevesburg the last time we rendezvoused with Flower."

"But that was before we announced that we were getting married," Lisa said.

"I've been in the intelligence business longer than your grandparents have been alive," Bindaal said. "Half of our business is finding solutions to problems before they arise."

"Buying wedding gifts is a problem?"

"You didn't strike me as the type to register, so, yes."

Nineteen

Hercules stopped to buy pancake mix on his way back from an early morning workout, planning to surprise Rayne and Sarah with breakfast in bed. But the lights in the apartment were all on when he walked in, and he could hear mother and daughter chatting in the kitchen. He hid the pancake mix in his gym bag for another time.

"Good morning, ladies," he announced himself as he entered the kitchen. "What are the two of you doing up so early on a Sunday?"

"Mom's taking me to a grand opening at the business incubator," Sarah replied immediately. "I get credit for career planning at school. You have to invite me the next time you open a new corridor or something."

"I thought you wanted to be an agronomist."

"I like growing tomatoes but selling them wasn't much fun. If you account for the time we spent, the tomatoes we grew cost way more than the ones you can buy in the market."

"But yours were sustainably farmed and organic," Rayne reminded her daughter.

"Yeah, but not everybody is willing to pay more for that every time they eat a salad or a sandwich," Sarah said, waving her spoon for emphasis. "In our last meeting with Botan, he explained that we hadn't included in our profit calculations the cost of the seedlings, the rental space on the ag deck with water and climate control, or the gardening tools. He said that you can make a living as a farmer, but it takes a lot of time and good decisions, while one bad decision can break you."

"So you're thinking about other careers?" Hercules asked as he prepared a bowl of cold cereal for himself.

"Well, I'm almost grown up, and I have to do something to make a living."

"After you finish university," Rayne said.

"You didn't go to university, and neither did Hercules," Sarah protested. "And I don't want to spend four years on Earth. It smells funny, and the people are weird."

"Your mother earned her degree through correspondence courses," Hercules reminded Sarah. "I'm the big dumb one."

"Who manages more employees than any other human on the Miklat," Rayne pointed out. "And nobody said you have to go back to Earth, Sarah. You could go to the Open University on Flower or any Stryx station, or even apply as a foreign student on an alien world."

Sarah sighed and managed to produce the long-suffering look of a teenager prepared to ignore her annoying parents for the next five years.

"Whose grand opening is it this morning?" Hercules asked, mainly to change the topic.

"The L'meuf," Rayne said. "A group of them came on board at Farling Four and asked if they could join. I couldn't get a clear explanation of their business plan, beyond the fact that it had something to do with advanced vocational training, but the Zarents are thrilled to have them. Snap explained that the L'meuf are practitioners of idiosyncratic technology, and it leads to interesting solutions."

"Idio-what?" Sarah asked, unable to remain aloof from the conversation.

"Idiosyncratic technology. It means that the L'meuf have a compulsion to create solutions that other species haven't pursued. That balance-beam scale you were using at the farmstand was one of their inventions."

"That was pretty cool, but I don't see what's so idio-whatever about it."

"Primitive scales work with a balance and counter-weights, but after a species develops an electronics industry, the weights are replaced by sensors in order to make scales more compact and quicker to operate," Rayne explained. "The L'meuf could build standard scales, but instead they chose to replace the counterweight with a complicated setup using an electromagnet. Snap said that all the Zarents are looking forward to seeing what else such a creative species can come up with."

"Which ones are they again?" Hercules asked.

Rayne suppressed a shudder. "They look like giant spiders."

"Do they speak English?"

She shook her head. "Translation pendants, and I can't hear them speaking, so maybe they produce natural electromagnetism, like the Zarents."

"The Zarents aren't natural," Sarah reminded her. "The Farlings engineered them."

Rayne blinked a few times. "You know, I haven't thought about that in a while, but somebody told me that when the Farlings created the Zarents, they borrowed the best elements from a wide variety of other species, both alive and extinct. Even though the L'meuf have a bunch of multi-jointed legs and the Zarents have tentacles, they're more similar to each other than to other species I've seen. And they can both do the radio frequency trick."

"You have to be careful making comparisons," Hercules said, smiling wryly at the memory of a lecture he'd been given by a Zarent apprentice who barely came up to his knees. "I've been told that humans have a fundamental perception flaw that makes us try to fit every new thing we encounter into categories that our brains created as our vision developed."

"Doesn't everybody do that?" Sarah asked.

"To some extent, but we take it to extremes. I guess our mental processes are on the slow side compared to most species, so it's an evolutionary trick that our ancestors used to escape danger. As soon as we see big teeth or claws, our brains are already telling our legs to start running without filling in the rest of the picture."

"My knees started shaking when the L'meuf delegation cornered me in my office," Rayne admitted. "But they're very polite, and they didn't try to cover me in a silk cocoon and suspend me from the ceiling even once."

"I like silk," Sarah said. "Can they make it for free?"

"I don't know if they can spin silk at all, and if they can, I'm sure it would be work for them. I can picture a young L'meuf telling her mother that if you include the cost of food and the time spent spinning, you just can't make a living spinning silk these days."

"Very funny," her daughter said, but she couldn't maintain her scowl and broke up laughing. "I guess everybody with parents has parent problems."

"That's one way of looking at it," Hercules said and winked at Rayne. "And you can come visit me at work any time you want, Sarah. You don't have to wait until the opening ceremony for a new corridor or deck. That's not what the job is about."

"What do you mean?"

"You spent three months working on the ag deck after school. Do you think that your mother and I got a good understanding of all the work you put in by showing up to buy something at the farmstand?"

"You're saying that the farmstand was almost like a graduation ceremony," Sarah said and nodded slowly in agreement. "Yeah, I get that. Your job is supervising the foremen who are supervising hundreds of construction crews, not presenting them with the final quality check score when the work is finished. But mom's job is mainly showing people empty places to rent and answering their questions."

"Is that the impression I've given you?" Rayne asked. "The showings in the bazaar and the incubator don't account for even ten percent of my time most days."

"You don't talk about your work, so how am I supposed to know?"

"I—" Rayne stopped when she saw Hercules making a face which either indicated that Sarah had a point or that a piece of granola was stuck between his molars. She ran a quick mental review of her work conversations at home and realized that her daughter's description wasn't far from the truth. "I guess I didn't want to bring my work problems home. You already put up with me disappearing into the bedroom for visor conference calls at all hours. I talk about showing rental spaces because the people opening businesses in the bazaar and the aliens visiting the incubator have interesting stories."

"Just because they're new to the Miklat doesn't mean that they're interesting, and even if they are, it's not their stories I want to hear," Sarah said. "I know that you ended up with the job managing the bazaar because everybody from Bits was already used to you handling the money as treasurer, and then the Zarents and the co-captains asked you to do the same for the incubator because you built up experience renting space in the bazaar. But I don't know what you *do* when you aren't walking and talking at the same time."

Rayne took a long sip from her rapidly cooling coffee, checked the time, and said, "We should get going. From now on I'll try to talk more about other parts of my job, but you have to remember that business transactions are confidential. I can't tell you how much somebody is planning to spend on inventory for their bazaar stall, or an alien consortium's target for return on their investment."

Sarah said, "Snap is here," and then lifted her bowl and slurped out the remainder of the milk and the cereal while the adults were looking in the other direction.

"I would have heard the door—Oh," Hercules said when he caught up with the ploy. "Have a good time at the grand opening. I'll be at Lisa's dojo getting beat up by a boxing bot."

"Is she back from the honeymoon already?" Rayne asked as she retrieved her purse and made sure that her tab was in it.

"I didn't know they went anywhere. I ran into her at the gym, and she invited me by."

"They didn't leave the Miklat. They stayed in the honeymoon suite at that new hotel that the Dollnicks opened. Kruik told me that it's a wholly-owned subsidiary of the Empire Convention Center chain, but they use the Nest Away brand for smaller facilities."

Sarah ran into the bathroom and her mother waited at the door, struggling with a natural tendency to tap her foot. Then her smartphone chimed, and she read the incoming text from Mouser saying that he was running late because he'd left the ceremonial ribbon-cutting scissors in his lab and had to detour.

The incubator plaza was teeming with aliens when they arrived, and Sarah began taking notes on her tab for the written part of her report. At first, Rayne thought that Bindaal must have run a special on hot stimulant drinks for so many of the incubator's tenants to show up, but then she noticed that they were all waiting for a turn to meet the L'meuf.

"I'm going to check that everything is ready," she told Sarah, who stopped writing long enough to acknowledge that she heard. Rayne worked her way around the edge of the crowd, passing in front of Bindaal's vegan restaurant. The Vergallian was working behind the counter and gestured for her to come over.

"I'll make my rent early this month," Bindaal said to Rayne. "It's the first time I've seen so many members of the advanced species in one place at one time on the Miklat."

"I didn't realize there would be so much interest in the L'meuf. Is their technology that good?"

"It's different, but that's not why everybody wants to meet them. Before the Stryx connected the tunnel to Farling Four, visiting them was expensive and time-consuming. Most of us have never seen a L'meuf, not to mention getting access to their markets."

Rayne frowned. "I thought they were here to develop a new learning technology, though it sounded a bit vague. Are they really traders? The Zarents will probably make an exception, but the idea of the business incubator was to start manufacturing and service businesses, not to create an alien version of the bazaar."

Bindaal set two tall glasses of dark purple juice on the counter from where a Drazen grabbed one in each hand and dropped a tip in the jar with his tentacle.

"There was a time when I thought that humanity had nothing to offer the advanced species, but tipping the owner is a good one," Bindaal said happily. "I've already made the acquaintance of the L'meuf and you don't have to worry. They really are here to develop a new product."

"Did you understand what it is they're working on?" Rayne asked.

"An adaptation of existing technology for different species. I gather they are starting with Humans since you're viewed as the lowest common denominator of sorts."

"Because all of the advanced species can eat our food?"

"I don't believe that's true outside of the tunnel network. The L'meuf asked for samples of the ingredients I use so they could test them for toxicity, and if they're careful about Vergallian vegan, they must have had some bad experiences with alien vegetables."

Rayne heard a snipping sound near her ear and almost got a pair of scissors in the eye when she turned. "Sorry," Mouser said as he jerked the scissors back. "I should have thought of that possibility."

"Almost doesn't count with impalement," she gave the standard gaming response. "Have you ever seen such a mob scene? All the aliens want to meet the L'meuf."

"As long as they didn't notice that I'm late. Is their space going to border the plaza, or did they get mobbed when stopping for breakfast?"

"They took one of the premier spaces that faces the plaza," Rayne said. "Since there were never L'meuf living on the Miklat in the past, there isn't any renovated habitat space for them, but the Zarents doubled the area of their rental for free and offered to build to suit."

"I see visions of a giant web in my head," Mouser said. "I suppose we should go let them know we're here even if they're in no hurry to cut the ribbon."

It turned out that the spider-like aliens had a sense of humor, because instead of a ribbon, they had stretched light netting to simulate a web over the entrance to their newly leased space. As Rayne and Mouser approached, the L'meuf all politely broke off the conversations they were holding with incubator tenants and straightened all of their legs to stand as tall as possible. Katya, who was wearing her hat, though she had dispensed with the uniform rather than modifying it for the final months of her pregnancy, waved Mouser over.

"They're ready when you are," she told him. "I already gave a speech welcoming them to the Miklat, so it's just you."

"That's pretty much all I had," Mouser said. "All right, I'll wing it." He offered each of the L'meuf a handshake, which they gravely returned with the manipulators at the end of one of their hairy limbs, and then cleared his throat, an agreed-upon signal for Kruik to start amplifying his voice. "Welcome to the Mik—"

"Halt," a woman's voice interrupted. "This is a travesty of representational government. Our primary was settled weeks ago, but your negotiator keeps putting me off on a final election date."

"This isn't the time," Rayne said, trying to keep a professional smile on her face as Mattie pushed her way through the crowd. "Why don't we—"

"No," Mattie cut her off. "The good people joining the Miklat's incubator should know that—" she jumped back a full space, crashing into a Verlock she had just cut in front of, though if the dense alien even noticed the impact, he was too polite to show it. "Giant spiders! Somebody do something."

"The L'meuf aren't spiders," Mouser told his rival for mayor. "They're an advanced species from the Farling Empire who we are welcoming to the business incubator. I was about to cut the ribbon."

"That's not a ribbon, it's a spider web. They're probably controlling your mind."

"I pinged Sabina," Katya told Mouser. "Drake is on his way."

"We'll talk with Kruik when the ceremony is over and schedule an election as soon as possible," Mouser said. "Please restrain yourself for just a minute and—"

"I should be cutting that web," Mattie said, pushing forward again, though she kept as much distance as possible between herself and the guests of honor. "Give me those scissors."

"This isn't going to stop," Rayne muttered. "She's unhinged."

Mouser didn't know whether to hold the scissors over his head where the short woman would be unable to reach them even by jumping, or to just give in and let her cut the ribbon to save further embarrassment to humanity.

"We are very interested in your concept of representational government," one of the L'meuf spoke up unexpectedly. "Will we be permitted to observe this election you speak of?"

"Outside observers," Mattie said, converting the alien's question into an offer. "I graciously accept. I invite all the oppressed aliens on board to watch my coro—my election to mayor. I pledge to you right here and now that in the next election, you'll have the right to vote for mayor just like humans."

"Why wait?" Mouser asked, getting fed up with the Oner's endless self-promotion. "Why not invite them to vote now?"

"Anything that will compel you and your Dollnick intermediary to schedule an election is acceptable to me," she shot back, and then ducked under the simulated webbing into the L'meuf's space. "I see you've called out your hired muscle to repress me."

"And I see I'm too late to prevent an interspecies incident," Drake said in frustration. "Come on out of there, Mattie. Everybody wants to finish the ceremony so they can go back to getting to know each other and having a good time."

"Not until the election," she said, retreating further into the space.

Drake started forward and then pointed at his ear. After a few seconds, he turned to Mouser with a puzzled look on his face. "Kruik is willing to hold the election now," he said.

"It's a trick!" Mattie shouted from where she was standing half shielded by a potted plant that might have been imported from Farling Four or the L'meuf's homeworld. "You can't just hold an election without preparing."

"Kruik can," Drake told her. "His thermal imaging covers every interior space in Miklat and he can use it to count a show of hands, or limbs. Mouser can announce the election and—"

"No. An incumbent has enough advantages. Let the co-captain make the announcement."

Drake shrugged and looked at Katya.

"Fine by me," the co-captain said. "Let's get this over with so I can take a load off my feet." She pointed at her ear for a few seconds and then said, "After I announce the election, the mayoral candidates can each speak for thirty seconds and Kruik will put your voice through the public address system."

"Five minutes," Mattie countered.

"One minute, and that's final," Katya said. "Do you want to go first or last?"

"Last."

"Mouser?"

"Makes no difference to me," the current mayor said.

Katya was silent for a moment, and when she started speaking again, her voice came over the public address system. "Attention everybody on board. This is Co-captain Katya Zerakova. We're conducting an election for mayor, which is a largely ceremonial position that has been filled to date by Mouser, the former Rules Committee Chairman from Bits. Running against him is Mattie of the Colony One movement who joined the Miklat at our last Earth stop. Mattie recently prevailed in primary caucuses held by the Colony One movement for their members. Each of the candidates will be given one minute to make a speech, and then we'll vote by a show of hands which will be recorded and counted by Kruik. Mouser?"

Mouser reflexively cleared his throat to signal Kruik, even though the Dollnick artificial intelligence was waiting for him to begin.

"I never sought the job of mayor, and I won't cry if I lose it, but my wife insists that I'm the best man for the job, so quitting isn't an option. If you vote for me, I promise not to give you anything, but I'll continue to listen to whoever takes the trouble to track me down in my shop in the bazaar or my lab. It's been an honor serving as your mayor these last two years, and I just want to remind everybody that we'll rendezvous with Flower next week for a two-day visit. Mouser out."

Katya pointed to Mattie with both hands, like she was working at an airport on Earth directing sub-orbital transports.

"Oners, Bitters, humans, and aliens," Mattie began in measured tones. "If elected, I pledge to represent all of you, equally, and without favoritism," she shot a glance at Mouser with what she no doubt thought was this telling blow, "and unlike my predecessor, I will push forward with winning a voice in the governance of the Miklat for everybody on board. I know you've heard that it can't be done, that we're merely guests on a private vessel owned by aliens, but if we stand shoulder to shoulder, everything is possible."

"Time," Katya said.

"I came to the Miklat without—turn the public address system back on."

"Now we'll vote by a show of hands," Katya announced, her voice heard all over the ship. "All in favor of keeping Mouser as mayor?" She raised her hand, and behind her, every alien in the crowd elevated a hand, tentacle, or whatever appendage they would use to get a teacher's attention in a classroom as little sentients. After five seconds, Katya lowered her hand, and said, "All in favor of Mattie?"

Mattie raised both of her hands and glared. "Just wait until he counts the Oner vote," she said.

Another five seconds passed, and then Katya said, "Bad news, Mouser. You're still mayor, and now that it's an elected position, you can't keep threatening to quit."

"This is a travesty!" Mattie cried. "You didn't even report the vote count."

"You don't want to know. I'm not sure what you said to the Oners in the caucuses, Mattie, but Mouser got more of their votes than you did."

Twenty

Belle walked up the aisle of the packed shuttle looking for an open seat, and her memory flashed back to her first tunnel network visit as an exchange student. All the young aliens going on the school's field trip had shifted their backpacks to the empty seat next to them, and in one case, a Horten girl even got up and moved so she wouldn't have to sit next to a clone.

"Over here, Belle," she heard Sabina call. "I saved a seat for you. Last row."

The co-captain shifted the hat she'd used to save the seat to her lap as the Gem approached, and turning to her left, added, "You owe me a cred."

Drake grumbled and paid his wife. "She's always early to everything. I detect a whiff of pre-arrangement."

Belle slipped into the open seat and fastened her safety restraints just as the shuttle began to move. "Thank you," she said. "My head must have been underwater in the Jacuzzi when the departure time of the first shuttle to Flower was moved up. Have you tried the new public baths?"

"I was just getting out of the ice bath during the announcement, and I noticed your head going under," Sabina said, flashing her husband a smug grin. "That's why I texted you a reminder when I didn't see you on the shuttle."

"If you were here early, why did you sit in the back row?"

"Mercenary training," Drake told her. "I did a stint flying plainclothes security on Frunge mining shuttles. If you want to keep an eye on everything without turning around all the time, the back row is the best place to be."

"I'm surprised your sister isn't on the first shuttle," Belle said to Sabina. "Or maybe I just didn't see her."

"At eight months pregnant, Katya is pretty hard to miss," Sabina said with a laugh. "But there's an event in the independent living cooperative where Rayne's mother is staying, so Katya is handling visitors to the business incubator for Rayne today. You know how important the incubator is to the Zarents."

"I'm still in shock that they allowed Kruik to run an election in the middle of the grand opening for the L'meuf business."

"First Engineer Miklat was rather amused by the whole thing. I gather that the little apprentices riding around the ship on their unicycles are always listening, so the Zarents knew where the election was headed weeks before the vote. It's ironic that as knowledgeable as Mattie was about political infighting, she was the last to know how unpopular she was making herself. Kruik told me that she got fewer than a thousand votes, and I guarantee that some of those were people who raised their hand at the wrong time."

The constant acceleration of the shuttle that was keeping them pressed back in their seats cut out. There was an audible whooshing sound as the passengers all inhaled and held their breaths while the shuttle spun around, and then deceleration started and everybody exhaled.

"Flower must be flying," Drake commented. "Kruik always spins his shuttles around to the left at the midway point."

Sabina tapped Belle on the shoulder and used a little head movement, basically pointing with her chin, to where one of the Hortens working on haptic gaming accessories in the business incubator was sitting between a young Dollnick and Lisa's wedding planner.

"They haven't made official contact with us, but Bindaal and Kyor both believe that the three of them are sizing us up," Belle said.

"You don't sound thrilled by the prospect of competition."

The Gem made a noncommittal humming sound.

"You're worried they won't be comfortable in the presence of a clone?" Sabina followed up.

"I think it will take a full generation for everybody to believe that we truly have given up cloning Gem," Belle said. "And they're clearly amateurs, which means a lot of mentoring work."

"If I know Kyor, she'll steer them all in the wrong direction," Drake said with a chuckle. "I can imagine her making them memorize made-up passphrases and secret handshakes."

"Secret handshakes would be funny," Sabina said. "Drazens do this thing with their extra thumb—you have to experience it."

The starfield visible through the portholes suddenly disappeared as the shuttle, still decelerating, passed backward through the atmosphere retention field that kept the air in Flower's core from escaping into space. The passengers all experienced the weird feeling of their weight shifting from against the chair-back to down on the seat as the shuttle accelerated in a spiral and then touched down on the deck with only the slightest jolt.

"We'll know humanity has arrived when we can build spaceships capable of that trick," Drake said as he released his safety restraints.

"It's not the shuttle," Sabina told him. "I doubt they even bothered turning on the engines for a trip this short. Kruik pushed us out of his hold with a manipulator field, and then Flower took over, pulled us in, and spun us up."

"My logical mind knows that, but my walking-around mind won't accept it. I can't see manipulator fields, and seeing is believing."

"Do you want to join us for dinner, Belle?" Sabina asked as they all stood. "We have to stop by Human Empire headquarters for a meeting, but after that we're free. I want to do some shopping and eat some good faux-Frunge food at the Blue Tea Café."

"I'll ping you," the clone said. "I have to check in with my colleagues, and these rendezvous are like vacation days for them since they don't have to go over to the Miklat to debrief sources, though I imagine they will all want to visit the business incubator tomorrow before we leave."

"—and I want to visit with Em, and with Flower," Sarah wrapped up the recounting of her plans for the day. "But Grandma first."

"I'm sure Grandma will be pleased to hear that," Rayne said. "Her independent living cooperative is putting on a play this afternoon and Dave has one of the leading roles."

"Dave is an actor? I thought he was a retired salesman."

"He worked as a scaffolding stand-in for Flower's first anime production," Hercules told her. "What was it called again, Rayne?"

"*Everyday Superheroes*. Dave stood in for M793qK who played the Evil Farling Mastermind."

"But I *like* M793qK," Sarah protested. "He's not evil."

"But he did a wicked good job of getting free publicity for himself so that everyone knew who he was when his tunnel connection scheme came to fruition," Rayne said, and let out a sigh. "I never felt bad about the aliens all being better than us at science and technology since they've had thousands of times as long as us after their industrial revolutions to advance the state of the art. But humans have probably been transacting business of one sort or another for over ten thousand years, and we're just as far behind in that."

"I don't think we're behind the aliens at all in business," Hercules said. "The difference is that our idea of long-term thinking is a few months or five years. The advanced species all live much longer than us, so they're much more patient when it comes to developing new products and markets."

"Kyor wiped the board with us in *Speed Trader*, and Belle, who'd never been in business, was runner-up," Rayne reminded him.

"Delphi was closing in on her the last few weeks, it's just that we ran out of time. And Kyor was in the art business. She must be a natural salesperson to have sold her sculptures to other species. Every time she suggested a trade to me, I could feel my willpower melting away."

"Do you think she used mind control?" Sarah asked, apparently excited by the prospect.

"She just has a way of putting things that makes you want to buy," Hercules said as they shuffled into the capsule. "And that's the longest I've ever had to wait for a lift tube on Flower."

"Everyone on the shuttle went to the nearest spoke," Flower said irritably through the capsule's overhead speaker grille. "If you'd followed instructions and spread yourselves around, nobody would have waited for over a minute."

"Humans are clumpers," Sarah volunteered. "Third Educator Miklat told us that when she substituted. And how are you doing, Flower?"

"I'm fine, Sarah. Em asked about you as soon as she got up this morning. I told her that you'd want to visit your grandmother first thing, but that you might be open for lunch."

"Grandma's boyfriend is in a play this afternoon, so I'll have to see that. Can you check if Em wants to come watch it with me?"

Flower was silent for almost half a minute before responding. "Em's father, Captain Pyun, is the guest of honor, so they'll be there. And Em says if you'll meet her at the Vergallian vegan restaurant in the food court for lunch, it's her treat."

The family exited the lift tube capsule on the independent living deck and took the familiar corridor to the common room where they'd arranged to meet. June was helping Dave struggle out of a lifelike Farling costume as they arrived, and Hercules immediately went over to help.

"Thanks," Dave said. "I forgot how much it weighed. Irene planned the dress rehearsal for the morning of the play so we wouldn't have to move all the scenery twice."

"Irene has started directing plays?" Rayne asked. "I thought she'd dedicated her retirement to making documentaries."

"She has, but the Grenouthian director told her that directing a live play was the best way to hone her sense of dramatic timing."

"What kind of play has a Farling in it?" Sarah asked.

"One that your grandmother wrote," June said, putting a hand on her granddaughter's shoulder. "You didn't think I'd spend my whole retirement sitting around and drinking tea, did you?"

"Don't you have to know a lot about the inner thoughts and plans of characters to write a play?" Rayne asked her mother.

"It's a documentary play," June told her with a smile. "About the origins of Flower's Paradise. I interviewed dozens of residents about their most meaningful experiences here, and right behind the social interactions came their brief encounters with M793qK."

Dave, who had just draped his life-like costume over a chair where it looked like a deflated Farling, began rubbing his forefingers together in front of his throat like M793qK's speaking legs. "Fixing damage and correcting design flaws in Human hearts is easy," he said in a voice that sounded a little like the doctor's external translation pendant. "Fixing human hearts that have been broken by lovers is beyond even my skills."

"Really?" Sarah asked. "I thought you could fix anything."

"The problem is that you don't take my advice," Dave continued in his role as the Farling doctor. "If you're going to sit in a dark corner and have dark thoughts, nothing I can do, short of reprogramming your neural network, can change that."

"So why don't you reprogram our brains?"

"Professional ethics, plus the Stryx asked me not to."

Several decks away, in the Farling physician's clinic, Sabina accepted the programmable cred M793qK handed her and frowned at the balance. "Am I supposed to split this with my sister?"

"That's just for you," the alien reassured her. "I'm not that bad at computing percentages. I'll give Katya her coin when she comes for her final prenatal checkup."

"That's one way to get her in the door." As if on cue, the door to the clinic slid open and Delphi entered. "Hi, Captain. You wanted to see me, M793qK?"

"Payday," the Farling said, and handed her a programmable cred. "I trust G32FX with my planet, but creds have a way of sticking to his manipulators."

"I've been wondering why you put G32FX in charge rather than one of your older retainers who have lived on Farling Four's moons all through your exile," Sabina said. "Do they lack business experience?"

"They lack Human experience. G32FX spent almost two decades on Earth. None of my higher-level retainers were willing."

Delphi rubbed at the balance shown on the programmable cred as if she was afraid that it was a trick and the numbers would disappear. "If I ever figure out bartering, I'm going to end up rich," she said. "Maybe I'll buy a LARPing studio for the Miklat."

"That will take a serious investment in vector processors since Kruik doesn't have anywhere near Flower's spare capacity," M793qK told her. "And if you have any of those baskets made of recycled wood from the Grenouthian's twelve-million-year clock left, I'll take them."

"I've got two left, but they aren't fancy," Delphi warned. "What will you do with them?"

"Make gift baskets for Grenouthians who are waiting for the opportunity to owe me a favor. They're sentimental about that sort of thing." The Farling rummaged in a cabinet while he was speaking and brought out a black medical bag.

"Making a house call?" Sabina asked.

"Wellness visit. I always visit the Miklat to check on the Zarents when I have the opportunity. I'll ask Kruik to pull up the container with my trade goods and grab those baskets while I'm there."

"I think they're in my cabin," Delphi said.

"Then I'll stop by your cabin and pick them up," M793qK rubbed out on his speaking legs as he herded the two women toward the door. "If I hurry, I can take the shuttle you arrived on."

"Shadow came over with me to get in line for Flower's LARPing studio. There's nobody in my cabin to give you the baskets."

"I'll let myself in."

"Is it productive to reveal your superior technological prowess just to pick up a few baskets?" Sabina asked as she followed Delphi and the alien out of the clinic. "I'd think you would be more worried about offending Kruik or the Zarents. Sometimes I really can't follow how your mind works."

"Then I would recommend you attend the matinee in the common room of Flower's Paradise after lunch," M793qK rubbed out on his speaking legs as he accelerated away from them on his way to the lift tube. "Dave does a surprisingly good interpretation."

"I came as soon as I could get free," Bill told Jake. "Where's Harry?"

"His wife is directing a play in the independent living cooperative," Jake told the man he'd replaced as Harry's assistant in the kitchen of the small cafeteria that doubled as a meeting space for alien intelligence agents. "He did most of the cooking before he left, but this decorative vegetable tray is taking far longer than I thought it would. I've never done one so big before."

"I'll start serving, you finish the tray."

"That stands to reason since I've never figured out whether you work in here or out there."

"I'm a man of many half-baked talents," Bill said with a laugh. "And if I told you the truth, I'd have to recruit you."

The small cafeteria was as crowded as Bill had ever seen it as the intelligence agents who were just starting out on the Miklat got to know their elder colleagues on Flower. Lume tried to put the young Dollnick agent at ease by engaging her in an eight-handed game of cat's cradle, but Ulah was so nervous in the famous spy's presence that the string became hopelessly tangled.

Razood sat across from Fonzil, who was breathlessly reporting on the strange wedding customs of Humans, a species that didn't even have the stamina to keep the reception going for the usual two sidereal days traditional in Frunge culture.

"They're living on the Miklat, and it's revolving so fast that a sidereal day is measured in seconds," Razood pointed out.

"But I was talking about Human Standard Time."

"Cheese and a grain-free cracker?" Bill offered, trying to tempt them with the platter of snacks that Harry had made up earlier.

"Thanks," Razood said, using his butter knife to shovel a dozen little squares of cheese. "Bill, this is Fonzil. The home office sent her out to get established on the Miklat. Fonzil, Bill runs the Human Empire's café for their school of government, but he also moonlights for M793qK."

"Mainly testing products for the *All Species Cookbook,*" Bill told the young Frunge who was staring at him with something like awe or pity. "Do all the guys have a new understudy?"

"Not Avisia, but that's because Bindaal is already covering the Miklat for the Vergallians," Razood said. "Oh, and the agent the Sharf sent decided to stay on Farling Four, and Yaem hasn't made the time to find a replacement. He's probably hoping that we'll do it for him."

"The Sharf station chief expects you to find a Sharf replacement for their agent who didn't stay on the Miklat?" Fonzil asked in disbelief.

Razood gave her a sympathetic smile. "We do things differently on Flower and it's carried over to the Miklat. Everyone takes turns writing Yaem's weekly reports since he's so busy running the anime studio for Flower and was never really interested in intelligence work."

"I'll leave the cheese platter with you for when Jorb gets here," Bill said. "Going by the look of that Grenouthian talking with the director, I better bring some vegetables out before there's a riot."

Jake was just putting the final touches on the large vegetable platter when Bill returned to the kitchen, and he looked up and asked, "Should I start the ramen?"

"Jorb isn't here yet," Bill said. "Better to wait. I'm going to bring the veggie platter out before the new Grenouthian decides he's a carnivore and eats one of us."

"I don't think their teeth evolved for ripping," Jake said, but he handed Bill the large platter. "By the way, when the new Horten looked in the kitchen and saw me wiping my chef's knife with a hand towel, he turned kind of green and left. I swear the towel hadn't been used."

Bill nodded. "I got a secure text from M793qK that he saw the Horten boarding the shuttle for the Miklat. Why he thought it was important for me to know is above my pay grade."

When Bill approached the Grenouthians with the vegetable platter, the director motioned for him to put it down and sit.

"I have to serve the meal soon," Bill told them.

"This is important," the director said and turned to his young colleague. "Tell him what you told me."

"I was curious about the obvious differences between the Colony One leadership and members aboard the Miklat, so I checked with Flower as soon as I arrived," said the Grenouthian, who had failed out of the diplomatic track due to his impatience with the twelve-million-year clock. "I followed up on analyzing the Colony One lottery results from your last stop at Earth and concluded that the drawing was rigged by the individuals who thought they could take over the Miklat by staging elections. They weren't even members of the movement a month before the lottery."

"Why are you letting him tell me?" Bill asked suspiciously. "It sounds like a story you could sell to the Grenouthian News."

"Making Humans look bad is one thing," the Grenouthian director said. "Making the Miklat look bad at this critical time is another. You should pass the information along to EarthCent Intelligence or the Galactic Free Press and let them decide what to do."

"Did you remember to enable your magnetic cleats?" Nigel asked Katya as they exited the lift tube.

"I don't need them anymore," Katya said. "I'm massing for two now."

"What does that mean?"

"You spent a decade on a Verlock academy world and you can't guess? Never mind, Snap is coming."

"Co-captain Zerakova, Xenoarchaeologist Nigel," First Engineer Miklat greeted them formally. "Please follow me." He spun a hundred-and-eighty-degree turn on his unicycle and headed back in the direction from which he'd appeared, away from the atmosphere retention field at the open end of the Miklat's core.

"I should have come down here more often the last few months," Katya told her husband. "I feel the right weight for the first time in ages."

"The baby is due in three weeks," he told her. "You can wait that long."

"First babies are often overdue, and it will take months of exercise to get back to my fighting weight. Remind me to buy a jogging stroller."

The most senior Zarent on the ship rode his unicycle directly at the metal bulkhead and disappeared straight through it. Nigel extended his left arm in front of his wife to hold her back as he poked at the bulkhead with a finger. "I'll never get used to holograms," he said.

"Try walking around in one of your virtual reality headsets," Katya suggested. "When you enable the exterior cameras for mixed reality, they don't see the holograms."

"Why is that?"

"Dewey explained that it has to do with different frame rates. He can't see holograms at all unless he makes an effort." She signaled for the mayor of the Miklat to remain seated, but Mouser had old-fashioned manners and he rose to his feet, at the same time offering her a large paper shopping bag with thin rope handles.

"Is it a jogging stroller?" Katya asked.

"A baby quilt," Mouser said. "Sophie's new hobby. It's going to be strange living on a ship with only one captain while you're gone."

"It's only for four months, depending on when the baby makes its appearance," Katya said. "Nigel will be teaching at our School of Government on Flower, and my mother will come for a vacation as soon as I send her a coded message informing her that she's a grandmother."

"And here comes the good doctor," Snap announced, swaying his unicycle on purpose to see around Katya. "Please, sit everyone. This meeting won't take long."

M793qK strode up to the table on his hindmost limbs and then leaned onto the inclined Farling couch, which tilted forward until all his limbs were off the deck. "You've outdone yourself," he said to the engineer. "This is better than the ones they make on Farling Two."

"Our apprentices studying ergonomics did it as their certification project. I just informed them that they passed."

"Do you have something for me?" Katya asked the Farling pointedly.

"When you come in for your checkup," he rubbed out on his speaking legs and then turned his multifaceted eyes on Mouser. "Congratulations on your election to mayor."

"Thank you, but it's strictly a ceremonial job," Mouser replied.

"Not anymore," M793qK informed him.

From the Author

The next EarthCent release will be **Earth on the Galactic Tunnel Network**, the seventh book in the **EarthCent Auxiliaries** series. I apologize to readers who haven't kept up with the spin-off series and are now faced with discontinuities in the main Union Station thread, but the plot lines have become integrated across all four series, and the timeline is given below. If you're new to the EarthCent books, you can start back at the beginning with **Union Station 1, 2, 3**, a discounted three-book bundle.

For notifications of new releases, sign up for the mailing list at www.ifitbreaks.com. You may have noticed that Amazon notifications of new releases have become random, they missed three of my books in 2022, lately they been sending two for every book. I also post new releases to facebook.com/E.M.Foner/ and respond to all temperate e-mail sent to e_foner@yahoo.com

Readers have asked me to include the complete timeline of the EarthCent Universe in order so here it is:

Destiny: Union Station
Date Night on Union Station
Alien Night on Union Station
High Priest on Union Station
Spy Night on Union Station
Carnival on Union Station
Wanderers on Union Station
Vacation on Union Station
Guest Night on Union Station
Word Night on Union Station
Party Night on Union Station

Review Night on Union Station
Family Night on Union Station
Book Night on Union Station
LARP Night on Union Station
Career Night on Union Station
Last Night on Union Station
Independent Living
Soup Night on Union Station
Assisted Living
Freelance on the Galactic Tunnel Network
Con Living
Empire Night on Union Station
Space Living
Traders on the Galactic Tunnel Network
Orphans on the Galactic Tunnel Network
Swap Night on Union Station
Slow Living
Artists on the Galactic Tunnel Network
History Night on Union Station
Bits of Anarchy
Double Living
Bits of Flower
Synergy on the Galactic Tunnel Network
Substitutes on Union Station
Bits of Catalyst
Elder Living
Royals on the Galactic Tunnel Network
Deal Night on Union Station
Intellectual Property
Bits of Business

Made in United States
Orlando, FL
07 March 2025

59245584R00157